Jacumba
Connection

Jacumba
Connection

David C. Taylor

E-MAGINATION PUBLISHING

Published in the United States by
E-Magination Publishing.

ISBN: 9780996987202

Library of Congress Control Number: 2015918789

Book cover art by: Jose E. Torres

Book cover design by: Katie Mullaly, Faceted Press

Interior design by: Katie Mullaly, Faceted Press

For my mother and father.

I finally found my hallelujah.

Who knew?

ACKNOWLEDGMENTS

Working with a writer in prison is difficult at best. It takes patience, creativity, and dedication. So I'd like to thank my teachers, colleagues, friends, and family, as follows:

First to the "Memoir Midwife" Stacy Dymalski and to Keltin Barney (You're the man!), my editors extraordinaire, thank you for your guidance and the extras on my behalf. The reams of paper. The runs to Staples for printer ink. Bonzi runs to the post office, and of course, the midnight editing sessions. All things you do to accommodate a writer in prison. Your smooth style guided me in the margins and taught me what it means to be a writer. Also, many thanks to my copyeditor, Elizabeth Evachuck, who soldiered through thousands of pages of my barely decipherable handwriting.

To Doug Hoffman, thank you for creating a website and blog so that my voice may continue to be heard in the free world, even though my physical presence remains locked away. And to his wife Corinne Nareau who made several passes through the book to ensure every "t" was crossed and every "i" dotted.

Many thanks to my book designer, Katie Mullaly, for taking all the work we've done and assembling it into something that goes far beyond my wildest dreams. Who knew that what started out as a pile of handwritten pages could end up as a beautiful book?

Speaking of which, thank you to Jose E. Torres for creating cover art that fully captures the essence of all 400 pages of my story.

I'd also like to thank Stephanie and the girls for their love and support on this project. And of course, big gratitude to my "Down Brothers" and independent readers: Adam Teague, Bill Gregory, Earnest Hearing, and Sam Grey. Thank you for your time, enthusiasm, and endless engagement in my personal story.

Lastly, and most importantly, my biggest gratitude of all goes to my mom, Ellen Taylor, the Queen of my Heart, whose unconditional love and unwavering support has brought me peace in a place of chaos.

--David C. Taylor

TABLE OF CONTENTS

FOREWORD

In the spring of 2014 my phone rings. "Hello?"

The voice on the other end is a woman named Ellen Taylor. She tells me, "My grown son has written a book and I need to know if it's any good." It makes sense that she'd reach out to me on the Internet because I've branded myself as The Memoir Midwife. I'm a film producer, story editor, teacher, and author, and as such I help people find, write, and share their stories. In other words, I'll help you give birth to your story, but I won't write it for you.

I quickly learn Ellen's son's name is David Taylor and he's greatly changed the lives of many people in his 50-plus years.

Well, heck yeah, I'm in! What is he? A humanitarian? An inventor? One of those new age thinkers who spouts pearls of wisdom that get turned into cat memes on Facebook. This is what I call real social work.

However, in David's case it's what the Federal Government calls human trafficking.

What? (Cue the needle scratch across the record.)

David is in federal prison for conspiracy, related to his conviction of smuggling undocumented aliens into the United States. At the time Ellen contacted me he was on year two of a 10-year sentence.

I wasn't exactly jumping for joy at the idea of working with a federal prisoner, but at the time I *was* jumping through hoops trying to navigate a devastating divorce that swiftly drained my bank account. And since I had sole custody of my two kids I didn't have a lot of time to devote to billable hours.

In all honesty, I agreed to read David's story purely for mercenary reasons.

Obstacle number one: The manuscript is handwritten on random pieces of paper. Apparently they do not have laptops or iPads in prison. *"Ellen, you have to get this mess transcribed before I can read it."* Honestly, I thought that would get me off the hook right there. However, Ellen rises to the occasion and when that beast of a manuscript is finally printed out on 8.5 x 11 paper it's 478 pages long.

I reluctantly start reading.

As expected, David's manuscript is a royal mess; full of typos, bad grammar, misspellings, and a shaky story structure at best. It meanders between first person and third person and has so much chit-chatty dialog you'd think the characters get paid by the word to speak.

And yet, I can't put it down. In all that jumble of a literary mess is a riveting, funny, poignant, character-driven story of a middle-class, white bread couple, who because of their own financial struggles, wake up one day entrenched in the human smuggling business.

At first the main characters break the law because they need the money. But in a very short time their cargo evolves from shipping a commodity to helping people embark upon a trip that brings about hope and purpose. As I read David's story suddenly these people have names and faces, families, hopes, and dreams that are not unlike mine. And the only baggage they bring with them are their own stories; stories that don't necessarily fit into the criteria of an immigration form, but nevertheless are just as important as anyone else's.

David's story reveals the war on illegal immigration told from a boots-on-the-ground insider, who just happens to be born a white, U.S. citizen in middleclass America. It's a perspective on immigration from which we've never heard until now.

I wanted to hate David's story. It would've made it so much easier to walk away from what was undoubtedly a weird situation in terms of a client. But for some reason I can't dismiss an authentic story... because it's truth. And that's all I ever want.

I come clean and tell Ellen, "There is something here that needs to come out."

So for the next two years we embark upon a creative process that is so wacky and backward, no one would believe me if I made it up. To help me streamline the process I enlist the help of another story editor (Keltin Barney) and a copyeditor (Elizabeth Evaschuk). Every time I send a re-edited manuscript to David, I have to reprint all 400-plus pages. David edits by hand, sends it back, we edit on the computer, reprint, and start the whole process all over again.

This all goes back and forth by snail mail, and the Feds inspect everything. Sometimes it takes weeks before the manuscript arrives at its final destination.

And if I want David to study a book, his mom has to send it directly from Amazon. Only approved vendors are allowed to mail anything to a prisoner, other than letters or pages.

And after over a year of not being able to email David, one day I was magically allowed to do so. I still have no answer for that. Email is spotty to this day.

David was able to call me three times to clarify some of our manuscript notes, but we were only allowed 15-minute phone calls. At 15 minutes on the dot the line goes dead. And every few seconds a recording reminds me I'm talking to a federal prisoner, which ironically eats up precious phone time.

Working with David in this manner routinely reminds me how we on the outside take our simple freedoms for granted.

But in spite of all that David finished his book. I helped Ellen start a small publishing company, E-Magination Publishing, which she used to turn David's pile of handwritten scribbles into the book you now hold in your hands.

As David's book project neared the end, I suggested he write a blog, because just like immigration, he now has an insider's view of prison. David agreed, and with webmaster Doug Hoffman's help, *PostcardsFromPrison.net* was born. I highly recommend you check it out.

In the end, helping David tell his story allowed me to regain my creativity during one of the darkest periods of my life. And by his own admission, committing his story to paper saved David's soul from spiraling down a black hole of the deepest, darkest despair. Even though he was in prison when he wrote *Jacumba Connection*, getting up every day to work on his manuscript gave David hope and purpose, which in turn *gave him* a reason to get up everyday.

We all have unique passions that burn within us. Although those passions are different for everyone, it's what we rely on to get through the worst challenges in our lives and bring about change in the world. It's a superpower that unfortunately remains dormant in far too many people. But when it finally emerges, it cannot be repressed. Not even by prison.

Even though I was reluctant at first to take on this project, I can now say with zero uncertainty, it's been an honor and a privilege to help David find, write, and share his story. I hope you enjoy reading it as much as this eclectic team of people miraculously came together to write and produce it.

Sincerely,

Stacy Dymalski
May 2016

WHAT IF...

If you were living in abject poverty, and your average income was just two dollars a day, but just across the river, or just across the fence, was advantage, opportunity, food, healthcare, and free education, as well as law officials that catered to minimal corruption, my question to you is this: Would you risk everything to put your family and children on the right side of that fence?

Of course you would.

Anyone in their right mind would try.

THE RIDE OF YOUR LIFE
Introduction

"Fly the highway but don't see the road signs, you can't read in between the lines…"

Blind Highway blares out of the Kenwood as Denice seductively blows a plume of smoke from her nose. It drifts towards the headliner of the big K-5 Blazer.

Charlie thinks to himself, *God, she's so sexy when she does that.*

"…but you would see the buckshot if you opened up your eyes."

Denice, a.k.a. Dee-Dee, gives her man Charlie a little wink and a smile as they crest the hill racing toward the little town of Jacumba. The Golden Acorn Casino is a distant shadow in the rearview mirror.

Like spheroids in darkness, the only light is in the full moon dead ahead, shining off the glossy black pavement. Surrounded by desert on both sides at 2:00 a.m. in the high desert above San Diego, the spirits of a thousand souls wander about, seeking freedom they'll never find.

Hundreds of jackrabbits race across the road from both sides, causing Denice to ask, "What's with all the freaking rabbits?"

Charlie slows down the Blazer, which is unusual for him. *Slow* is typically not on Charlie's radar. "Beats me," he answers.

The night wind blows off the desert from Imperial Valley through the open window on Dee-Dee's side. Creeping along on the glossy blacktop, Charlie gives a low whistle. "Baby, this is some spooky shit. You hear that?"

Denice turns to face him. "Like a moaning on the wind. I can feel the sadness." She shakes her head, "Ghosts of failed attempts to cross."

Coming up to The Bridge of Sighs, an eighth of a mile from the Jacumba Elementary School, the two-way radio crackles to life: *Five for the ride, señor.*

Charlie keys the mic, "Ten-four," he replies nonchalantly. "Thirty seconds to Wiley."

Wile E. Coyote (or just "Wiley" for short) is the best in the business; fearless and tough as the desert he calls home. Years of the six-mile run from the Mexican border, through the hostile desert of the Kumeyaay Reservation, to the sleepy little town of Jacumba has turned his body into hardened brown steel. Mescal's his only true friend – besides Charlie and Denice.

Charlie flashes his lights three times as he comes round Fortress Hill to the front of the school. Right on cue, five shadowy figures run down from the top of the hill. Denice jumps out two feet before Charlie brings the big K-5 to a halt. She runs around to the back and drops the tailgate.

"*Pronto amigos. Ándale*, for chrissakes." She slams the tailgate shut as Charlie raises the electric tinted rear window. Denice jumps back into the passenger seat, smiles at her man and commands, "Haul ass, lover boy."

Charlie's already burning rubber, as he shifts into second gear. He looks in the rearview mirror at the wide-eyed, exhausted men in the back and says, "Okay, boys, hands and feet inside the vehicle at all times. We should be arriving in Los Angeles inside of two hours. Enjoy the ride and welcome to the Jacumba Connection."

Denice rolls her eyes. "Very funny Captain Clown." Throwing her left arm over the back of the seat, she turns to the group and says, "Hey, y'all hungry? You like Jack in the Box?"

Charlie cuts in, "Oh, sure, maybe they'd like a taco, honey. Jack's got tacos." And then under his breath, "Jesus. And she calls *me* Captain Clown."

"This ain't the first time it won't be the last, you fly down that highway going nowhere fast."

THE HUNTING GROUND
Prologue

Indian Gaming Facilities. That's the politically correct verbiage for Native American-run casinos, which are the perfect hunting grounds for illegal alien trafficking and drug smuggling brokers.

People gamble for all sorts of reasons: excitement, financial gain, self-abuse, obsessive-compulsive disorder brought on by one's addiction to one's own physical chemistry. Endorphins versus adrenaline, a classic cocktail brought to you by the almighty gamble.

Bet a dollar on your machine and 5cc of adrenaline races into your bloodstream as you anticipate your big win. Then the wheel...slowly...spins...to the top. *LOSER!* Your pancreas adds a little insulin to the mix. Suddenly you're over it; and not just because of insulin shock, but because now you're a mere twenty-three dollars away from blowing this month's mortgage.

Perfect.

Time to bet *another* dollar. Please, please, please, toss in a little more adrenaline. Your arms nervously roll around to the back of your head as the wheel spins. When that third seven creeps to the centerline, Mother Nature's morphine kicks in. Sweet. Like Charlie Sheen: "Winning!"

That happy rush envelopes your better judgment, so you collect your 800 bucks, hit the head for a couple tokes, and plan your next run at another machine for the big jackpot. After 18 hours of this chemical roller coaster your decision making process is toast. Not only have you lost this month's house payment, but your credit cards are maxed out and you're left sitting in front of a mocking machine, smiling at you after consuming every last cent you have.

As you mindlessly thumb through a pamphlet entitled *Responsible Gambling*, your thoughts turn to the idyllic, blissful marriage you *used* to have before you made the decision to gamble away the diaper money.

Enter the smuggling broker who can smell misery and spot a dark horse across a smoke-filled casino. He saunters over to the high roller in Reeboks and says, "No luck? Hmmm. You got a car? A truck? SUV? You want to make a thousand bucks in two hours?"

The image of your wife with a butcher knife in one hand and your penis in the other looms in your frontal lobes. This is a no-brainer. You look to the heavens and mouth the words, "Thank you, Jesus," and even thank your sinister broker for the chance to commit a federal felony.

The trap snaps shut. *Bam!* The sound bounces around your empty head and echoes out your ears.

But no one else hears it.

✠ ✠ ✠

There are five major casinos and two smaller ones in San Diego, California. At least one has an 18-hole golf course. Many have six-story hotels with VIP suites, swimming pools, and movie stars. Some are just glorified to-go holes with smelly, nappy carpet and abusive drunken Indians.

The Golden Acorn in Campo, California, is a combination casino and truck stop. It caters to the commercial freight industry that services San Diego from the Imperial Valley (a.k.a. the salad bowl of America) and all points in between.

Located at the top of the grade on Highway 8, south of the beautiful Cuyamaca Mountains that run parallel to the old Butterfield Stagecoach Line, the Golden Acorn resides on a well-traveled route that predates the Union Pacific Railroad. This enticing gateway to prosperity saw thousands of settlers who attempted the daunting task of completing the "pass" through the desert, by going up and over the boulder region, and through dry-ass uncertain mountains. You can still see the ghostly track from the expansive parking lot/gas pump area of this hilltop Indian gaming facility.

It pays for these tribes to have their own casinos. All this revenue has been a blessing to the tribes; most have spent wisely, subsidizing new healthcare facilities, childcare, schools, and other social programs. And some do a good job of reflecting their native culture while relieving you of the burden of carrying around too much cash while on the reservation. A few casinos even have large shopping malls with Gap stores and arts-and-crafts boutiques that sell Native American pottery made in China.

The Golden Acorn casino is off the beaten track for the "runners," but still caters to a decent crop of not-so-lucky, downright desperate targets. *Kind and helpful lifesavers* (better known as brokers of the game) harvest the down-and-out from the Golden Acorn's loud, exciting interior like migrant workers picking ripe tomatoes.

This is not to imply that any of the tribes condone criminal activity of any kind. On the contrary, they are vigilant against any form of corruption, ranging from organized crime to petty theft. In fact, they employ a collaborative of cameras to watch what's going on. However...these cameras have no microphones. Imagine that? And because they do not hire a squad of lip readers to mindlessly stare at security screens, it is safe to say, *it's safe to play* the broker game at The Golden Acorn.

But that is a story for a later chapter in this saga of money, loss, crime, sex, VIP gambling, drugs, hot-tubbing, and *crying-in-your-beer* drama.

And it all begins with Charlie and Denice DeVille – that's "DeVille" as in Cadillac, baby.

YIN TO MY YANG
Chapter 1

Charlie and Denice were a team in the true sense of the word. Few couples can spend almost every waking moment within arm's reach of each other without ending up knee-deep in divorce court or worse.

The love they shared ran the gamut of emotion, commitment, and trust. Their relationship continually evolved into something better with each change in, shall we say, *lifestyle*. Both in their 40's and in excellent shape, they'd raised their children past their 20's and gently booted them out of the nest. Now they could finally abandon the nine-to-five, middle-class, my-lawn-is-greener-than-your-lawn, PTA-ish neighborhood. Now they were free to partake in *something* a little more exciting and bold, if not downright crazy.

The bonds of trust and the longing for adventure were forged by years of hard work, dodging financial bullets (instead of real ones), and raising three daughters, which included dealing with a multitude of boyfriends and ex-boyfriends. Hard to tell which is worse? Imagine at 1:00 a.m. you awaken to BINK, BINK, BINK on your bedroom window. You patter to the window only to find some young man, pants around his thighs, heroin eyes, a ring through his nose and an eyebrow, throwing pebbles at the glass. Of course Charlie's response was to raise the window and shout, "Hey, genius, wrong freakin' window. Didn't do your homework, did ya? My girls don't date the brain-dead so beat feet before I shoot you in the dick. If you even have one."

Charlie was known in the neighborhood as an old-school kind of dad. If you wanted to date Mr. DeVille's girls, it was *"Drivers license and proof of insurance please. Your ride got current registration? No Japanese fast and furious crotch rockets. Harley Davidsons are acceptable with clean DMV. A firm handshake scores important 'man points' and a little sit down with a 'tell me a little about yourself, son,'"* kind of lecture. You passed if Mr. DeVille said, "Have her home by 12:30, do not turn off her cell phone, and make sure you compliment her mother on the way out the door or there won't be a second date."

The fact that these girls weren't his biological kids meant nothing to Charlie. He loved *his girls* with the overprotective ferocity of a lion, but at the same time he provided the soft-spoken heart and strong shoulder that Daddy's little girls need to grow up feeling safe and secure.

For those who have never lived with four women under one roof, their combined cycle is one of the great mysteries of the universe. It's a fact: a group of females living as a family unit will get their freaking periods all at the same time, almost to the hour. *"So shut up and leave me alone, dammit."*

Charlie will tell you that there are a few days every month that he was not in control of the girls or his household. Period.

The DeVille family circus was a happy, warm, and inviting place the other 26 days of the month.

So the bonds of love ran deep in all directions. Charlie would step in front of a bullet for Denice and vice versa.

Having both been born and raised in San Diego, California, Charlie and Denice were the hip parents. Their house was where the cool kids hung out.

Charlie made his living with his hands. He could build or construct anything he could break, blow up, or tear apart. Not that he could have ever been a success in any white-collar career. Instead of hacking away at a keyboard, he loved twisting wrenches, pounding hammers, sawing wood; basically creating anything handmade – a true motor-head and Renaissance man combined.

Denice was raised Catholic in San Carlos and surfed her way through high school. Charlie was raised Episcopalian and lived just ten miles away in Fletcher Hills along the canyon edge of El Cajon (where home base is now).

But in the way of magic and universal good things, their paths would not cross until years later...at San Diego Harley Davidson, no less. A great place to start a ride into the sunset.

LIFE IS SHORT - MAKE IT SWEET
Chapter 2

So we jump ahead about 10 years. Charlie and Denice have sold their little, white-picket-fence, suburban dream, even throwing in the lawn tractor and hedge trimmers at the closing table.

If you stay abreast of things like the Southern California real estate market, you learn that 10 years equity in a 1,700 square-foot home with a large yard ends up being a nice chunk of change. Enough, in fact, to outfit the two of them with some of the niceties they'd always dreamed of.

To start, they bought a 30-foot Airstream travel trailer, and then Charlie set about restoring a 1990 K-5 blazer with a removable fiberglass top.

Needless to say the outfitted Airstream was crammed full, but you could not tell how bloated it was until you opened a cabinet. Which Charlie was never allowed to do, owing to his inability to put said items back in the same box from which they came.

Charlie and Denice leased a perfect little commercial space from Timmy One-Hit's mother, a friend of the family since forever. She was a widow now, blessed wealthy by Timmy's dad, who also left Timmy a fat trust fund. Though it had only taken him a mere three years to smoke his fund away.

But even so, Charlie and Denice loved Timmy and took care of him on and off. Tim's mother was extremely grateful and proved to be very loyal by returning the favor later when Denice and Charlie ran into some rough patches.

But at this point, times were fabulous.

Right after closing on the old house, Charlie began working on Denice's Camaro. When Charlie had completed the '71, split front bumper, muscle car, it shook the pavement at idle. Safeway Foods was only a mere 8.6 seconds away.

Living out of a commercial space takes a special kind of tolerance for the inconvenient. But once they were on the road it was bliss. Of the things they loved most, traveling to casinos with RV parks and nice three-star hotels was tops on their list. If they got on a winning streak, they could comp a VIP suite. If they lost, they cozied up in the Airstream and then it was on to another destination, be it Las Vegas or Sturgis, North Dakota, or anywhere in between.

It was on these trips that Denice discovered her uncanny ability to win at the one-dollar Blazin' Seven machines. Charlie's take on it, should anyone ask was, "She's got a lucky horseshoe in her ass. I know, 'cuz I put it there. If she sits down, she wins. It's that simple."

Charlie and Denice were well-known at Barona and on a first name basis with just about everyone, from the VIP concierge to the cashiers who knew and loved them. When they won, everybody won. They tipped like crazy. Charlie and Denice were very superstitious about that. Every gambler has their lucky talisman, such as a rabbit's foot, special hat, or whatever. Denice's was in her ass (according to Charlie).

Everybody loves a winner. And to show their gratitude, the casino suits took pictures of the victors standing next to their winning machines before they were reset. Denice and Charlie had been in this position so often, they had a bedroom in the Airstream with one wall covered in Polaroids and 8 x 10 color glossies of their triumphs.

Friday and Saturday nights were crazy in the casinos, even the VIP high rollers were packed in. Around 4:00 or 5:00 a.m. the machines were audited, meaning all the cash was removed and the machines reset. Federal and state regulations mandate a certain rate of return for each dollar inserted, but when it pays, that's the gamble.

Realizing the video games were audited every 24 hours, Charlie and Denice found a way to improve their odds of *getting lucky*. They kept an eye on the big spenders and which games they were playing. At the same time, they would spend their gambling money slowly until 3:00 a.m. Then they would hit those stuffed machines, knowing they had to pay out before 5:00 a.m. at the latest to meet regulations.

They called these machines *fatties* as in "I watched that dumb-ass put 11 one-hundred-dollar bills in that triple diamond machine, spit a booger on the glass and walk out."

"Cool. You got a wet nap in your purse? I'm going to toss it twenty, talk nasty to it, and see if I can make it cum." *WINK. WINK.*

On this particular night, Charlie strolled over to a machine, sat down, pulled out a cancer stick and did his best *Andrew-Dice-Clay-lighter* thing. And as was customary in casino etiquette, he looked over at the guy sitting next to him (the poor schmuck's face was paved with bad decisions) and said, "Wassup? Winning?"

The guy positioned his forefinger and thumb at 90° to form an "L" at his forehead, indicating he was a loser.

"I feel your pain, man," commiserated Charlie. He then extended his hand. "Charlie." The guy tentatively shook it. "Like this fancy carpet? Yeah, I bought it," joked Charlie.

"I hear ya," the loser replied. "Been payin' the light bill here forever. Enjoy the AC, it's on me." He then stared blankly at the machine. "Got a bazillion dollars in this piece of shit."

"They're like video crack whores," agreed Charlie. "Whether they have a flat screen or pretty face, they'll leave ya with your pants around your ankles."

"Nice meetin' ya," said the loser, obviously ready to move on. "Charlie was it?"

"Yeah. Right back at ya."

"K. Hey, and just so you know, I'm a sign painter. You need a sign, here's my card."

After coming up this side of 500 big ones on the fatties, Charlie called the sign painter dude. "Hey, you still up here at Barona?"

"Yeah, my son's coming up. Thinking about waiting for him. Besides, headlights ain't working. And I don't need a ticket on top of being a broke dick dog."

"Hey, my wife and I love The Uninvited. How much to paint 'Love Bus' on my Airstream?"

From that day forward, the RV was appropriately called The Love Bus: *"It's a honey-dripping love vibe on a funky little bus…"*

THE LAW OF UNINTENDED CONSEQUENCES
Chapter 3

If you stop betting, you never have to lose. But all winning streaks must eventually come to an end. It was a slow death for the DeVille Family Trust. Not quite like a bad stock investment or a low yield portfolio, it just couldn't sustain Charlie and Denice's *life's-a-gamble-when-you-ramble* attitude forever.

It started with: "I'm sorry, Mr. DeVille, but your card was declined."

"Run it again."

"Yes, sir."

Charlie glared at his wife. "You pay the bill?"

"I thought I did," she answered.

The waitress returned with a stern look. "Do you have another card, sir?"

"Leave it. We'll pay cash." Charlie looked to Denice for help. "How you fixed for cash?"

She handed him two twenties. He slipped the bills into the black leather check valise. "Hey, babe, maybe we should take a walk back to the Love Bus, jump on somebody's wi-fi and find out what the hell's going on."

"Good luck with that," she answered. "Up in these mountains?"

As they exited the smoke filled circus atmosphere, the sky was painted in violet and orange. The smell of night blooming jasmine gave the promise of spring. They both inhaled deeply, tasting the crisp evening air. And as gamblers do, they lit up a smoke.

Sitting on a bench tucked back off the trail to the campground, they watched the sun sink into the western sky. Both knew the answer to the question Charlie had posed in the café – they were running out of mad money, draining the last golden drops from their fund fountain.

Charlie looked over his right shoulder at Denice. "How close are we to fiscal oblivion?"

Denice sighed. "I can hear the bomb whistle from where we're sitting."

"Should we even bother to Google it?" he asked sarcastically.

That was Charlie's action word for research, depending on his mood. *Go fucking Google it.* Very seldom did he talk that way to his Pumkin, and never when it came to cash flow.

His inquiry brought an unwanted response. "To tell the truth, honey, we're screwed. Let's face facts. We can't retire at 42. That's a gamble in itself."

"Well. Too much analysis means not enough time to live," summed up Charlie.

Unfortunately that philosophy would come back to haunt them as, at that very moment, a cyber thief was knee-deep in their 401(k). And like a ringmaster, the culprit expertly diverted dollars from their crazy-ass circus to his PayPal account.

And with that, the party was over.

It was time to circle the wagons.

✠ ✠ ✠

The conversation on the drive to home base was tense. "How the hell did this happen?" he asked. Charlie wondered if he should update his resume.

"I'm not sure," countered Denice. "But paying bills online, slingin' plastic all over hell's half acre. Not to mention those cheesy ATMs in every casino. Someone must've...Shit I don't know." She turned both palms up and shrugged her shoulders.

Charlie pounded his fist onto the wheel. "Okay, well, we'll fall back ten and punt. Regroup. We'll drop off the Love Bus and go see Mr. Moneyman at *Melon, Morrison and what-the-fuck*. Find out what our options are."

"By options, you mean what?"

"You know, call the cops. File a report. Have a nervous breakdown, I don't know. Jesus, honey, we can't just pretend it didn't happen." Deep down Charlie felt his manhood had somehow just had its ass kicked.

Denice turned away from Charlie, stared out the window, and with a kind of guilty childlike voice said, "Not my fault, babe, please don't yell at me."

And as if Jesus were the disc jockey, right on cue Billie Holiday started to sing *Cry me a River* on the radio.

✠ ✠ ✠

Walking out of the attorney's office, the sky was a noncommittal gray. Maybe rain, maybe not. The concrete jungle of downtown San Diego, with its horns blaring and panhandlers begging, the smell of moist concrete and exhaust fumes was a perfect backdrop to receive bad news. No ifs, ands, or buts. They were a short one-month away from holding their own sign that read, *Will work for food.*

The conversation with their moneyman, Mr. Morrison, went like this:

"Mr. and Mrs. DeVille," adjusting his glasses upward on the bridge of his nose, "I'm afraid we have some rather bad news."

Charlie mumbled sarcastically, "Great."

Mr. Morrison continued, "There's been a breach of security in the credit line side of your 401(k), which as you know, can be accessed through your credit card."

Denice fidgeted in her chair, hung her head chin to chest, stared at the ten-thousand-dollar Persian rug, and let loose a small sigh.

Morrison leaned back in his ergonomic office chair and concluded, "This could be a multitude of things. Cyber theft is the new version of highway robbery. These guys come at us from every angle, from every country on the planet. We've got a slew of IT people trying to dodge bullets and build firewalls while running this new breed of conmen into ground. At this point...I just don't know."

Silence.

"However, our investigations are closing in on the apex of the break. There seems to be a problem surrounding a credit card purchase at...let me see here..." He looked down at a folder on his desk. "Lee's Truck Recycling."

Denice looked sideways at her husband and said, "Lee's place? Really, Charlie? Really? You know Lee's a crack head."

"Hey, he's not a crack head. He just smokes some meth once in a while."

"Well, that's comforting," Denice replied tartly.

Charlie defended his honor. "Probably not one of my best decisions, but he had the best price."

Denice crossed her arms over her chest. "Oh for God's sake, don't be a moron, Charlie. Now is not the time."

Mr. Morrison, holding up both hands palms out in a gesture of retaining-calm, spoke with a positive inflection in his voice. "Look, who knows? There may be recourse. There's a chance we might find the bad guys." But then eager to dodge liability added, "But, honestly, I would not count on it."

On the way down the hall to the elevator Denice stopped and said, "Give me your credit cards."

"What?"

"You heard me."

"Don't treat me like a child."

"Then don't shop at the local drug addict's using our credit card."

"Are you saying this is my fault?"

"What I'm saying is you don't think things through."

Charlie thought about that for a moment. Reaching down to the lizard part of his brain he could not find a way out of this one. "You're probably right," he finally relented. *Damn, I hate it when she's got a point.*

✠　✠　✠

On the ride back from *Melon, Morrison, and Bad News* Denice suggested, "Let's make the rounds and call in markers," which is casino lingo for hit the big five Indian gaming facilities and retrieve monies they lent to other desperate souls just like themselves.

"Sounds like a plan. How's the horseshoe?"

"Ask me later, when I sit down at my favorite machine."

"Okay, let's go to Viejas and find fat Larry."

Scary Larry was into them for about five dead presidents, specifically Ben Franklins. Which makes no sense, since Ben Franklin was never president, and was definitely too smart to be your garden-variety politician.

"You think the sweaty bastard will have it?" Charlie asked.

"Yeah," she answered tentatively. "But you'll probably have to turn him upside down and shake it out of him to get it."

Scary Larry. Larry the Fairy. *That* Larry. Now *there* was a guy who knew the meaning of "fall from grace." An ex-vice president at a La Jolla savings and loan, he was an easy mark to spot in a crowded casino; ugly green suit, red tie, sweaty neck stains on his *used-to-be-white* shirt. Lost his white-collar job in the banking industry, because they frown on meth addicts who gamble and pay for sex.

Larry moved to Jacumba to be closer to the *real* love of his life – casinos.

The parking lot was crowded as they found a spot for the Blazer.

"It's Friday. Three more hours and the vampires emerge," said Charlie stoically.

"Let's find Larry before the full moon rises."

Camacho Cortez, the partially insane proprietor of Hotel Mexico, thought he was the reincarnation of Pancho Villa. In his head the whistle from the film *Gunfight at O.K. Corral* ran on a continuous loop. His floppy Indiana Jones hat did nothing to shield his face from the intense desert sun. But his huge, droopy, Deputy Dog mustache covered the lower half of his face like SPF 1,000.

He walked through the unpaved dirt streets of his village, seven miles from the United States border, with that tune bouncing around inside his noggin, looking all-the-world like a gunfighter; including that obligatory stupid hat and $1,100 over-the-top snakeskin boots.

His father was Lopez Cortez, head of the Cortez Cartel. Infamous smugglers, the family transported everything from people to guns to drugs over the borders of South America and on up into the U.S. Historically, they were the best in the business.

Camacho, being the firstborn son and next in line to fill his father's shoes (which were $3,000 ostrich skin boots, by the way) was a hands-on, upper-level operative. He ran the Hotel Mexico Bar and Grill, a two-story adobe and stucco affair with an arched doorway. Windows, crowded with neon signs, fronted a small patio. The signs promised cold beer and air-conditioning, a promise they routinely failed to keep. The entire structure was encased in a lime green and bright yellow lacquer slathered on so thick it could withstand the effects of a low-yield atomic bomb.

Set back from the dirt road of Main Street, the blue and yellow Corona umbrellas on the patio fluttered in the breeze. And if you looked closely, a decapitated pig's head rested on a table. You could smell the rest of the doomed animal cooking on a spit around the side of the hotel.

Yes, *carnitas* was on the menu 24/7. Camacho loved his roasted pork.

The hotel accommodations took up the entire second floor of the bar and doubled as a staging area for thousands of people past and present, preparing for Mr. Toad's Wild Ride to the border fence. Mr. Toad being Macho Camacho Cortez, and the wild ride being his beloved four-wheel-drive Ford Bronco.

Camacho's cousin, Pelón, tended the bar. Bald as an eagle and missing his left eye (a direct result of an encounter with an unruly customer sporting a long fingernail), Pelón stood under a three-bladed ceiling fan that moved so slowly it circulated no air at all. As Camacho entered the bar he slurred, "Eh, it's hotter than your sister when she sits on my mustache." He preened his mighty facial hair and continued, "Pour me a shot of Patron and a cold *Dos XX* lager, Cyclops."

"Funny, Little Man," Pelón responded sarcastically. "My sister would come nowhere near you or your filthy mustache. Ugh. Your mouth smells like an Iguana lives in there."

"Quiet, you fool. I have more hair on my handsome face than you have on your entire head. Bald men should not be allowed to speak."

The sun was starting to set. Twilight gave way to the pink and red from the neon signs flicking *Corona*, *Patron*, *Tequila*, and cold *cerveza*. They glowed off Pelón's shiny pate. It looked to Camacho like Pelón had his head in the microwave and that it was just about to burst.

Outside the wind blew and swirled dust around a '62 Impala that belonged to a customer currently asleep under a table. It was a hot, arid wind, perfect for the procreation of cacti and snakes. It shrieked in between boulders and warmed the hearts of a million scorpions.

"Pelón, the weather is perfect for the run. How many upstairs?"

"Nine. Two will not make it."

Camacho's face twisted, his brow raised. "Why is that?"

"They are gay." Pelón's one good eye had the special powers of insight into the hearts and minds of men.

Camacho laughed, "You are gay, too, *señor*? It takes a gay man to know a gay man." He was on a roll and would not stop. "Your father was gay or you would have hair."

Pelón replied calmly, "I'm just warning you, they shall perish in the desert."

Holding his index finger straight up at the ceiling, Camacho grumbled, "Just because you play butt darts does not mean you can't follow a coyote across the desert. You are an imbecile."

Pelón remained unflappable. "I have seen it with my eye, *el jefe*."

To indicate that there was no further discussion required, Camacho smoothed his 'stash and queried, "Jesus, Mary, Joseph and the donkey, are the people ready or not? Are they all here? Have you checked with your *all-seeing* eye?"

Doing his best Lon Chaney impersonation Pelón replied, "Yes, Master. I will load them in the Bronco before the stroke of midnight."

"That is a perfect accent for you, Cyclops. Now quit this foolishness and let's have another shot." Camacho slapped the bar with his hand to punctuate his command.

✠ ✠ ✠

The deal goes down like this: You place an international call to a number in Mexico City from your location in the good ole *U-S-of-A*. Someone from Ramona Flores' office answers. You provide them the name of the loved one you wish to magically appear in a shopping mall parking lot somewhere in Los Angeles, California. The friendly operator gives you an account number and a code. You electronically transfer $2,850 into the account. When the transfer is verified your confirmation is a five-digit code. You make another international call to your loved one, wherever they may be in Mexico, and give them the code. All they need to do is find their way to Hotel Mexico, smile at Pelón's one good eyeball, and hand him the code. Then it's *FOLLOW ME TO AMERICA*.

That $2,850 buys a guaranteed "crossing" no matter how many times it takes, providing the seven-mile bonsai, off-road trip to a hole in the fence, where Wiley Coyote drags you through six miles of sand, cacti, and scorpions. Then, if the trip doesn't kill you, you get picked up just past the Kumeyaay Reservation by a driver/runner for a clandestine cruise, thick with Border Patrol and checkpoints, to a meet-up in L.A.

One million things can go wrong running this tricky gauntlet those in the business call the *Jacumba Connection*.

WHERE RUBBER MEETS THE ROAD
Chapter 5

Charlie put the K-5 in park, leaned over to his right and kissed Denice for good luck on the mouth, like lovers do. Looking her in the eye he said, "You and me baby, till the wheels fall off."

"Atta boy, handsome. Give a girl some hope."

He winked, "Maybe later, baby. Right now we gotta find Larry."

Denice thought, *If he wasn't my man-candy, I just might bring his ego down a notch.* But instead she simply said, "Promises, promises."

Her sassy grin lit up her whole face and Charlie thought to himself, *If smiles were dollars, I'd be the richest man alive.*

They pushed the big heavy glass doors to the casino open and entered. Their senses were immediately assaulted with blinding lights, *bings, bongs,* and crazy melodies (some engineer, no doubt, who thought a stupid tune spewing from a one-armed bandit would make you want to put more money in it), as well as the smell of 1,000 different perfumes, mixed with smoke, and cheap buffet aromas. Lovely.

But to Charlie and Denice it smelled like money. Walking hand-in-hand she said, "Let's start in back and work our way to VIP."

Charlie stopped to have a smoke, looked at Denice, and motioned toward his pack. "No, thanks, hon. I'd just wind up burnin' somebody in this crowd."

Charlie smiled knowingly. He'd seen it happen more than once. Guys trying to cop a feel of Dee's 38 double D's turned sideways in a crowded aisle. After which they would just happen to get burned by Charlie's cigarette *on accident*. Even if the accident was five minutes later.

Denice didn't like setting Charlie off by snitching on misdemeanor drive-by perversion. She handled these pervs just fine on her own, and had since high school. But anything more serious than a minor groping and Denice would tell Charlie. About three seconds later the pervert would be introduced to the colorful casino carpet and the wonderful world of good manners. Dumb-ass.

They found Larry on the dollar poker machines. He was sitting on the end closest to the wall. His suit jacket resting on his lap, a smoldering cigarette dangling from his fat, porky lips. He slapped the touch screen with such a forceful *thunk* you could hear it over the circus din.

Beads of sweat collected around Larry's hairline and the back of his neck. Charlie thought he could smell burnt meat. *Probably this idiot's brain cells.* He approached Larry from his left side, and Denice stood behind, holding her nose.

"What's up, Larry?"

"Busy right now, man." Larry replied without looking away from his machine.

Glancing at Larry's money-line, Charlie noticed Larry was up $263 and was betting two dollars a hand.

"So here's the thing, Lar, Denice and me, we're runnin' low on fun chips. So that requires me to ask you for the five Benjamin's you owe us."

Larry closed his left eye as the smoke curled up into it, which caused him to drop ash in his lap and onto his jacket.

"Ain't got it. Not right now, anyway."

"Looks like half of it's on your machine," piped in Denice from behind.

Larry shifted in his seat, which apparently made it easier for him put his foot in his mouth. "Hey, Chuck, tell the tramp to put a sock in it, would ya?"

Words cannot express what a huge mistake that comment was. Charlie could hear the "snap" inside his head. Denice's eyes rolled as she slowly shook her head from side to side. She took half a step back, knowing full well that Larry had put a match to Charlie's fuse.

Charlie grabbed the pointy end of Larry's tie with his right hand and the knot with his left, and pushed Larry back until his head slammed into the wall, his fat body conveniently shrouding the action from the eye-in-the-sky cameras. Then for all he was worth, Charlie yanked on the pointy end of Larry's tie.

Two things happened: Larry's sweaty collar flat-out disappeared into his fat neck. And then a gurgling sound emanated from his contorted pie hole.

Without missing a beat, Charlie again pulled Larry's tie and re-slammed the lout's head against the wall with a thud that wrung the poor guy's bell – which brought a smile to Charlie's face.

Charlie glanced at his baby-cakes and quietly said, "Hit the button and cash him out, babe."

Denice's hand flew to the cash-out button and gold coins spewed into the tray with a *ding, da-ding, ding*.

Turning his attention back to Larry, Charlie commanded, "Now listen up here, bitch. Apologize to my wife."

Larry's eyes bulged and rolled back into his head, like he was trying to look at Denice. But all Larry could manage was a *cough*, a *gag* and some pathetic choking.

"Honey," Denice offered evenly, "he can't say shit. You're choking the life out of him."

Charlie snickered. "Oh. Yeah." He loosened his grip slightly.

Larry struggled to speak. "Um (*cough*), Sorry, Dee. Don't know what I was (*cough*) thinking."

Denice had a paper bucket in her left hand and was quickly digging coins out of the receiver tray with her right. "Okay, Larry, well, Charlie's kinda protective. You know that. I don't know why you'd call me a tramp. Sorta stupid on your part."

"You still owe us $237, asshole," Charlie reminded Larry. "Now reach into those fat-assed Dockers and pay the lady." Denice held the paper bucket about six inches from Larry's face.

Charlie released his grip completely and stepped back just enough to allow Larry room enough to dig his hand into his humongous pants.

Sitting there with his red tie on sideways, Larry whined, "That's all I got, man. Don't take it all!"

Charlie laughed out loud. "I was only askin' you to share. Just a hundred, so Dee could put her horseshoe to work. But no, you had to go and get your needle stuck on stupid."

Rubbing his head where it had been introduced to the wall, Larry tried to collect himself. "Look, I know how you can make $1,000 in two hours."

"I'm listening," Charlie said.

"Runnin' Mexicans to L.A. Easy. You put a couple of 'em in your truck and..."

Charlie slapped Larry on the back of the head like a child trying to steal candy. "Look, dumb-ass, I just want what you owe us." He looked at Denice. "Count me out 36."

She did, and he tossed the coins into Larry's tray. "You still owe me 300. Funny how you didn't have to kick *my* ass to borrow it. Maybe you can come up on 36. Otherwise you take *your* fat ass to L.A. and get the money to pay me."

Denice sympathetically put her hand on Larry's shoulder. "Try to behave yourself, hon," she said. "Don't be testing everyone's patience. Remember, not all girls are tramps. Just the ones that sleep with you."

Charlie roared with laughter. "Ha! Burn. She got you, bud. Burn!" He turned to Denice. "Good one, honey."

Charlie and Denice walked away confidently. "Yeah, that was smooth, honey," Charlie complimented his wife. "Burned him. Ha ha. Lard ass."

They wandered over to the Blazin' Sevens and saddled up. Charlie turned to watch his Pumkin play. Unfortunately, Denice's horseshoe wasn't working. She looked over at Charlie. Her husband was lost in thought, staring blankly into the Cosmos. She knew that stare well, the internal wheels in motion. Searching for an answer to their current crisis.

"Whatcha thinking about?" she asked her man.

"The lease payment on home base. Timmy's mom's pissed. She wants the rent."

Denice pulled a smoke from her purse. As usual Charlie's lighter was aflame, as she brought the cigarette to her lips. "Any ideas?"

"Not a clue," Charlie confessed.

"Not easy being king, eh, hon?"

Charlie smiled. He put the lighter back in his leather jacket. "Heavy is the head that wears the crown." At the moment he really did feel like a tragic character.

Denice smiled empathetically, moved by Charlie's rare show of vulnerability. "What now, babe?" she asked casually.

He shrugged slightly. "Let's cruise up to the store at Live Oak Springs and get a ten-dollar phone card. How much do we have left?"

Denice checked the DeVille fortune. "Sixteen-seventy-six. And three dollars in gold tokens. But we need smokes, too."

"We got zero without a phone," he reminded her. "So after cigarettes we're lookin' at...complete poverty." Charlie slapped his knees with both hands, stood up, and offered a hand to his lamb-chop.

Denice snuffed out her smoke, grabbed his hand and said, "Let's make like horse shit and hit the trail".

They headed toward the exit. Once they went through the revolving doors, they saw it was already dark outside. The night was hot and dry. The lights of the casino cast ominous shadows across the parking lot. It was desolate and windblown. Out in the distance the blazer looked like a ship on a reef with a broken back, standing alone out there forlorn and stranded.

Much like Charlie and Denice DeVille.

FIVE FINGER DEATH PUNCH
Chapter 6

In the casino parking lot Charlie opened the door for his wife. Denice stepped behind him to jump into the truck. A figure stepped out of the darkness. At this point all Charlie could see was the business end of a Desert Eagle chamber for a .357 pointed at his forehead. Behind the big ol' pistol was a rather small wanna-be gangster. Saggy pants. Black hoody. Obviously scared shitless.

"Give me your money, motherfucker, or I'll split your skull."

His cold black eyes bounced back and forth from Charlie to Denice. *Cocky little bastard,* was the last thing Charlie thought before going on autopilot.

As the dirt-bag's eyes move back to Denice, in literally the blink of an eye, Charlie's left hand came up palm out, he grabbed the barrel, twisted it counter clockwise as he pushed down and away. The only sound was the snap of bone as the trigger-guard broke the asshole's index finger.

Charlie planted his right foot behind him to steady himself. His punch started out low and compressed as it climbed his spine, and then thundered through his right shoulder. It gained momentum down his forearm and virtually exploded through his clenched fist as it crushed the thug's left orbital socket, ruining the poor jerk's face an instant before he hit the ground like a sack of smashed moldy melons.

Denice slid past Charlie, took three quick steps around the prostrate body and kicked the big ass handgun away and out of reach. She turned to face Charlie, who was holding his painful right hand.

"Oh dear...Oh my...This...This is just terrible," she stammered in a panicked whisper.

Charlie looked down at Denice. "Christ Dee, he was gonna kill me."

"No, no it's not that. It's...Oh god, my panties are soaked. That was...It was...I swear you could take me on the hood of this car right now!"

Charlie looked from his hand to the hood and back to his hand and in a childish voice whined, "My hand really hurts, Dee."

Suddenly two tribal police officers silently drove up to them in a fancy electric golf cart, thus cutting short any options for sudden car hood sex. Both officers got out, one was on his Motorola talking to dispatch. The other with his hand on his holstered nine-millimeter. They took in the scene. It was pretty evident what went down. Denice excitedly explained the five-finger death punch while the officer checked for a pulse and, finding one, said, "Better call EMS, Lloyd. Get an ambulance out here. He's still breathing."

Lloyd shook his head. "Man, that's some bad medicine right there."

Charlie has a big, ugly, gorilla inside of him. He keeps it chained down tight, right behind his give-a-shit switch. He brings it out only in emergencies.

Don't. Poke. The gorilla.

✠ ✠ ✠

The twelve-mile trip from Viejas to Live Oak Springs was uphill; the *grade,* as locals called it. Beyond the main drag there was a winding road that continued up that steep mountain, where hang gliders dared the dirt switchbacks to ride the desert thermals like human falcons.

As you crested the mountaintop by car, the main road slipped slowly into a small, bowl-shaped valley, with the freeway running east, directly through the center. Kitchen Creek Road was on your right and at the base of the high mountain, on your left as you entered the valley, was the ominous Border Patrol checkpoint.

Above Kitchen Creek, atop the mountain peaks on the right, were the dirt roads of Anderson Truck Trails – a labyrinth of roads used by dump trucks hauling sand, granite, fieldstone and rock for the cement industry. At night all you could see were the glow of the neon signs, alerting you to the Casino truck stop of the Campo band of Kumeyaay Indians. Better known today as the "Old Highway 8" exit, it's part of the Butterfield Stagecoach Road, which was used by thousands of settlers to cross the mountains to get to the Pacific Ocean.

This exit was where Charlie and Denice realized they had less than a quarter tank of fuel left. "Sweet," Charlie grunted sarcastically, looking at the gauge. "Almost outta gas. Let's pull in here to the Acorn and do a hot lap around the casino floor. Maybe we can hustle up some gas money."

Charlie looked at Denice, as if he had let her down. But then, trying to hide behind false hope he added, "If wishes were horses, beggars would ride." One of his father's many pearls of wisdom bestowed upon the three boys Charlie's parents raised with moral fiber in Southern California – a place traditionally short on morals or fiber.

As Charlie drove around the parking lot Denice commented, "Place looks kinda empty."

"Just our luck," Charlie replied. He had already written this day off to failure.

After he parked he came around to open Denice's door. She stepped out into the crisp mountain air. "Honey, grab my purse please?" She put on her sweater.

"Why? It's empty." But as he picked it up he stood corrected. "Guess not."

Denice's purse was always large, always packed, and always it seemed to Charlie, bottomless. He would ask, "Got any Chapstick?" Denice would then rummage around in her cavernous purse, digging deep, and excavate not one, but two kinds. "Cherry or Mentholyptis," she would offer. "Or I have some Vaseline."

As they made their way through the *porte cochere*, and passed the entrance doors, the place was hauntingly quiet – only a few patrons, half asleep, sitting at the machines.

"Gotta pee, handsome." Denice suddenly announced. "Back in a flash."

Charlie loitered at the entrance of the ladies' room, standing guard in case some perv rushed through the door to check out his wife's panties around her ankles.

Standing sentry, waiting around for their women to do whatever it is they do, is a mindless thing *men do*, Charlie thought. Maybe in our instinctive memory we worry about getting eaten by some wild animal while taking a leak. Plus, it would've been hard to run with panties around your ankles. *Did they even wear panties back then? Hmmm. Probably not.*

"This place is a graveyard," Charlie concluded when Denice returned. "Let's blow this off and get to Live Oak before the store closes."

Charlie gently slapped her pretty little backside on the way out of the ladies' room. As they exited, she rolled her hips with that hooker stroll that women do when they want to be noticed and followed.

✠ ✠ ✠

Live Oak Springs was a quarter-mile down old Highway 8 towards Jacumba. A beautiful little retreat nestled in the midst of lush oak trees, consisting of both short scrub oak and majestic California White Oak. A general store with two old-fashioned gas pumps stood at the entrance. After that, six small A-frame cabins lined up in a row, each complete with its own Jacuzzi and upstairs loft. The hot tub combined with a little Franklin stove was merely a prelude to a wonderfully romantic evening.

Farther up the hillside was the restaurant, run by a lovely couple that kept a hearth fire burning and served excellent home-style meals with a smile.

Even farther up were mobile homes for visitors that fell under the spell of clean, fresh air, and the secluded nature of this place – due to the fact it was bordered on two sides by the Kumeyaay Indian reservation.

If you went far enough up the hillside, where the road turns to dirt, and followed it another quarter of a mile you'd find a small, silver, single-axle trailer sitting on a small slice of Indian land, and one crazy Croatian named Valentino.

Charlie pulled the K-5 into the store parking lot, jumped out looking back through the open door, and said to Denice, "Gimme all your money, honey."

She dove deep into the huge chasm she called a purse and extracted fifteen dollars. "Don't spend it all in one place."

"Very funny," he said, as he stuffed the bills in his jeans.

Inside the store he confidently laid his money on the counter. "Ten-dollar phone card and a pack of Marlboro lights, please."

"That'll be sixteen-seventy-seven, please," replied the young man behind the counter.

Charlie stood there dumbfounded. "You're shitin' me, right?"

The clerk replied equally dumbfounded. "No, sir. With tax it's..."

"Hold up slick," Charlie interrupted. "I'll be right back."

As Charlie approached the truck he made a *roll-down-your-window* motion to Denice. She complied.

"I need the sixteen-seventy-seven," he said to her.

"What?"

"Tax."

Again she went to the magical purse and started pulling out the top layer, which included camping supplies, toothbrushes, and extra panties, all in search of the bottom of her purse.

"Jesus, babe, come on," Charlie pleaded impatiently.

"Just a minute, it's in here somewhere."

How many freakin' times have I heard that before, thought Charlie.

As Denice rummaged toward the bottom of her purse, Charlie listened to her mumble into her open handbag. "What happened to my normal life, huh? This is just…pathetic…" She continued as she pillaged her purse, but Charlie couldn't quite make out all of her muttering, something about "scrounging around for quarters." But the one thing Charlie did understand was Pumkin's body language, which clearly stated, *Batten down the hatches, baby, a storm's a comin'.* "I miss my house, my, my stuff…" Denice continued on the verge of tears. "I miss my kids…my babies, dammit!"

She finally stopped digging and turned her head towards Charlie, who was leaning on the door, looking through the window opening. Her eyes misted over. "What happened to the life I had where my husband didn't have to hurt people… on purpose? Is this my new normal? Oh Charlie, I think I'm gonna cry!"

Charlie confirmed, "Too late, Pumkin," and reached through the window to wipe a tear from her cheek. He brought it to his tongue and thought, *a drop of truth serum…salty, and it tastes like failure.*

For the first time in their relationship Big Chuck had nothing, zip. No snappy come back. No words of wisdom. All he had was, "I love you, Pumkin." And her tears on his lips.

With a dash of somber resignation in her eyes she handed Charlie some more change. "The sum total of our wealth," she sniffed. "Except for three tokens."

Charlie looked down at the miniscule pile of coins, brought his eyes up to meet Dee's and said cynically, "Well babe, this is a place we've never been before. Just. Bitchin'. Fab-u-lous." He dismissively turned on his heel and went back into the store, frustrated.

After a few minutes, Charlie came back out and jumped into the driver's seat. "Looks like we're campin' in the back tonight." He pointed to the rear of the K-5. With the seat down, there was plenty of room, and Dee always stocked blankets and pillows, just in case a nap was called for, or they were on a road trip.

✠　✠　✠

Under a pitch-black sky backlit by the celestial glow of the Milky Way, crickets and katydids competed to fill the night air with song. The stillness mixed with starlight came close to erasing their thoughts of being broke. Charlie parked under a huge old tree, wondering what stories the old man could share. Three hundred years was nothing to a mountain oak.

Denice prepared the sleeping arrangements while Charlie slid the rear curtains closed, locked the doors, flipped the switch for the RV batteries, and turned on the dome lights.

When all was secured, they lay together in the cozy blankets, just the two of them against the world. "I love you, Pumkin," Charlie whispered. "I'm so sorry I…"

Denice turned, inches from her man's face. "Don't even, Charlie," she commanded. And before he could say anything she quickly added, "Do you remember when we first met? We were both looking for that *can't-go-to-sleep* kind of love that keeps you awake at night because you can't stop thinking about the other person. It wasn't about endless money."

"Yeah, I remember," answered Charlie. He smiled at the thought. "We had to save up to go to a movie. We ate Ramen noodles three times a week."

A little chuckle escaped Denice as she reminisced, "No cable. We watched whatever old movies happened to be on that fuzzy, old RCA."

Charlie was right there with her. "Burning popcorn on that piece of shit thrift store popcorn maker," he continued, as he nuzzled Denice. He was so close to her now he could smell her minty breath.

She reached up and moved a strand of hair out of Charlie's face and whispered, "I can still see you running outside in the rain to adjust the antenna. Looking like a wet puppy, smiling when the picture was finally perfect."

Charlie was silent, going back in his mind. A bigger smile slowly spread across his stoic face.

Denice continued to voice her thoughts. "*That* was struggle, handsome. Shoes for the girls, you working two jobs. Looking back, we were happy. We came through okay. We always find a way."

"Thanks, babe." Her confidence in him gave him hope. He kissed her forehead, her cheek, and finally her lips. "Till the wheels fall off..."

She smiled and replied quietly, "Till the wheels fall off, handsome."

✠ ✠ ✠

Dawn broke with rays of pure sunshine through the windshield and into Denice's eyes. With the sound of Blue Jays skittering in the trees, and the smell of a fire burning in a fireplace somewhere, she greeted the dawn with "Shit, I need a freakin' tampon."

"Huh?" Charlie stirred, trying to show support, even though he was half asleep.

Denice was once again delving into the maw of her beast-of-a-bag that to Charlie looked like the open mouth of a killer whale.

"I can't freakin' believe I don't have a freakin' tampon." Charlie's Dee-Dee, his little lammy chop, did not believe in using the F-word. Dropping the F-bomb was taboo, mostly because of raising the girls. They copy everything you say. Every parent learns that the hard way. When at some perfect, quite, awkward moment your little princess says, "Fuck, I dropped my crayon." Or "Pick up my fucking crayon, please," to her preschool teacher, that's always a pleasant parent-teacher conference.

Charlie smiled and said, "You don't need to swear, potty mouth."

"Shit, shit, shit." She looked lost, like a little kid who couldn't find her Barbie lunchbox. "Oh Charlie, I'm sorry. I need a thingy, a pad or…You know…a poon." Her eyes welled up with premenstrual tears.

"Don't you worry, I'm on it, babe. I'm gonna walk into that restaurant, sell that man a service on his equipment, or wash dishes, or whatever. Just let me get my pants on."

"Think it will work?" Denise asked desperately.

"Watch me pull a rabbit out of a hat," her man replied without an ounce of worry.

There was no question that Charlie could turn on the charm when he needed something. Plus, he was a consummate professional when it came to all things mechanical, like restaurant equipment, water heaters, air conditioners, furnaces, motors, or anything that needed to *run*.

With all his assets, he knew he practically had Denice's much-needed tampons in his back pocket.

He walked into the restaurant, went up to the guy who looked like he was in charge and, extending his hand, announced, "Hi, I'm Charlie DeVille."

To get the ball rolling he always opened with a firm handshake.

"I'm Ron," replied the man pleasantly. "How can I help you?"

"My wife and I are stuck like Chuck in your campground." He went on to tell Ron about all his qualifications, his present dilemma, his desire to pay for the overnight spot and the status of the DeVille fortune. But the big emphasis was on the *no-tampon* problem.

Thank God for Ron's wife, Lily. "Oh dear," she empathized. "That's not good."

Charlie wheeled and dealed. "Ma'am, I'm not asking for a handout. I'll work for breakfast and a box of tampons."

"Bless your heart, Charlie," Lily responded.

"I'll service your equipment, wash dishes, or burn a biscuit. No, actually I can't cook, so don't let me near a griddle."

They all shared a laugh.

The way of a charitable world is when God's grace befalls the good and the planets line up in perfect order, which seems to be rare indeed, but sometimes it happens. Charlie walked out of the restaurant with the key to cabin #2 (the Honeymoon Suite), accompanied by the promise of a country breakfast and a temporary job. And last but not least, half a box of regular Kotex tampons.

As Denice saw Charlie approach she rolled down the truck window and looked at her man eagerly.

Charlie smiled wide. "Jim Dandy to the rescue." He slid the box of tampons through the window while holding up the key to their cabin. "How about a bath in a Jacuzzi?"

"Oh. My. GOD! You're kidding. How?"

"Livin' in the moment, babe. Let's just relish this little victory for a second." He stood frozen in time. "Okay. I'm done. Now let's roll."

Denice squealed with delight as Charlie hopped into the K-5.

It was a ninety-second drive to the cabin and a hot bath.

THE NIGHT BELONGS
TO WILD THINGS
Chapter 7

The people above the bar had a million questions: "When are we leaving?" "Does the AC work…? It says cold air-conditioning. Where is it?" "You ever thought of tattooing an eyeball on your eyelid, or flames on your bald-ass head?"

Pelón (which means bald in Spanish) was used to the nervous interrogation by the people that had either waited all their lives for this moment, or were pissed they had to try again.

"Okay everybody…Get naked," Pelón requested. This brought a bevy of groans and one giggle from the gay guy. "No shit, *amigos*, drop trou."

Pelón needed to check to make sure no one had any heroin, cocaine, or meth taped to their bodies. Hotel Mexico did not cater to drug traffickers. That was a whole different operation. Their clients in L.A. wanted family members safe, but sometimes bad guys would try to talk their code-holders into some sneaky stuff in an attempt to make some extra cash. Unfortunately this undermined the safety of family members.

After a quick search of the seven Latino men, everyone dressed and mulled around aimlessly until Pelón blurted out with much enthusiasm, "To the bar, my friends. Where we will toast to the Blessed Virgin for a safe journey."

Pelón was so theatrical it bordered on corny, but with his "all seeing eyeball" in consideration, it came off almost credible.

Down in the bar the Gypsy Kings were rockin' the box, a vintage Wurlitzer, the Latin big band sound smooth as silk. The three-bladed ceiling fans that hung almost motionless were reminiscent of a Mexican version of Casablanca. *Of all the gin joints in all the towns in all the world, she walks into mine.*

Pelón lined up nine shot glasses on the bar, filled to the brim with Cuervo 1800. Camacho came through the backdoor, his mustache glistening shiny from pork fat.

"*Amigos*, tonight I guide you. No, I take you on the first leg of your journey. We are on a dangerous mission, *amigos*. Raise your glass with me."

Each man grabbed a glass. Pelón raised an eyeless eyebrow at the giggling gay man, but let him drink also. Camacho toasted, "Here's to the Virgin Mary who reproduced without sinning. May we sin without reproducing." He raised his shot glass over his head. The others just looked at each other in complete shock.

Pelón had a stupid smile, full of ad-hoc Mexican dentistry. You could taste the awkward silence. Camacho looked each man in the eye. And without a trace of irony said, "What? We do not need luck? We do not need the Virgin's blessing? You are with me, *amigos*. The best in all of Mexico."

Camacho's ego was almost too large for the small bar. But it was obvious his buoyancy made the group feel safe. The tension broke. It was all laughter and smiles, handshakes and backslaps. The mood was once again festive. Everyone tossed back the Cuervo as Camacho boomed, "Follow me to America." He spun one-hundred-eighty degrees on his right heel and took off out the back door.

Pelón herded the men out like sheep into the hot arid night where the stillness was absolute. Only the hum and crackle of the neon signs out front pierced the darkness.

Camacho's Bronco was huge. It sounded like a NASCAR racer, and more than made up for his "stature-challenged" penis. The four-wheel-drive truck was a perfect tool for Camacho to ply his trade. He had never been stuck or broke down on any run.

He kept his Bronco in immaculate condition. If by some rotten stroke of luck, you were to vomit on the ride to the fence, which happened more often than you'd think, he'd stop, turn around, pull his side arm, and say, "Out. Get out NOW. This is a do-over for you. Walk back, you son-of-a-bitch. You will clean my truck and we will try again. Smells like rotten *carnitas*. Do not eat next time, you hear? If you find your way back, stay away from the BBQ." At which time he would queue up the two-way radio and alert Pelón to the pedestrian status of the guy and his new diet.

The run to the fence in pitch-black darkness was a precisely-timed, choreographed piece of smuggling. In this business timing is everything. There are many unseen eyes and ears, from ranchers to homeowners to private pilots, all paid well for their vigilance. The comings and goings of U.S. Border Patrol and Mexican *Federales* are monitored and recorded, analyzed and compiled, with stealth and accuracy.

The network of people involved in a safe crossing is incredible. That's because all smugglers share information, but not product. The need for precise timing is exactly the same whether you're trafficking guns, drugs, or humans. But the morals and value systems differ when you're shuffling humans across the border.

Priority number one is to know the Border Patrol's schedule. There is an inherent 15-minute delay during each shift change when everyone exchanges info about the day's observations. Coyotes cue microphones on two-way radios; that's when people literally crawl through holes in the fence, and, in some cases, gamblers-on-a-losing-streak load someone's loved ones into the back of the family van.

An action-packed race against time occurs during this dangerous dance, thus requiring nerves of steel. Confidence and control are the smuggler's best traits. If you're prone to mistakes and don't have a poker face, you won't succeed. There are so many variables and so many quick decisions to be made in that 15 to 20 minutes that it takes an almost mechanical state of mind to live to collect your money.

Camacho pulled the Bronco up next to the hole in the twelve-foot chain-link fence. The 50-mile-an-hour ride took less than 11 minutes. Once the Bronco jerked to a stop, frightened men anxiously jumped out of the vehicle and crawled, one at a time, through a recently cut hole onto Reservation Land.

On the other side, Wiley Coyote accepted his charges for the second leg of the three-part journey. His head constantly darted from side to side. Like an owl, Wiley did not need night-vision goggles.

Nor was he afraid of the natural elements.

As usual Wiley wore lineman boots that laced up 18 inches over his shins, covering thick leather leggings. These items protected his lower half from diamondback rattlesnakes, common to the California desert. Some up to seven feet in length, their powerful, venomous fangs could end a man's career in the blink of an eye.

There was no moon in the night sky – there hardly ever was during crossings – only the stars as Wiley's guide. But that didn't matter because he was a pro and his people knew it. Which is why they immediately tuned in when he started his instructions with "Listen up my friends, and listen closely…"

NAKED TIME
Chapter 8

Denice was buck naked, sitting on the edge of the small Jacuzzi with her feet dangling in the steaming water. A small, but toasty fire in the Franklin stove warmed the cedar-scented air of the A-frame cabin. The only windows were at the peak of the A-frame, the same level as the loft, private, cozy and delicious. Two small candles added to the luxurious camping atmosphere.

While looking at his wife, Charlie thought to himself, *Sometimes the Creator's handiwork demands thankfulness from the hearts of we mortals. So beautiful, so smart, so tan, at times this spectacle can take your breath away.*

Except for the string. Dammit.

Denice noticed her husband's leer as he slid naked into the bubbling cauldron. She knew him so well. As with a lot of loving relationships, they read each other's thoughts and finished each other's sentences. At this moment, she thought about rewarding Charlie with that one thing he loved more than fast cars. More than jackpots. More than any other activity known to man.

"You've been a very good boy Charlie," she cooed.

"I have?"

"Yes. My knight in shining armor. And as your queen, I have a reward for you." She slipped into the water and looked up into his eyes. "Don't you worry 'bout that string, handsome."

No more words were needed, nor could be said by Denice. Sometimes Charlie thought his cup runneth over. Life was good, sooo freakin' good.

"Oh, yes, what a good boy I am," he whispered lustily.

Life doesn't get any better than this.

✠   ✠   ✠

Lying on the antique comforter and the too-soft mattress, Charlie and Denice listened to the serenade of the night: chirping crickets, the hoot of an owl looking for its mate to share a kill. This is when Charlie and Denice shared their innermost thoughts, after the tension and stress of the day was shed.

"I like Lily," Denice shared. "She seems nice. Dinner was excellent, and she made me feel welcome."

"Yeah. And Ron's a cool guy," Charlie continued. "We'd be ass-out without their kindness. I'm going to give him double his money's worth."

"Lily said they're short on cash, so the trade is good for them. Ron can't do it all. She said he's no electrician nor plumber."

"Well, we'll see how it goes, Pumkin." Charlie kissed Denice's forehead, her cheek and finally her lips like he had every night for 21 years.

Sleep came quickly for them both.

The next few days went by in a hurry. Charlie and Denice worked in the restaurant, campground, and cabins. They ate their meals in the restaurant and slept in the honeymoon cabin. But this sweet interlude couldn't go on forever. The weekend was only two days away and all the cabins were booked.

"You want to go to the casino and have a look around?" asked Denice, well aware that they needed to find another way to get some cash.

"Sure," replied Charlie unenthusiastically. He also knew they needed a Plan B. "Maybe play duck, duck, goose with all the people that won't pay us back?"

"Just try a little charm, Charlie. More flies with sugar and all that."

"You do know that flies start out as maggots," Charlie reasoned comically.

"We all have to start somewhere," Denice replied in that monotone *I'm-not-impressed-with-your-attempt-at-humor* voice that women do so well.

The Acorn Casino was packed on this Wednesday night, and resonated loudly with the din of dropping coins. The low hum of voices competed with the piped in muzak, and the atmosphere was charged with everyone's desperate hope of quick money.

And then there was Larry, bingo was his game-o.

"Looky there, hon," Charlie nodded toward Larry. "A cash cow."

"Moo," responded Denice.

Charlie spread his arms out like wings, "I'm gonna swoop over there and pounce on his wallet."

"Thank God he's not wearing a tie," said Denice, remembering their last encounter.

Charlie walked up and stood behind Larry, looking over his shoulder. The money line was at eighteen dollars. "Rollin' like a big dog, eh Lar?"

"Holy crap, you scared me, man. I'm broke, dude." Larry noticed Denice behind Charlie. "Hi, Dee-Dee," he said respectfully, not wanting to make the same mistake twice. "Let me throw this 18 bucks into the abyss, and I'll meet you at the café. I want to talk to you guys."

Charlie and Denice exchanged surprised glances. "Okay, Lar," said Charlie happily. "But you're buyin' the coffee."

They found a table near the back, sat down and waited for the fat man. They only had to wait moments. Larry had cashed out to pay for coffee.

"Hey, guys. What's up? So, about that money. Ain't got it, but look, I got a real good deal for ya." He looked around nervously. "I got, like, 10 people in my garage waitin'."

"For what?" asked Charlie, unimpressed.

"A ride to L.A., $300 each, you take three, that's $900."

"And how do I get paid?" inquired Charlie, slightly interested.

"Cash on the barrelhead, soon as you drop, the guy will hand you the cash."

Denice hadn't said a word up till now. "I thought you clowns got $500 each?"

"I gotta get paid for storage," Larry held up both palms to show he wasn't lying through his meth teeth.

"How come you don't take 'em?" asked Charlie.

"My Mustang's a piece of crap, and besides, the whole town knows me. I'd be busted in a heartbeat."

Charlie thought about this for a second. "Okay, Lar, the wife and I need to have a pow-wow, so give us some space and we'll come find you."

Larry rose to leave. Charlie tapped his index finger on the table. "You're buyin' the coffee, remember?"

Larry laid eight dollars on the table, fumbling with the few dollars he had left. "This shit is easy. I'll even run up and check the status for you."

"The status? The status of what?"

"The checkpoint. Unless you want to go down the backside."

"Whatever, Lar." Charlie let out a long sigh. "Just give us a minute." Larry nodded and walked away.

Charlie slumped down in the booth while forks scratched plates and the conversational hum of diners filled the air– winners and losers, all of them. "Well baby, I never thought I'd ever consider this shit."

"Are you now?" The words swirled over them like a tornado, one that hadn't hit the ground yet.

"Desperate men do desperate things."

"You need to rethink this Charlie." Ah, the voice of reason, like the angel whispering in your right ear. Even so, Denice knew better than to draw a line in the sand. "You and me Charlie, till the wheels fall off. But I gotta tell you this ain't a great idea."

"Ya think? But it's cash. Lots of it. Five or six hours, there and back, one time. Two times and we're good for a spell."

Denice tapped out a smoke, looked at the pack with three left in it. Charlie's lighter went *click, flick, flame*. Denice took a long drag, exhaled and said, "Okay. Let's do it, handsome."

Charlie breathed a sigh of relief.

✠　✠　✠

They met Larry at his house in Jacumba.

A little background on Jacumba: It's the oldest smuggler's town in southern California. Jacumba is the last little town on Old Highway 8, heading east from San Diego towards the Imperial Valley. It consists of an elementary school, a post office, a small store, and 16 blocks of residential homes, some with wheels. A few of them are nicely re-modeled, vintage 1950s ranch style homes, but most of the dwellings are just tiny, ticky-tacky postwar housing. The standout feature in town, however, is the spa. Once a trendy mineral spa to the movie stars in the days of the Rat Pack, now it's just a tired rundown pool.

Jacumba also has an airport. That is, if you consider an unmonitored strip of dirt on which planes come and go unscheduled an airport. There is no tower, no gas pump, no tarmac, just easy access to a very flat, well-maintained, landing strip. This is one of the many mysteries of Jacumba, as no one's ever witnessed any maintenance equipment grading the airstrip.

To the south exists *No Man's Land* – an area belonging to both Mexico and the Indian tribes. To the west sit mountains in which the Border Patrol roosts like a gaggle of buzzards, watching, always watching, just like they've done since the day the agency was conceived.

Sandstorms, heat, monsoons, and neglect have removed any shine the town once had. Scrub oak and Acacia are the only native trees left. The roadsides into town are filled with a billion boulders piled up by the hands of God, smothering the cracked pavement on both sides back to Interstate 8 east, and out of town.

But everything in Jacumba changes at night. In the expanse of the high desert, with any kind of moon, shadowy shapes form like those you swear you saw in your open closet as a child. The sleepy little Spanish stucco town by day becomes a chilling and haunted wasteland at night.

Doomed spirits wander the desert searching for something they'll never find: human beings too slow, too old, or too weak to keep up, abandoned by their coyotes; the timid, with bodies locked in fear, left behind. It's a trail of broken dreams spawned by failed attempts at a shot at the American dream.

There is no record of these lives lost, shattered and broken, on top of this mountain. But you can feel them. You can hear them on the wind. You can sense their presence in your soul.

If you ask any old-timer, he will fill your ear with story after story of success and failure, of love and hate. Even so, the tempting, all-too-glamorous life of big-money smuggling far outweighs the deadly consequences of potential loss in the sweltering desert of Jacumba, California.

Looking at Larry's rental house, you could not tell there were 10 nervous, sweating, hungry Mexican nationals packed into his garage, dreaming of the sunny skies over Los Angeles. The house was 1960s pea green with a pitched roof. It had a detached garage and breezeway, which led to a single-story ranch style so common of that era. The property sported a gravel yard instead of grass, nicely complimenting the three dead barrel cacti that graced the front, arranged at one time like flowers. A three-foot chain-link fence around the property kept wild dogs out more than family pets in.

Charlie and Denice pulled into the crumbling driveway ahead of Larry. Fat Larry was always late, always in a hurry, except in front of a gambling machine.

The neighborhood was like any lower middle class street, except for the eyes. Everyone was watching. Everyone. No one called the sheriff or the Border Patrol. It wasn't that kind of watch, it was *awareness*. In Jacumba, it was important to know, just to know.

Larry pulled up as Charlie was considering pulling out.

"Larry, what the hell, man?"

Inside the garage two families and three single young men were hunkered down in any dark, humid hiding place available. "Someone's here, someone's here," they whispered. The youngest peered through a crack between the door and jamb.

"It's a big Blazer, man, that's our ride."

The oldest member, Mr. Martinez, said, "Easy, *mijo* and *cállate*. You don't know who it is, relax."

Many families save for years to send their sons and daughters to America. The freedoms and opportunities we take for granted are dreamed about and worked towards, sometimes for a lifetime, just for the chance to earn and send money home to the village.

These are not drug dealers, criminals, or ex-cons. These are working class people, seventy percent are young adults who worked months in Mexico just to afford Levi's and decent shoes, if they could find work at all.

"Look there! Gordo, in the Mustang."

Mr. Martinez calmed everyone down. "Okay, okay. When they come in, the women and Pablo go first. Agreed, Simone?"

"We can't have the girls using this nasty bucket for a toilet."

"I don't know why that fat man won't let us in the house. At least let my Aunt Lucia in to use the *baño*."

"You want a bubble bath, too?"

"Shut your mouth, son, and be thankful to Jesus."

Inside the garage, excitement filled the air. So close. Imagine yourself in a strange country, but you don't know how to get where your American family is. You don't even know where you are. And since you came by foot in the dark, there is no way back. It's terrifying, you have no choice but to depend on people who don't speak your language, and for the most part are concerned only about getting paid and not getting arrested.

"Sorry, man," justified Larry, "had to find you some gas money and get a hold of Ramona. I'm hooking things up for the drop."

"Alright, Lar. Let's get a move on. This place creeps me out."

"Yeah, it's Jacumba," like that explained it.

"Can we go inside, gentlemen?" Denice broke in. "I gotta pee."

Larry keyed the deadbolt, and they entered the house. Charlie and Denice looked around and then at each other. Pigsty. Denice headed to the restroom with a look of terror.

"Hey, Chuck, follow me," instructed Larry.

"Don't call me Chuck, fairy."

"Don't call me fairy, Chuck."

Charlie scowled at the fat man and then followed him through the breezeway into the garage. The first thing Charlie noticed was the smell, then the faces. The combined odor of chaparral, human sweat, and that nasty bucket. Charlie did not speak Spanish, but he didn't need to in order to know that these people had been through hell and back. His heart ached for them immediately.

"*Señor*, we ask you to take the women first."

"You ain't runnin' shit, *amigo*," scoffed Larry. "Just sit tight and we'll let you know."

"Jesus, Larry. What the F's wrong with you?" asked Charlie incredulously.

"What?"

"You don't gotta be such an anus, man."

"Keep your voice down. This is your cargo. Nothing more."

Charlie again looked into the desperate faces and his heart bled.

Back in the house Charlie was not as cavalier as he had been before his trip to the garage. "Let's get this show on the road, Larry. You gonna check status, or whatever the hell it is you have to do?"

"Yeah, let me hit the head first and then I'm outta here."

Charlie knew that meant hit the pipe, the *pizo*, the glass dick. Meth smokers like Larry needed to wrap their lips around it every half hour.

Denice emerged from the bathroom. "God dang, Larry, you ever heard of Pine-Sol? They make this gizmo called a toilet brush, for chrissake."

"Kinda busy," replied Larry on the very edge of mocking Denice. "Ain't had time."

"Busy being an asshole," Charlie added.

"Whatever, Chuck. Those illegals are lucky I didn't stash them *under* the house."

"Just gimme the gas money, you turd, and then go check on whatever it is you have to check on."

Larry handed Charlie forty-six dollars.

"What the fuck?"

"You'll get paid at the drop. That'll get you there."

Charlie shook his head in disdain. "Beat it, Larry, before I change my mind, or before Dee-Dee changes it for me."

Larry slithered into the bathroom, slamming the door behind him.

Charlie shot Denice a disgusted look.

✠ ✠ ✠

Charlie had already gassed up at the Shell on the frontage of Highway 8 on their way to Larry's house. Since they would be going west, not east, the nearest gas station was in Alpine, halfway down the grade.

Larry, after checking the status of the checkpoint and finding it closed, waited in his car as Charlie opened the back door on the passenger side of his truck. It was dark outside, no porch lights and zero streetlights in this neighborhood.

Denice opened the garage door, revealing anxious faces. Larry sighed. "*Cinco*, man. Only *cinco*."

Martinez replied, "Ladies, come on." He then pointed to his nephew and the two youngest of the men, "You and you." He looked at Miguel, his nephew and in a calm voice said, "Don't worry, *mijó*. We will watch the Dodgers play. You and I. Just like we talked about. I'll see you at Auntie's house."

Five dark figures stepped out of Larry's garage, into the crisp night air, and quietly loaded themselves into the Blazer.

Larry looked at Charlie through the driver's side window of his car, "Have 'em lay down thru town, past La Posta. Once on the grade you're cool if the checkpoint's still closed. The Border Patrol's snacking on donuts at that time, and won't be hiding in the bushes."

"Okay," replied Charlie. "I got the address. Carl's Jr. parking lot on Atlantic in Bellflower."

"Keep your cell on," commanded Larry. "I'll call if there's a change. Good luck and haul ass. You got my last dollar."

"Don't worry, dick smoker. We got this."

Charlie got into the driver's seat, and Denice joined him in the front passenger side. "Everybody down," Charlie instructed while looking in the rearview mirror. Denice turned around in her seat and motioned with her hand, smiling at the frightened women. With a shy smile back, they all curled up on the rear seat, the men in back behind them.

"My heart's beating like a drum." Denice anxiously whispered to Charlie.

"I hear ya, babe."

Charlie shifted into focus mode.

Years of teamwork kicked in without one word being said between them. Denice scanned the road ahead, behind, each crossroad, every driveway.

"There really should be a manual for this," said Charlie.

"Yeah," replied Denice stoically. "The FBI probably already has one."

The smell of fear and unwashed feet hung in the air. They turned onto Highway 8 West and there it was – the Border Patrol checkpoint. It was dark and empty, but cameras perched on the archway over the road like predators waiting for their prey. Charlie looked at Denice and took a deep breath. Denice turned around and whispered, "Everybody stay down."

Charlie put the Blazer in gear and then drove forward. As the checkpoint drew closer everyone held their collective breath. Closer...Closer...And then...

They proceeded through the checkpoint, no hidden border patrol, no camera flash, no trap.

On the other side Charlie let out an exhale of relief. "Yeah, baby."

Denice turned around to the wide-eyed bunch in the back. "Everybody okay?" she asked, looking at the nervous smiles. "You can sit up now, were good to go."

Lucia, one of the women, translated to the others, then asked, "How long to L.A., *señora*?"

"About two hours."

A street light suddenly flooded Lucia's face and Denice noticed her hooded, bloodshot eyes. The Hispanic woman pointed at Charlie and asked, "Is he your *esposo*? How you say...husband?"

"Yes, he is," replied Denice. "Kinda cute for a white guy, wouldn't you say?"

"He's nice. Not like fat man. That *gordo*. Your *esposo* yelled at him for being bad."

Charlie caught her eye in the rearview mirror and said jokingly, "You mean Captain Ugly Pants? Yeah, he's got a black belt in asshole."

Lucia shrugged her shoulders. "I do not understand, *señor*."

Denice interjected, "Don't even try, girlfriend. Just laugh and pretend he's funny."

Lucia smiled. She didn't understand, but she didn't need to. *This is a nice couple*, she thought. *Not like the fat man*. She clutched her picture of the Blessed Virgin that Mr. Martinez had given her, and felt safe for the first time in days.

Charlie and Denice knew just about every street, road, and highway in southern California. They'd already figured a way around the checkpoint on Highway 15 in Temecula near the Pechanga casino. Charlie had framed houses out in that area, and was raised in Escondido, 15 minutes back down the interstate. Side roads were the key.

Denice was the perfect navigator. Years of pulling the Love Bus all over hell's half acre and back (looking for campgrounds, casinos, and places to skinny dip – one of the prime California pastimes for your average Cali girl) made Denice just as familiar with the lay of the land as Charlie was.

After doing the *duck-and-dodge* around the checkpoint, it was clear sailing to Bellflower in Los Angeles, California.

Everyone in the K-5 breathed easier.

☩　☩　☩

Pulling into Carl's Jr. they saw the custom coach van, silver with red stripes. They sidled up next to it, and Charlie nodded at the Latino gentleman with the Lakers basketball team logo on his ball cap. When the guy stepped out of the van, Charlie saw he was middle-aged, older than Charlie had expected. He wore a windbreaker, Levis and pointed-toe boots. Not Justin's, like Charlie wore, but flashy, nevertheless – and shined up like a diamond.

The man was smooth, all right. Charlie could tell right away this guy was a pro, and respectful, too. He removed his hat to greet Denice, his hair black as onyx.

"Good evening, ma'am."

"Good evening to you, *señor*," Denice responded, equally respectful.

"I trust all went well?" He looked at Charlie.

"Smooth as glass, sir," Charlie replied, as if he were addressing an important official.

The man opened the side door of his van while Charlie opened the side door of the K-5 Blazer, with two feet between the vehicles. The transfer was quick and flawless, but more importantly seen by no one.

The gentleman reached into the side pocket of his windbreaker and extracted a wad of bills wrapped in a thick rubber band. "Five times five is 25."

"All day long," Charlie replied grabbing the cash, and then added, "Five more up there, relatives of this group. The checkpoint was closed earlier. I know it's late, but now's good for the wife and me to—"

"Run again?" the man said, finishing Charlie's sentence.

"Yes, sir," confirmed Charlie. "While the getting's good, if you get my drift."

The man studied Charlie cautiously.

"Name's Charlie." Charlie extended his hand. The man looked into Charlie's eyes for a second before clasping hands.

"Okay, Charlie. You think maybe five hours?"

"Give or take, sir. Larry will let you know when we leave the mountain."

"Fine. I'll make the call. Be safe, Charlie." The man touched his hat with his finger in sort of a salute.

Charlie jumped in, started the truck and handed Denice the cash. She started counting as they pulled out of the parking lot, "Twenty, 40, 60, 80. One, 20…"

Charlie looked at his wife. "That was so freakin' cool."

"Twenty, 40, 60," Denice continued counting, ignoring her excited husband. "Fifteen hundred, plus the three Larry still owes us."

"Damn. That was so easy, so slick baby, oh my God. But did it make you horny?" Charlie could just not help himself. He had a penis, after all, and sometimes it spoke on his behalf.

Denice laughed. "Kinda. Hold up, let me check." Denice stuck her hand down her pants. "Yup. A bit moist down there. But Jesus, Charlie, come on. Plenty of time for that later."

"Promise?"

"Yeah, I promise. As a matter of fact, you're a lot more attractive now that you're rollin'."

Charlie leered at his wife like she was wrapped around a pole on a catwalk. "Honey, I don't want it at all unless I can have it twice, Sooo...let's do it again."

She seductively smiled and replied by recounting the fat stack of cash, "Twenty, 40, 60, 80, one thousand..."

CAN'T TOUCH THIS
Chapter 9

Fourteen hours later Charlie and Denice happily set up camp in room number 307 at the Barona Casino without a care in the world. Denice snored away like a farm animal, while Charlie perused the room service menu. After meeting up with Larry, they pocketed a total of $3,300, which was now in the electronic room safe waiting to be introduced to room service and the Blazin' Sevens.

Their new profession was as stressful as searching for landmines or performing any bomb squad detail. They were both completely exhausted.

Suddenly Denice was awakened by a loud knock followed by the shout-out of "Room service."

"Just a moment," replied Charlie, as he slid into a terrycloth robe, compliments of the concierge.

Charlie opened the door. "Come on in. Thank you. Just put it next to the bed, please."

"Yes, sir."

Charlie tipped large, the man smiled. "Thank you, sir." Charlie understood from his dad the importance of tipping your service employees. They talk. The maids, the chef, the wait staff. Want a booger in your cheesecake? Stiff room service on their tip.

Denice sat up on the fluffy pillows. "For little ol' me?" she cooed.

"You're my queen, remember? You said so back in the Jacuzzi," said Charlie, reaching under the covers for any delights that might be waiting for his attention.

"Charlie, do you ever think of anything else?"

"I think I'm hungry, does that count?"

The smell accompanying the covered silver trays held the promise of a country breakfast with all the trimmings in true California style, including ice cold Mimosas, the morning cocktail of champagne and orange juice for those who detest tomatoes, celery, and that nasty Tabasco sauce.

As luck would have it, the blanket kept slipping down off Denice's naked chest, as she tried to adjust her tray.

"You sure know how to treat a girl," she said, awkwardly adjusting the covers.

"Right back at ya, Pumkin."

"Oh my God, this is so good."

Charlie pulled the blanket down. "You got that right," Charlie leered.

She pulled the blanket back up. "Hey, honey, were you scared last night? I mean, we were breaking the law."

"You want the truth?"

"Of course," she replied.

"Okay. That shit scared me so bad you could not have jack-hammered a needle up my ass."

"Me, too," confided Denice.

"For real?" replied Charlie mockingly.

"Stop it, Charlie, be serious."

"Alright, alright. You know, I have to say, it was a kick in the pants. What a rush. Balls out, middle of the night, sexy lady as co-pilot. Big cash payoff. More fun than Six Flags. Yes, it scared me shitless. A couple of times I wanted to cry, like the time when CHP blew past us, lights flashing. But damn, it was fun."

Denice looked at her man like he was ready to jump off a cliff. "That is so sexy," she finally said.

"Really?" Charlie replied hopefully.

"No." She pulled the blanket up to her chin. Twenty-one years and he still could not figure her out.

Well, no means no.

So after scooping every morsel off his plate with a delicious slice of buttered sourdough toast, he rose from his perch on the bed, grabbed his Mimosa, went to the sliding glass door and looked out on the golf course. "I should learn to play golf," he said.

"With who?"

"You."

"When pigs fly the Concorde."

"I love *Caddyshack*." Doing his best Bill Murray impression, Charlie quoted from the movie, "Cinderella golfer. Gonna use a nine iron. It's in the hole."

"You just wanna tear up some grass in your pimp-daddy, off-road golf cart. Charlie, you're not a yellow pants-and-pink-shirt kind of guy. You don't even own a pair of white shoes. So soon as you're done daydreamin' we need a game plan. And not a golf game."

Charlie thoughtfully looked out on the golf course. Denice was right, as usual. He would never be happy as a Sunday golfer. Clinking glasses at the club, talking about redoing the guest room, bragging about which colleges everyone's kids are going to.

"And by the way," Denice interrupted his reverie. "I don't think we should use Big Blue if we run again."

"You're probably right. We'd be in a world of hurt if the Feds took it. Larry said they could keep it if they wanted."

Slipping into her skintight chinos, and then laying flat on the bed, struggling with the zipper, she added, "When I was looking for my purse I saw your 38 under the seat. You know I hate those things. You need to put it back in the Love Bus, ASAP."

Charlie pulled on his shirt that said, *Nut up or shut up.* "Okay, babe, will do. We need to get some money to our slumlord anyway."

"Right, we'll hold back $1,500. One thousand for Timmy's mom, and some for Ron and Lily at Live Oak Springs."

"Sounds good," replied Charlie. "I'd feel real good about handing Ron 500 bucks and telling him the work's on us."

Charlie watched Denice lace up her sandals and thought to himself, *even her painted toes are sexy.* "Let's take $600 down to the casino and leave the rest."

"Okay. Lunch at Kenny Rogers' favorite steakhouse?"

"Perfect. We'll split $500, hold back $100 for lunch."

Denice stood up, applying some lip gloss, and announced, "I'm ready to roll, handsome."

Charlie did the last minute accessory check; smokes, lighter, room key, sunglasses, tip money, valet ticket, and wallet. "I'm good, got your horseshoe?"

"What do you think?"

"I think if it's in your ass, you should know."

"Very funny, Chuck."

"Hey! Don't call me Chuck."

They took the elevator to the casino floor.

Let the games begin.

✠ ✠ ✠

The phone rang in Dee-Dee's purse and, seeing *Captain* light up on the caller ID, she handed it to Charlie. "For you. It's Captain Ugly Pants."

Charlie took her phone. "What's up, Dickweed?"

"Any luck, Chuck? I can hear the sound of money dropping. Where you at?"

"Barona."

"K. My sister lives in Alpine. I can you meet you there tonight."

Charlie pulled the phone from his face, turned to Denice on the next machine. "Larry wants to talk to us at his sister's place in Alpine."

"I guess so."

"Good God, I have to meet her, just to see." Charlie brought the phone back to his ear. "Okay, Captain. Got the go-ahead from headquarters, what's her 411?"

Captain Ugly Pants gave him her address and they agreed on 7:00 p.m. Before they hung up Charlie added, "Hey, go by Mario's Italian restaurant and pick up a pizza. Sausage with extra cheese. Dee and I will bring the Red Trolley Ale."

Mario's Little Italy had the best pizza in the western hemisphere. But it was located in one of the most remote parts of California. Definitely worth the drive.

✠　　✠　　✠

Larry's sister, bless her heart, unfortunately looked like Larry's twin, but 30 pounds heavier. All 30 of it between sagging breasts and knocked knees. Black rim librarian glasses sat atop a nose badly in need of plastic surgery, or at least putty to fill in the pores. She opened the door to her generic second floor condo and said with no amount of enthusiasm, "Hey, guys. Larry's not here yet, come on in."

Charlie followed her inside with two six-packs of the dark ale under one arm.

"My name is Shelley, and this good-looking stud is Johnny."

If "stud" means five-foot-three, no neck and man boobs, then Charlie was shaking hands with one. "I'm Charlie, and this lovely young lady is my wife, Denice."

"Enchanted, Denice," said the troll of a man, as he took her hand.

Charlie was on the verge of busting out laughing. Enchanted? *Enchanté, Mademoiselle.* Who was this bozo? "Want a beer, Johnny?" asked Charlie. "How about you Shelley?"

Johnny grabbed one right out of the six-pack, put the cap to his canine teeth, and pried it off, making Charlie and Denice wince. But Shelley cocked her head to the side with admiration. It appears that scraping enamel off your teeth classifies you as a stud in Captain Ugly Pants' family.

Larry came barreling through the door with two scrumptious-smelling pizzas, obviously hot out of the oven. "Hope you're all hungry, these cost a fortune."

"God, you're a cheap bastard," Charlie said. "I could shove a lump of Christmas coal up your ass and you'd shit out a diamond before New Year's."

"Good seeing you too, Chuck." He smiled at Denice. "And how are you, Mrs. DeVille? You look lovely this evening."

Charlie thought, *Atta boy Lar, now your learnin'. Nothing teaches good manners like a good ass whooping.*

Denice handed the captain a beer and said, "Thanks, Larry." She offered a bottle of brew to Shelley.

"No, thank you," said Shelley with a giggle. "Johnny bought wine."

Denice figured the box was in the fridge. She thought it'd take at least two liters thru a spigot to make Johnny look like a stud. "Nice touch," said Denice tightly.

"Thank you," answered Johnny from the kitchen, not realizing Denice was being facetious.

Everyone sat in the living room, two pizzas on the coffee table, lids up and with paper plates and cold beer.

"I want to talk to you guys about runnin' again," started Larry.

"I'm listening."

"I don't want to keep filling my garage. Wiley, that's the coyote, he's got people stashed in the rocks above the school waitin', and another load coming to the fence. I gotta tell Ramona how many I can move. Ya feel me?"

Charlie looked at Larry with a pained expression. "You been hanging out on Euclid Avenue, Larry? Don't ever ask me to feel you again."

"Right. Sorry. Um, anyway, let's come up with a plan."

"Do you golf?" asked Charlie.

"Huh?"

"Dang it, Charlie, be serious," interjected Denice. "Larry's right. We need a game plan."

"The Captain's got methlexia, he can barely generate a brain wave, much less a working plan, Pumkin."

You could smell rags burning as Larry mulled that over. It was too much for him to process, so he just skipped over it and asked, "Are you guys up for this or what? I need to know."

Charlie and Denice looked at each other. She saw the quirky little smile on the corner of her husband's mouth.

"We're in, balls deep," confirmed Charlie.

"Cool," Larry responded evenly.

"But let's be smart about this and rent a vehicle," Denice added.

"In whose name?" Charlie asked.

"Let me handle that," offered Larry. "I'll hook it up at the casino. But it'll cost us 40 or 50 bucks."

"Fine," answered Charlie. And then in a surprising moment of mental clarity, Larry added this little gem, "My daddy told me if you sail it, drive it, fly it, or fuck it...rent it."

It was at that exact moment that the stud, Johnny Rotten, asked, "Anybody got a handgun for sale?"

That shut conversation down completely. Everyone in the room was trying to figure out where that came from and why.

Thinking that Mr. Man Boobs felt left out of the conversation in front of his "Shelley Belly," Charlie answered, "I do."

"For reals?"

"Yeah, stud, for reals. Real bullets. Real holster. Real snub nose, the whole shebang."

"How much?"

"Four hundred, cash," Charlie quickly replied.

"It's a deal, when can I take delivery?"

"I'll have it delivered UPS."

"Righty-oh," Johnny said.

Denice giggled.

Charlie pondered, *Jesus, who is this clown?*

✠　✠　✠

The rented Suburban was parked in the Viejas Casino parking lot, gassed up and ready to roll. Denice jumped out of the K-5 and into the huge SUV. It was top-of-the-line with three rows of leather seats and that new car smell. Denice adjusted the seat, reached in her purse, pulled out her favorite CD, and lit a smoke. Following Charlie back to home base, her thumbs tapped out a beat on the huge wheel to The Uninvited.

FREE FIRE KILLING ZONE
Chapter 10

Back at the fence, Edgar Escobar Sanchez a.k.a. Wiley Coyote addressed the group, "Listen up. You follow me in a single file line, always." He pointed at the biggest man and said, "You bring up the rear. Don't let anyone stop to rest until I say rest."

"*Si, señor.*"

"The trick is my friends, to watch the feet in front of you and step in their tracks. If you trip, fall, or get hurt, we leave you where you sit. *Comprende?*"

Nervous eyes looked around at each other. The coyote instructed them, "If I lay down, you lay down. No talking at all. Only listening and only to me." The group nodded in agreement. "Do not ask for water. I have only two canteens. I will give you water when I say it's time." Some looked at the ground, most already thirsty from Mr. Toad's Wild Ride in Camacho's Bronco.

Wiley continued, "Pay attention, *amigos*. It is a matter of survival. If you fall behind, your chances are slim to none. People die out here. It's freezing cold at night and hot as hell in the day. There are no landmarks, and plenty of *gringos* looking to steal the money you have in your shoes."

That was just an added bonus to the gauntlet run by these people. As in all places in this cruel world, there are predators looking for the weak. The stragglers, they have the advantage of fear on their side. Robbing illegals is a major problem in this line of work, and especially in Wiley's job. That's why Wiley carries a 9-mm Beretta with a 14-round clip as a side arm. Should you come across him and his charges in the high desert, your best option is to hide or turn and run. Wiley Coyote is much like a rattlesnake – silent and deadly. If you provoke him you end up feeding real coyotes, perishing in the desert.

"We should be in the town of Jacumba before daylight. We'll hide out until your ride comes to take you to the City of Angels. No rest till I do. Do you understand?"

They all looked at their shoes and nodded in the affirmative. Wiley turned around, faced north and walked a fast pace into the dark desert landscape.

✠ ✠ ✠

Denice followed Charlie into town. After meeting Timmy's mom and giving her half of what they owed, she kindly removed the huge lock on Charlie and Denice's home base. Charlie pulled the K-5 into the building and shut off the engine. Denice pulled down the rollup door and went to the Love Bus to get some clothes. She then went to the mountain of carefully packed boxes along the wall for luggage and jackets, boots and more crap than they would need for an expedition to Mount Everest.

Charlie packed the rental with two-way radios, cell phone chargers, as well as some man stuff like a Taser, lighter fluid, and black shoe polish. Denice packed four suitcases, and stood holding four pillows and two blankets. Charlie could barely see her face.

"Jesus, babe, they have stuff at hotels."

"Not my blankee, and these are feathered goose down, people drool on hotel pillows, honey." Like Charlie should've figured that out.

"Two pillows and one blanket, blankee, whatever."

She stomped her left foot like a petulant child. "You're sleeping on the drooled ones, Charlie DeVille."

Must've pissed her off, Charlie mused. *She only uses last names when she's mad.*

Charlie strapped luggage to the rack atop the Suburban for that *family vacation* look. After Denice was completely satisfied, and she had twice as much crap as they needed, she called Larry.

"Larry's Bar, poker in front and liquor in the rear," answered Larry smugly.

"Oh my God, you're disgusting, Larry," Denice replied. She handed the phone to her husband with two fingers like it had herpes.

"Good one, Lar'," said Charlie into the cell phone. "You're battin' a thousand."

"Sorry, Chuck, I thought it was you, man."

"She'll get over it. I think," Charlie smiled at Denice. "So Captain Ugly Pants, you've got our marching orders, right? We're ready like Freddie."

Larry was tangibly excited. "Man, we're good. We're set. Meet me at the Golden Acorn."

"Roger dodger, over and out." Charlie handed the phone back to Denice, who replied with a mystified, "Roger dodger? When did you join the geek squad?"

"That's old army stuff. My dad was in a tank platoon, he said stuff like that."

"Well, if that's a quote from Big Daddy DeVille I'll accept it. But don't say it again."

"Since when have you succeeded in monitoring my mouth?"

They pulled into the truck stop side of the casino parking area, near the gas pumps. Lots of outdoor cameras to protect the big rig drivers who always left their trucks running.

They found Larry on a carousel of triple diamond machines and took a seat on each side of him for a little pow-wow. Denice put in a twenty, bet two dollars, pulled the handle. Triple bar, triple bar, and a diamond. *Bam.* Three hundred dollars. Charlie made a horse noise, blowing air through his lips like a huge fart, and said a little too loudly, "Horseshoe, baby. Horseshoe."

Larry shook his head saying, "I was just on that machine."

"Thanks for loading it, Captain. Atta girl, baby doll."

Denice wiggled her butt, smiled at the boys and pulled the one-armed bandit again.

Larry said, "Okay, it's looking like first thing in the morning at 5:00 a.m., shift change. You'll get a page here at the Acorn. They'll say 'Go' and you'll pull into the elementary school. You know where the Bridge of Sighs is?"

"No, not really," admitted Charlie.

"You know where that little cement bridge with the little arches in it is?"

"Yeah, right before the post office."

"That's the one. When crossing it, flash your headlights three times. Wiley will hit ya on the radio with the number of people and if they're ready. You don't hear him, don't stop just drive through town past the airstrip, turn around, come back on Interstate 8 to the Acorn, and we'll try again. But don't trip. This goes down smooth almost every time."

Charlie processed this information quickly. "Cool," and pulled the slot machine's handle.

It was just about dinnertime and, thanks to Denice, they were flush with cash.

"What do ya say we head down to Live Oak and make Ron's day?"

Denice replied, "Excellent idea, I'm starving."

They arrived at the restaurant, greeted by smiles and the smell of rib-eye steaks mixed with Lily's perfume. Ron and Charlie shook hands, and Denice and Lily hugged and touched cheeks like movie stars do. All very hip.

Charlie reached into his inside jacket pocket and pulled out five one-hundred-dollar bills and an unopened box of regular Kotex tampons. He gave the bills to Ron and the box to Lily. It was one of those Kodak moments. Ron stood there with money in hand, not believing someone had actually returned his kindness.

Lily was red-faced and lost for words.

Charlie broke the ice. "Could we get a steak here for that?" pointing to Ron's hand.

Ron shook himself out of his reverie and said, "You bet your ass. But Charlie, this is way too much. What about all the work you've done?"

"Look, that was on us, brother. Help to support the resort. And the big picture, the family business."

Charlie did not call anyone brother without deep respect. Denice was a little shocked he had use that word, having only known these folks less than two weeks.

Lily put her hand on Charlie's arm and one on Denice's shoulder and said, "Bless your hearts. I just knew we'd be fast friends. I told Ron the day we met, you would not be like the others."

Ron choked up. Charlie was lost for words and not trusting his voice.

Sensing her man on the verge of an emotional moment, Denice came to the rescue. "Let's party!" she announced. "I'm buying the first bottle."

"Well, we are kind of slow right now," Ron said while looking around at the empty tables.

"A bottle of your best wine and four glasses, sir." Charlie shouted.

The fire crackled, the wine was superb, and the conversation was even better. The steaks arrived, medium rare, and were consumed with the avarice of true carnivores.

The place started to fill, so Ron and Lily had to take their places as proprietors, which left Charlie and Denice to share a candlelit table and a slice of homemade Boston cream pie.

"I'm stuffed," said Charlie. "That was a meal fit for a king."

"It's nappy time," replied Denice. "Let's go park and catch a few winks before it's time to run."

"Okay, baby, I'll pull up to the truck stop. We'll sleep there."

"Sounds good, let's say goodbye to Ron and Lily." Denice left a fifty spot on the table knowing they could not pay for their meal after having already given them the five hundred.

They hugged their new friends and promised to see them soon. On the way out Charlie said, "Probably be needin' a cabin in a couple of days."

"Your credits are good here, my friend."

"Roger that."

Denice looked at him askew and murmured, "Roger that? What is with you today?"

☩　☩　☩

"Mr. DeVille to the white paging phone. Mr. DeVille, white paging phone," a disembodied voice cried out of the sound system.

"It's go time," Denice said.

Charlie went to the four phones on the wall across from the café. He picked up the white one. The woman's voice on the other end said, "Mr. Charlie DeVille?"

"This is Charlie."

"You have 17 minutes, this is a go. Please hurry." The line went dead.

☩　☩　☩

Wiley had everyone nestled into a rock formation on the hill above the school. The tension was thick, the clients coiled like springs. Daylight was only an hour away. No one spoke. The quiet was unnerving. Wiley was frozen in place, looking towards the west, looking for a teal green Chevy Suburban.

✠　✠　✠

Charlie and Denice came upon the Bridge of Sighs at 50 MPH, looking east towards the hill behind the Jacumba Elementary School for any sign of Wiley. Just past the bridge, Charlie flashed his bright lights three times, and out of a pile of boulders, atop the hill, a group of people dashed down in a single file line. Denice opened the door as they hurled themselves into the big green machine.

Charlie looked over his right shoulder and gave a thumbs up to Wiley Coyote standing proud atop a boulder, releasing his charges to the last leg of the Jacumba Connection.

✠　✠　✠

Just past the Shell gas station, you can drive under Highway 8 to go west towards San Diego, or you can turn right on the on-ramp going towards Borrego Springs and the desert floor.

"Turn right," commanded Denice.

"What?"

"Turn right, now," she reiterated.

There was a Border Patrol unit a quarter-mile behind them. Charlie took the exit east, accelerated up the ramp and onto the interstate. In this direction, the grade was extremely dangerous. Steep by any standards, it drops over 4,000 feet to the Imperial Valley floor at 16 feet below sea level. The road turns to a two-lane highway with occasional passing lanes and runaway truck ramps. It starts as a long, straight black slash, winding narrowly through gigantic boulders left from a glacier in some long-ago ice age.

The highway turns into a steep drop with switchback turns, weaves in and out of boulders standing like sentinels on each side of the highway. When the road would disappear behind them Charlie would accelerate, putting distance between him and traffic. The big Chevy engine was up to the challenge. Charlie said a silent thanks to Captain Ugly Pants for choosing this particular vehicle.

Everyone was still down on the floor, only Denice was up and turned around backwards, scanning the road behind. At the base of the mountain the Border Patrol pooled in a group of four cars behind a tanker truck. Trucks operate their jake brakes when coming down the steep grade, using engine compression so their brakes don't catch fire. It helps them descend slowly. At the base of the mountain, Highway 8 is a straight, flat, black ribbon disappearing into a white sand void, with a 70 miles per hour speed limit. By the time the white and green Border Patrol cleared the semi at the bottom of the grade, the teal green Suburban was on vacation and long gone.

That would be their second lucky break in less than an hour.

Denice's bad feeling about the checkpoint at Kitchen Creek was right on the money. Had they turned left they would've found the checkpoint open and swarming with officers working a double shift, and no shortage of attitude.

"Luck certainly was a lady tonight," mumbled Charlie to no one in particular.

"Okay," Denice told the cargo, "everyone can sit up now. Please put on your seatbelts."

The cargo must wear their seatbelts. It's a nasty enhancement to a trafficking charge if your Mexican nationals are not wearing their seatbelts. Go figure.

"Okay, babe, good job," complimented Charlie.

"Thanks handsome, that was close."

"I'm pretty sure he turned off at the Union 76 station by Denny's," Charlie said. "He could've red-lighted and chased us. Who knows?"

"No, we're good. He never had a chance at our plate."

"Right. Don't have too much time to analyze. Here's what I'm thinking: We'll find a Motel 6, or something, and check everyone into a double room. Then we can figure out the best route to L.A. from here."

"All right, sounds like the best plan. How about Blyth, or maybe Indio?"

Charlie looked in the rearview mirror and noticed a couple of smiling faces. He said, "Anybody speak English back there?"

"I do, *señor*," came from a handsome face covered in dirt and sweat.

"Okay. Here's the deal. We're trying to get you there, but a little change of plans here. We're getting a hotel room and slow this roll a bit. Y'all need a shower anyhow."

"Charlie, don't be rude," reprimanded Denice.

The young man replied, "*Señora*, your man is right. We stink. No one here has had a bath in almost a week. At least not one with soap."

Charlie nodded toward Denice, "You're not the only one with ESP."

"Charlie, being able to smell is not ESP." Denice rolled her eyes.

✠　✠　✠

The Indio Desert Inn and Travel Lodge was a one story L-shaped motel. Surrounded by Palm and Manzanita trees, it was fronted by a gravel parking lot. The building itself, painted hot pink in the 1950's, had faded into non-existence. If it weren't 110° and dry as a bone outside, you'd expect to see a herd of plastic pink flamingos, standing on one leg.

Charlie parked on the blind side of the office that sported a pink neon vacancy sign, entered, and rang the bell on the counter. A woman with more wrinkles than a Shar-Pei promptly answered. With a small cough she barked, "Help you?"

"Need a room. Two beds please."

"How many occupants?"

"Three," he lied.

She moved the slim brown cigarette to the right side of her mouth, thus torturing her right eyeball for a bit, and slid the form across the counter, "Fill it out, then sign right here, hon."

Charlie signed it as *James Dean, Topanga Canyon, Los Angeles, CA. License plate number PTE DRPR.* He slid the form back, put a Pall Mall to his lips, did his *flip-click-flame* routine, punctuated by his best *James-Dean* smile. She glanced at the form, and with that *everyone's-a-clown* grin raised her right eye toward Charlie. "That'll be fifty-nine-seventy."

Charlie laid three twenties on the counter.

"Room 107." She handed him a key with a two-by-four piece of framing lumber on it. The number 107 was burned into it.

"Really? Come on, I've seen gas station restroom keys smaller than that."

"Well hon, I've seen guest forms with less bullshit on them than that. So I guess that makes us even, *Mr. Dean.*"

✠   ✠   ✠

After nonchalantly moving the group from the Suburban to the room, the group instantly broke into hushed conversation. Had either Charlie or Denice spoke Spanish they would've heard,

"I'm gonna have a truck like his."

"I was told we'd have to ride in the trunk of a car."

"This is a nice room."

"I'm first in the shower."

"Good idea, you smell like a goat."

"And you don't?"

Charlie and Denice were having their own conversation quietly at the small table in the corner of the room. "We need to explore the roads out of town, look for checkpoints."

"Next time maybe we should have a, what do you call it?" questioned Denice. "A spotter car?"

I'm not leaving you here with these guys alone and I'm kinda trapped if you take the truck."

"Okay, first let's look at the map."

✠   ✠   ✠

Always fight your battles on familiar ground. In this game, knowing is the battle. Combat is about time schedules, territory, and the number of opposing forces. Good *intel* is imperative. If you approach the game in this manner, the chances of collecting your money increase tenfold. That's the endgame – safe passage through the enemy's maze to the money.

Step one: Recon your adversary's position. Find the checkpoints.

Step two: Learn their schedules and the time factors.

Step three: Misinform the enemy. Assume all communications are penetrated. Use the art of disguise to create subterfuge, buy time and advantage. For example, dress like a tourist, drop a valium, commit to your poker face 100%, and convince yourself you're not committing a crime. Oh, and have your big-breasted wife wear low cut tops through the checkpoints as a diversion. That works well too.

So now it was just a matter of knowing when the checkpoints were closed.

First trip out, Denice brought back food: *carne asada*, *burritos* with sour cream and guacamole, Spanish rice and refried beans with cheese. Even sides of jalapenos and salsa. The meal was met with quiet cheers and much gratitude.

"It's open," Denice told Charlie, referring to the border checkpoint. "And it's in the middle of nowhere. I went right through and drove five miles, turned around and came back to town. Stopped at Casa Del Rio, figuring we'd feed the gang."

"Dammit." replied Charlie. "Looks like we'll be here a while."

Denice set their meal on the little corner table. The group, all with wet hair and stinky clothes, were using the bed as a dining room table.

After the tasty Mexican food and warm showers everyone was dog-tired. Charlie and Denice had a short pow-wow and decided to wrap it up. They'd try again at daybreak.

And with consideration for the other occupants around them, Charlie and Denice tried to find sleep amongst seven snoring *amigos*.

As the first rays of sun lit up the little town of Indio, Denice pulled back into the Desert Inn and Travelodge. The big Suburban on unpaved gravel sounded like crackling fire. She opened the door with that Cheshire cat smile, "It's closed," she told Charlie. "I backed in. We can load them from the rear. You go out and start the truck while I open the back. Then come to the passenger side, leave the motel door open, and when the coast is clear, everyone into the truck, quick as they can." Denice looked to the group and asked the English speaker to translate to the others.

The room was a flurry of motion inside. Charlie started casually loading the truck looking at nothing, seeing everything. Denice lined up the group behind the door before heading towards the truck. Charlie got in the driver seat, motor running. Denice opened the back, came around to the passenger rear door, and looked back at Room 107. She then nodded her head, and everyone ran out and piled into the back, laying down or at least out of sight of the windows. Denice closed the back and jumped into the passenger-side front.

Charlie pulled out to the Main Street, Highway 8 business loop, and proceeded through the three stoplights and out into the rolling dunes of Indio towards Palm Springs. Once through the deserted checkpoint, it was clear sailing to Los Angeles. One hundred and twenty miles to Palm Springs, Cabazon, and the Morongo Indian reservation and gaming facility. Through Coachella Valley and up into the San Jancinto mountains, past the ghostly windmill farms. Then down into L.A., via Highway 10 west. Another $3,500.

✠ ✠ ✠

The silver van meeting them was driven by a handsome and smooth gentleman named Julio Garcia, an old-school retired member of the Latin Kings street gang, reportedly respected and connected. He operated on so many levels you never know if he'd be in a baseball cap or an Armani silk suit.

A trusted family member of Mrs. Ramona Flores, he was the number one face of the Syndicate. He carried two cell phones, one strictly international prepaid with no SIM card, the other, with an AT&T family plan.

"Good to see you again, Mrs. Charlie."

"Please, call me Dee-Dee, my name is Denice, but my close friends call me Dee."

Charlie said, "Most of my friends call me lucky or asshole, depending."

Julio extended his hand and Charlie shook it. "I can see why they call you lucky." With a wink at Denice and a smile at Charlie, he reached in his pocket, pulled out the wad of cash, and handed it to Charlie. "Inside is a phone number. Program it in. Call it at 8:00 a.m. tomorrow. It is a direct line to the boss, Mrs. Ramona. We have concerns about your friend, Larry."

"Hey, hey, he is just an acquaintance. He approached us. Won't hurt my feelings at all if he fell off the edge of the earth."

"We are hearing bad things about his treatment of my people. And I understand you all stayed in a hotel last night?"

"No. It was a motel."

"And you had *carne asada*?"

Charlie patted his stomach, "I freakin' love *carne asada*. My wife makes the best Spanish rice, and you ain't lived until you've wrapped your lips around her chicken *tamales*."

"I can't tell you, Charlie, how many jokes come to mind," said Julio with a smile.

"We gotta get drunk sometime," deadpanned Charlie.

Julio shook his head. *This Anglo. He was all right, maybe boss lady made a good decision?* "Call at exactly eight, my friend.

We will see each other again, I'm sure." He pointed at the big green Suburban and said, "Rubber side down, *amigo*."

"That's the only way I roll. May good fortune be with you, *amigo*."

"Yes. With us all, *compadre*."

Charlie did not know that he had just been paid the highest compliment a white man can receive from a retired shot caller in the infamous Los Angeles Latin Kings.

Valentino looked like Snidely Whiplash without the top hat. Same aquiline face with a hooked nose and beady black eyes above a pencil-thin mustache. He was bald as an egg. He stood nipple high to most women, and believed in his heart they all found him irresistible. He never tied one to a railroad track that anyone was aware of. He lived above Live Oak Springs in a small camping trailer, and he knew just about everyone on the mountain, on and off the reservation.

Valentino had a mentally challenged cousin, named Robert, a.k.a Peg-Legs, currently living in downtown Jacumba.

Valentino can tell you more than you'd ever want to know about Jacumba and its sordid history. He was once the best coyote on the mountain, but found himself in a rather nasty situation, conspiring with Robert, who had gone the wrong direction with a duffle bag full of blow. The owners of the duffle bag ran poor Robert down and broke both of his shins with an aluminum baseball bat.

The duffel bag scenario is, without question, the most dangerous act on the mountain and carries the most time, in terms of criminal penalties. If you have more balls than gray matter, it goes like this: You wait in hiding near the checkpoint until that all-important 15 to 20 minutes of Border Patrol briefing takes place. Then you *bonsai* it, which means you run for your life, hell-bent for leather down a dirt road out of Jacumba, and head south to the fence near the airstrip. It is not THE fence, but merely a rickety barbed-wire annoyance.

You run to a pre-determined spot with a pickup truck that has a sliding cover over the back. You throw the duffle bag into the back of the truck. It is always an army issue duffle bag, and it'll always be full of some various narcotics. Then drive the truck back the way you came, out of town and through the open checkpoint in broad daylight.

As you go through, you try to maintain a goofy grin, knowing there's a 10-year federal narcotics trafficking charge with your name on it in the back of what might be a stolen truck. From a distance, binoculars or naked eyes track your every move as you go through. Then these questionable characters follow you through the checkpoint and into the valley, where you drop off the bag and pick up your $500.

The whole thing from start to finish takes 45 minutes, unless, of course, your poker face fails you. Border Patrol agents are highly trained to recognize tension and nervousness. In that case, it could take you about 10 years to get home.

If you make it to El Cajon and don't stop at the drop (which is usually some fast food parking lot), like Peg-Legs did one fine afternoon, the bad guys following you will easily outrun you. *They* have a full tank of gas. Guess what? You don't. The truck they gave you had less than one-quarter of a tank to start with – just enough to do the deed. Not enough to run away with their precious cargo.

If you're stupid enough to pull that stunt, you'll never run again. Literally. Just ask Peg-Legs. Rumor has it that Valentino talked him into trying to make off with the duffle bag. Bad move.

It's a well-known fact that between Valentino and Peg-Legs you still would not have a complete hypothalamus, the judgment part of the human brain.

Charlie met Valentino working at Live Oak Resort. Val emptied trashcans, swept porches, cleaned the two public restrooms and showers, odd jobs like that. Charlie and Denice invited him to supper one evening while they were staying in the honeymoon cabin. Valentino had a stray dog look about him that made one want to take him in to feed and water him.

While dining from Styrofoam plates, filled with tasty morsels from Ron and Lily's kitchen, Valentino regaled his audience with stories of Jacumba and days gone by. His memory spanned over 40 years back to the glory days of the mineral spa, Hollywood's secret love nest. You would not know that there was a large clandestine nudist colony behind the mountain outside of Jacumba. According to Val, it was popular with the swinging couples of the 1960s jet set. Far from the cameras of the true detective stories Paparazzi, celebs living on the edge could land in a small plane, and enjoy a tryst at the spa or intimate moments at the naked bar, toasting each other: *To our wives and sweethearts, may they never meet.* It seems Jacumba has always been a place of bad behavior.

So when Charlie and Denice were looking for someone to *run point*, they approached Valentino for some sage advice and possibly a name.

That name was Elwood Tucker.

Shaking hands when they first met, Charlie asked Elwood, "Is that Elwood like in *The Blues Brothers* or do you just go by Woody...like an erection?"

"I've been known to drive through malls, if that's what you're asking."

"So, it's true on both accounts," Charlie said. Right over the poor kid's head. It takes a sharp mind to spar insults with the head that wears the crown.

Denice interjected at this point, before a possible stare-down ensued. "We're looking for a driver, somebody to run interference and scope out the road ahead of us."

"I can do that."

Denice continued, "We need somebody to attract attention should we get into a jam. Someone to pull the heat off us and basically sacrifice themselves and their driving record, should we have a problem. You won't ever have people in your ride and we'll provide the car. We'll put sacks of cement in the trunk. So it looks like you're *driving dirty* (as in carrying Mexicans or drugs). If we're followed, or there's Border Patrol in the bushes, they follow you instead of us. You get pulled over? They don't find diddly. Easy money."

"How much easy money?"

Charlie said, "Depends on the run, we'll start with $250 a run. We'll provide the vehicle, walkie-talkie, food and hotel, the complete package."

Woody's eyes grew large, a smile spreading across his young face. He then said, "I get a walkie-talkie. Fuckin' A, I'm your man, dude. When do we roll? Do I get it now?"

Denice asked, "Do you get what now?"

"The radio, man! The *breaker, breaker, Scout One to Papa Bear*." Woody beamed.

Charlie looked at Dee, "Holy shit."

Denice laughed, "At least he's enthusiastic."

If Elwood made a perfect sacrificial lamb, then let's talk about the wolves. The brave men and women of the United States Border Patrol have one of the most difficult jobs in law enforcement. After September 11th, the Feds finally gave them firearms. Prior to that, they could only yell real loud, "Stop in the name of the law." Mostly, they just herded people into large buses.

In the early 2000s the Border Patrol's job description expanded to zero tolerance with zero training. In the years leading up to and including Charlie and Denice's time, prosecutors would not indict or prosecute a driver on an illegal immigration case until that person was (or persons were) arrested three times. Drugs or guns are completely different animals, perpetrated by a completely different group of smugglers and smuggling organizations. Bottom line, you get the least amount of prison time for illegal immigration, which means the lowest danger-to-dollar ratio.

That's not to say it wasn't or isn't still dangerous. There are 100 ways to get killed, 1,000 ways to screw up, and one million things that can go wrong. But if you're smooth, quick on the uptake, with an organized mind and a hole where the risk management part of your brain used to be, you can make a shit-load of money.

✠　✠　✠

The call to Ramona was placed at 8:00 a.m. sharp. Arrangements were made to meet at the Viejas Casino, in the buffet for lunch. The dining room had the most spectacular fireplace and lodge pole seating area. The fireplace was made of Fieldstone masonry and was three stories tall. The fire pit area was as tall as a man and 10-feet wide. The food was better than at Barona casino. You could have prime rib and horseradish at 10:00 a.m. On a Friday or Saturday you'd have to wait two hours for a table. But on this midweek afternoon, Charlie and Denice walked right in, found a table and ordered two coffees. They explained to the server they were waiting on their other party.

The wait was short. Ramona and Julio walked in and up to the table. Ramona was dressed in a light blue pantsuit and sensible shoes with a small black clutch purse. She had black, shoulder length hair. Julio was wearing Levi 501s and a comfortable looking sport jacket over a black T-shirt, probably silk. Charlie noticed the ever-so-slight bulge under his jacket. This was not surprising, nor did it cause him alarm. He stood up smiling and extended his hand.

"Good to see you again, Julio," as they shook hands.

"Likewise to you both."

Charlie motioned towards the table and invited, "Please have a seat," as he continued shaking Ramona's hand. "Good afternoon, ma'am. This is my wife, Denice."

Ramona spoke flawless English, having been obviously educated in the United States. (University of Southern California, they discovered later.)

"It's nice to meet you both."

Charlie inquired, "Business before pleasure? The food here is excellent and I wouldn't want to spoil it by talking with my mouth full."

"Sounds good, Mr. DeVille."

"Please, call me Charlie."

"Well, Charlie and Denice, we have much to discuss, and as always, best never over the phone. We transport family members. Our business is to reunite families. With citizenship taking five years, and the waiting lists, years to get a green card, we have a mostly exclusive *niche* market."

Ramona's eyes went back and forth from Charlie to Denice. She spoke earnestly and with conviction. Julio sat twisting his coffee, watching and surveying without moving his head, except to nod in agreement with Ramona's words.

"It has come to my attention, through your success and compliments from our customers, our *people*," she emphasized, "that you provide superior service. You seem to understand what we're doing here and what we're trying to provide."

Denice interjected at this point, "You make it sound so corporate, almost legal."

"This business is fifty percent illusion and fifty percent balls, to use a rather descriptive metaphor."

Charlie joined, "I use that metaphor to describe mine, as well. We're all adults here."

Denice kicked Charlie under the table so hard in the shin that Charlie had to mutter, "Damn, honey, that hurt."

"Be serious, Charlie. For once."

Ramona interrupted the little love spat with a comment,

"No, Denice, Charlie's right. If you're smiling and laughing, no one expects you're committing a crime. It is the shroud of deniability that creates the illusion of innocence."

Charlie's comedy was an invisible shield to protect the man inside the smuggler – a kind of a canvas cover over life's moral compass. So of course it made complete sense to him. He looked his wife in the eye and brought his right hand up in the shape of a gun, cocked his thumb and made a clicking sound with his tongue, and said in his best Will Ferrell impersonation, "Stay classy, San Diego."

Everyone chuckled and the mood became light and breezy.

Ramona continued, "We want the two of you to handle our specialty runs. Large orders, VIPs, and infants." All the while, Ramona looked at Denice with a raised brow.

Denice replied, "Infants and children?"

"Yes, infants and *very* small children, they cannot be moved by coyotes."

Julio chimed in, "Pelón is not good with children. His single eyeball would terrorize the poor *niños.*"

Charlie and Julio laughed, as Denice and Ramona shook their heads. In some way, they bonded at that moment.

The pace of the conversation accelerated as women are inclined to do when talking amongst themselves. Ramona said, "This requires you to drive into Tijuana with a car seat in your trunk, and drive the child across the border, back into the U.S. I understand you have a daughter and an infant grandson?"

"Yes, Renae is my oldest. But we call her Nae-Nae, or sometimes Nae for short. And my little grandson is a doll. His name is Brandt."

Charlie interrupted her, "Jesus, don't get her started. She'll cover the table with pictures and talk your ear off."

Ramona looked at him and explained, "There's always time for family. And I love children. We are all about family, and that time will come. But for now my question is, can we work together and not let our arrangements become known to, shall we say, the *Larry's* of Jacumba?"

Denice looked at Charlie. "Don't even start with the Captain Ugly Pants stuff," she warned.

"I've already forgotten who he was." Charlie then looked at the Big Boss, and in a very serious tone said, "Let's talk money."

Julio took over at this point.

"Infants pay $1,000 cash, from the San Ysidro International border to Chula Vista. Two infants at a time pays $1,000 each. If your daughter decides to do the run, we can provide a dark skinned gentleman, a U.S. citizen, to play the father. He would authenticate the dark skin of the children. If you choose to run, you must do it alone. Charlie is too white."

"Call me Casper the Friendly Ghost," Charlie wisecracked.

Denice had stunning olive skin, given to her by her mother who was a beauty of Hispanic descent. Her family was from Mazatlan. She could pass as an older mom or a younger grandmother.

Julio was taken back to his old school days in the gang, where he had watched a member named Casper die from a bullet wound, bleeding to death in his arms as they waited for an ambulance. It was a senseless killing by a rival of the Latin Kings, just another reason to retire as O.G. (original gangster), respected as such for surviving the streets of L.A.

After a moment of silence, for the memory of his friend, Julio continued. "VIPs are just that. You do not need to know who's who. There are some things you cannot question; you will not receive an answer. You'll always be informed of the risk, and never will there be drugs, weapons, or felons fleeing Mexican justice. If extra precautions are needed, due to the rank of a family member, you will be notified and paid accordingly for these people, we'll say $2,000 with a bonus. That means they ride alone and you will protect them at all times."

Ramona asked for their phones and Denice slid them across the table to her. "This one is okay. But throw this one in the toilet," she said, referring to Denice's AT&T phone. Ramona pulled out a brand new iPhone and handed it to her. "This is programmed with the numbers you need. Use only this phone for company business. We will call you on only this phone, or paging phones at the Acorn or Viejas casinos, also the Pechanga and Morongo casinos. Should you get pulled over, drop it in your 48-ounce Thirst Buster. I have one in my cup-holder at all times." Ramona gave a wink. "We will contact you tomorrow with the plans, that is if you agree?"

"Does the Pope wear funny hats?" Charlie asked rhetorically.

"As a matter of fact, he does," replied Ramona with a hint of good-natured sass.

"Let's eat," concluded Julio with a grin. "I'm starving."

LITTLE RUNNING SQUIRREL AND THE BIG YELLOW BUS
Chapter 12

Elwood moved out of his small one bedroom apartment on Mollison Avenue in El Cajon. He had rented an 18-foot Ryder moving truck for this purpose. It had a big, brand-new, diesel engine and an air-conditioned cab. Bells were bonging inside Charlie's head one millisecond after seeing Elwood load it.

Charlie saw it as the ultimate people-moving machine. He imagined one up at the drop, loaded down.

"Earth to Charlie, Earth to Charlie," Denice said, snapping her fingers in front of his face.

"Look at it, honey, like Fort Knox on wheels. It's like a big catering truck. Catering to immigrants, a bright yellow school bus. To school you on how to move a town of people."

"Settle down, handsome. It's just a moving truck."

"I wonder what Elwood's doing with it when he's done?"

"Ask him."

"Bet your cute little ass I will."

They had to go to Elwood's apartment because he wasn't answering his phone, and to show him the Maxima they had bought from Big Chief Acorn, a.k.a. Corn Hole. After the meeting with Ramona and Julio, they went to find Larry to extend the rental on the green Suburban. In the interim, they ran into Big Chief Acorn in the casino parking lot.

"Hey, you guys. What's shaking? What're you doing at my casino?"

Big Chief Acorn was a deranged Kumeyaay Indian who took the whole *Sovereign Nation* thing a little too far. He loved to question white people as to their reasons for being in *his* country, on *his* land, breaking *his* laws, and all that. This did not mean much, as he was not the chief of the tribe. His erratic behavior was more related to that week's drug of choice. Charlie started shying away from Corn Hole's presence after he discharged a handgun out of Charlie's passenger-side window.

Here's how it went down: As Charlie gave Corn Hole a ride home one day, they came upon Corn Hole's female cousin's husband. Corn Hole believed the guy had gotten rough with Little Running Squirrel. "Why'd you smack Little Running Squirrel? You piece of shit," the old Indian accused.

"I did not touch the bitch." Ouch. Wrong answer.

Corn Hole pulled a Glock out of nowhere, pointed it out the window, and *BOOM! BOOM! BOOM!* The window shattered and Charlie found himself in need of a clean pair of drawers.

So when Corn Hole asked if they wanted to buy a car, Charlie's first instinct was to tell him, "Nope. No, thanks. We're good. Thanks though. Nope, we're broke."

However, Denice interrupted with, "What kind?"

Charlie rolled his eyes.

"A Nissan Maxima, the white one right over there." He pointed at a nice front wheel drive, luxury midsize four-door car.

"Nice. How much?" asked Denice.

"Six hundred dollars," Corn Hole quickly replied.

"That's all? Shit." Charlie said excitedly.

Sticking out his chest, Corn Hole said, "My casino owns it. The Border Patrol arrested the owners right here. My country now owns it. Six hundred dollars."

"Pay him, honey." Denice said.

"Yeah, like you let me carry the money?" laughed Charlie.

"I meant, hand me my purse, babe."

And because of that weird transaction, they were at Elwood's old apartment in the new *point car*, the Maxima, equipped with a walkie-talkie on channel 14 and a Radio Shack *bear scanner*, which is a street name for a police band radio receiver. The plan was to keep the big green SUV. But now that Charlie had laid eyes on the Ryder truck, yellow was his favorite color.

"Elwood, I came to give you a hand and show you your new *Hooptie*. Complete with police scanner and, wait for it, a walkie-talkie."

"Far freakin' OUT, dude." Sitting in the car he checked out all the knobs and buttons, fiddling with this and that, questioning Charlie.

"Electric seats?" asked Elwood.

"Yeah," Charlie smirked.

"Air-conditioning work?"

"Yup."

"Radio?"

"Yuuup."

"Sweet!"

"Yes. And all you've got to do is let me use that Ryder truck for a couple days after you're done with it. I'll even pay the bill."

"Hell yeah, bro. It's on my mom's credit card anyway."

Charlie winked at Denice and turned to Elwood, "Perfect, dude."

They spent most of that afternoon into the early evening moving Elwood's crap into storage and cleaning his bachelor pad.

"I can't believe these assholes evicted me."

"What for?" Charlie asked.

"Noise. A couple of parties. Um, my ex-girlfriend kinda freaked out."

As they were leaving for the last time and walking across the pool area, Charlie noticed the light-weight patio furniture.

"You still got the key to the pool gate?"

"Yeah."

"Keep it until tomorrow."

They made the last trip to the storage unit and then traded vehicles. Charlie's mind was awhirl with crazy ideas. Denice said, "I'm hungry, how about Los Ponchos?"

Charlie picked up the walkie-talkie.

"How about it Wood Man, you out there?"

"Ten-four, Big Daddy DeVille."

"Meet me and the little woman at Los Ponchos on Second Street."

"Ten-four, right at Highway 8 on-ramp."

"That's the one. Bring the pool key and we'll buy you a burrito."

"Roger that."

Charlie spun his head quickly around and looked at Denice, "There, you see? *Rodger that.* I'm not the only one."

"Yup. You and the Wood Man, Charlie," she replied casually.

Charlie keyed the radio, "Over and out."

"What, no *Roger dodger*?" asked Denice mockingly.

"Naw. His name is Elwood," Charlie shot back.

Charlie and Elwood went back to the apartments on Mollison in the Ryder truck, while Denice took the Maxima to Sycuan Casino to exercise her horseshoe. The boys were on a mission of stealth and mischief, namely, stealing all the pool furniture; including the tables, umbrellas, and lounge chairs. They quietly loaded them into the Ryder truck, and then went directly to home base. Charlie and Elwood laid out the furniture in the back of the Ryder, using deck screws to attach the furniture to the wood deck of the box truck.

Standing back, inside home base, admiring their handiwork, Charlie knew Ramona would be impressed. The truck was now perfect. A roll-up backdoor, it also had a side door with pull out steps. The door was the size of an entry door in a house. The roof of the box was yellow fiberglass, which allowed the sun to shine in, hence, the umbrellas. Looking at the whole picture, if Charlie had two elbows on his right arm, he'd have patted himself on the back.

Denice was impressed, yet concerned, with the outcome of their mission. "I can't believe you, Charlie. You actually stole the pool furniture?"

"Borrowed it."

"I've never known you to steal anything."

"Elwood did it." As if that made it okay.

She stood back with her hands on her hips, staring into the back, there in the Sycuan Casino parking lot at 2:40 a.m.

"That is so damn cool. Oh my God. Brilliant. Crazy. But very cool." She kissed him on the cheek and cooed, "That's my man."

Charlie rolled down the back door and followed her into the casino. It was one hour before audit time. The magic hour. Charlie ran to catch up with her and said, "Hold your horseshoe, wait for me."

Denice hit Ramona's speed dial number. "Hey, girl. We're good for 20."

Ramona replied, "No way."

"Yes, way."

"Stand by. Let me call the hotel."

"Okay, hon. Have a nice day," Denice hollered back.

Charlie flashed on what a smooth operator his new partner in crime had become. He wondered if this was the same woman who was Scoutmaster, PTA mom, and softball coach? Charlie and soccer mom, Denice. Husband and wife team wearing many hats. These days, with sunglasses and a disguise.

The next afternoon, they woke to the ringing of their cell phone. On the other end the caller said, "Looks like rain."

Denice looked out the window of their hotel room.

"Yeah, it's drizzling here."

At the other end of the phone Ramona replied, "Can you hang at the Acorn until 5:00 a.m. tomorrow?"

"Sure."

"Page us."

"Gotcha."

"Pray for rain."

Charlie, overhearing said, "If she's on her knees, she won't be praying."

"Dammit, Charlie," Denice scolded in disgust.

"All men are pigs, replied Ramona."

"I hear ya, girlfriend."

"Bye."

"See you."

Smugglers pray for rain, snow, and sand storms. Maybe an outbreak of Border Patrol E. coli. When the weather is bad, the men and women of the U.S. Border Patrol do what most police do – paperwork and scarf doughnuts. They do not stand in the rain or ask motorists questions like *Where are you headed? Do you have any fruit? Is everyone inside the vehicle an American Citizen?* Being that California is classified as an agricultural state, they monitor the coming and going of fruit, as well as illegal immigrants. But at their core, they're Federal employees like the TSA, and at last check they had a 94%

failure rate, and that was without standing in the rain. Border Patrol/fruit police.

It was a blessing from the smuggling gods. It was raining cats and dogs when they heard, "Mrs. DeVille, white paging phone. Mrs. DeVille, white paging phone, please."

Denice stepped up to the phone, "This is Mrs. DeVille."

"One moment please."

CLICK

"Nineteen," said a disembodied voice, and then the line went dead.

It was *go time*.

They moved quickly out the side entrance past the gas pumps, to the truck parking area. They jumped in and fired up the diesel engine, turned left onto the old Highway 8 down towards Jacumba, to make the connection. Forty miles an hour over the bridge, with the windshield wipers on high, Charlie flashed his brights three times and then the radio in Denice's hand came alive.

"Nineteen for the ride, Crazy *gringo*."

"Back at you, Wiley."

The line of people was barely visible in the downpour, slipping and sliding down the hill behind the school. Denice jumped down, ran around to the driver side of the box, and pulled out the folding steps. As she opened the door, the first person arrived.

"Go, go, GO!"

It took less than 90 seconds to load them in. Denice jumped back up into the cab of the big yellow truck, now transformed into a combination bus and pool-side limo. Charlie started jammin' gears, pulling out into the rainy night.

In the smuggling biz, it just doesn't get any better than this. The radio came alive again. "Hey. Crazy white boy, you kiss Denice smooth on the lips for me. We set the world record today."

Denice keyed the mic, "Wiley, you may kiss me your damn self when we get back."

Charlie said, "On the cheek, those are my lips."

"Be safe, my friends." And then Wiley disappeared from the airwaves.

The rain came down hard as ever as they flew through the checkpoint.

"How 'bout it, Wood Man?"

"Gotcha, bro. On visual."

"Ten-four. Kitchen Creek exit?"

"Right behind ya, boss." He handed the radio to Denice and shifted into overdrive, cresting the hill to the downside of the grade.

Denice spoke, "I think we're cool, Woody. Just follow us for a while."

"Ten-four, Mrs. DeVille."

Denice looked over at her husband, "Remind me to tell that dumb-ass not to use my last name on the goddamn radio."

"Check us out, baby doll. You hear Wiley? World fuckin' record!"

"Stop it with the F-bombs, honey."

"Sorry," Charlie apologized.

"You have such a potty mouth."

"That's not potty mouth, babe. That's a shit-eating grin." Charlie's bright smile spread from ear to ear.

The rain continued as they approached the Temecula checkpoint, spanning all four lanes of Interstate 15. The Maxima passed them going up the incline, two miles before the checkpoint.

"It's clear, boss. Shut down tight. Not a soul in sight."

"Well, rock on, Wood Man. Take us to L.A."

"Ten-four."

✠   ✠   ✠

They pulled into the Century City Mall parking lot, having called Ramona after clearing the Temecula point. She alerted the families of the 19 people they had in the back of the truck. Pulling up to the Nordstrom's side of the huge mall, you could not tell that there were 17 separate cars, SUVs and trucks, all waiting for the magic bus to arrive.

They backed up to the curb at the far reach of the lot. Ramona appeared in Denice's window, as Charlie shut off the engine. Charlie opened the side door, and Ramona stepped up into the box truck.

Her clients were playing cards at the two tables, lounging in poolside chairs, and drinking cold Pepsi from the ice chest.

"Gin," said one of the men, laying down his card. "You lose, *vato*."

The smile on Ramona's face was priceless. Or rather it was worth $9,500, plus a $500 bonus, for a cool ten grand.

✠ ✠ ✠

Word had already reached the mountain. They had broken the record and returned victorious. Trading back the Ryder truck for the Maxima (not wanting it seen on the mountain) Elwood took it to his new place, along with 500 bucks and bragging rights. A victory dinner seemed in order, and their first choice was, of course, the Live Oak Springs restaurant.

It was still raining, but not as hard as when they were pulling in. The place was busy and so were Ron and Lily. Charlie and Denice were shown to a table by the window, and they placed their drink order. The hostess was new. Charlie asked her, "Will you please tell the chef that Mr. and Mrs. DeVille are present for an unparalleled dining experience?"

A few minutes later Ron appeared at their table, asking,

"Hey, guys, how are you?"

Charlie smiled, "Tippy-tappy, with a song in my heart. How about you and the missus?"

"We're good. Speaking of good, I've got some freshly baked salmon steaks, along with fresh asparagus and white sauce, baby red potatoes with a dash of garlic."

"Love it, sounds delicious," exclaimed Denice.

Charlie smirked, "I'll take 10 of those and a bottle of your best white wine."

"I'll have the waitress bring you a salad."

"Okay. Hey, can we get a cabin? Have any vacant?"

Ron, rolling his eyes, said, "For you guys, no problem. I'll have Lily bring the key over so she can say hi."

Dinner was excellent as always. They finished a bottle of a tasty, Napa Valley Chardonnay, and a piece of key lime pie. Lily was as good with pastries as Ron was with the entrées.

Lily brought over the key to the honeymoon cabin, the registration form, and the dinner ticket. "Hey, you guys. Kiss, kiss." she said.

"Dinner was scrumptious," complimented Denice.

"Thanks. Don't worry about the form, it's just a tax thing. Just put your name and the date, we know who you are."

Charlie filled out the form: *Elvis Presley, Graceland, Memphis, Tennessee*. License plate number: *DGY STYL*.

Charlie included a one-hundred-dollar bill and a twenty-five-dollar tip. He then looked at his lovely bride and said, "You know, Pumkin, luck runs like a renegade and I'm feelin' pretty enthusiastic about running-a-muck as a VIP."

Denice, feeling jubilant, agreed. "A little time-out-of-mind sounds fabulous right about now."

Quick on the uptake, Charlie reminded his wife, "Acorn has no VIP services, so flip a coin; heads Barona, tails Viejas?"

Denice called it in the air, "Tails!"

And tails it was. So it was a mad dash with the cash to the VIP Room at Viejas.

Here's the deal: If your glass is half full...there's room for scotch!

✠ ✠ ✠

Charlie and Denice strolled into the VIP Room and there she was. Her name was Luwana, but the men called her

"Luscious." The women called her "that slut." Denice called her "out of bounds," seeing as she had parked her perfect posterior on the machine next to Charlie, who had, it seemed, made her laugh – a husky sound filled with sexual tension. The atmosphere around Luwana vibrated with it. Like a human tuning fork. Luwana emanated juicy pheromones that agitated Charlie's gorilla just enough to rattle its cage.

The thing about Luwana that was most alluring was her scent. She smelled like night jasmine and good sex, slow-hand sex. Her essence made other women turn their heads and sniff the air, looking for the source.

She had a dusting of freckles below her dark eyes that pull you in, and this crazy little strut that turned heads. Sashaying through the packed casino like a little pink bulldozer, the crowd automatically parted at her approach. Just to watch her go by, hijacking your imagination, left you flustered – and if you were a man, a little frustrated.

Denice DeVille was not happy about any of it.

Seeing Charlie make Luwana laugh brought Denice's irrational and aggressive green monster of misunderstood jealousy to the surface.

Denice plowed through the crowd and, standing behind Charlie with one hand on his shoulder. "I'm back honey." She then turned to Luwanwa and added sweetly, "What's up 'Do-Ya-Wanna?'"

Charlie thought, *Good lord, here we go again.*

"My name is Luwana, ass-bite."

"Can't find any single men to flirt with?"

Charlie turned sideways in his chair and looked up at Denice, "I sat down next to her, so cool your jets, Dee," trying hard to disarm the monster. But Denice heard none of it, deaf to the truth.

"Fuck that. Every time I turn around this tramp is making eyes at you."

Charlie stood, hit the cash out button, collected his ticket, and said, "Outside. Now."

Charlie was disgusted when Denice would not disengage her humiliating behavior, trying to cause a scene. Charlie grabbed her elbow and physically dragged her towards the exit.

"Charlie, dammit, you're hurting me."

"Not yet, but keep it up."

"Stop it! You're embarrassing me..."

Charlie hit the exit door with his right foot, pushing Denice into the cold night air. He let go of her elbow and, through clenched teeth answered, "Embarrassing *you*? What the hell's wrong with you? I'm your goddamned husband."

"You know that tramp was coming on to you," Denice accused.

"So what?"

"So you're my husband. And, for the record, it looked like you were having a pretty good time. You had a big smile on your face."

"You're acting like she was sitting on my face. You telling me I can't talk to a beautiful woman unless you're standing right there?"

"Oh, so now she's beautiful?"

Exasperated, Charlie said, "This is stupid, I can't believe we're having this ridiculous conversation...again! Let's get out of the doorway."

Charlie took the lead and Denice followed. He found a bench and sat down. Denice sat on the other end. Charlie put a smoke to his lips, *flip-click-flame*. Offered it to Denice. She refused, but pulled one out of her purse. That spoke volumes to Charlie. Shaking his head, he waited a moment before continuing, clearing the anger, or at least trying to. "You don't trust me. And that's the shitty part, aside from the fact that we've been around this block a hundred fuckin' times."

"It's not me, it's her. She could give a shit less if you're married or not."

Charlie, trying to keep the anger under the surface, lowered his voice so she had to pay attention.

"Hey. Newsflash. I actually do give a shit. There's a tan line on my ring finger."

Sticking his hand up to her face, "See? This stupid shit has got to stop. You know I could give a shit less what people think. But when you act foolish, it makes me embarrassed for you. It's humiliating for both of us."

Denice exhaled a plume of smoke into the air, "Well, guess what? *I'm* not embarrassed. Everyone knows she's a slut."

The anger welled up in Charlie like a southern thunderstorm, "It's not about her, it's about *you*. You trusting me, godammit! I've never in all these years given you a reason not to. Not once!" Charlie angrily flicked his cigarette out onto the road.

After a minute, Denice said, "She makes me look stupid when you make goo-goo eyes at her."

"Oh please, you're acting like a fifteen-year-old. You're a grandmother for God's sake. And besides, just so we're clear, it's a compliment to you when a woman makes a move on me."

Denice sat there, deaf, dumb, and blinded by jealousy. Charlie looked at his wife's face, "You still don't get it, do you?"

Silence.

"Another newsflash for you; this bullshit is why your first husband left you."

"Fuck you!" Denice screamed.

"That's the point. You're the only one fucking me, in more ways than one!"

THE UNIVERSAL SMILE
Chapter 13

After some awesome makeup sex, the morning after the whole Luwana debacle came too soon. Sleepy-eyed and smiley-faced, Charlie and Denice rose in their Live Oak cabin to freezing wet sleet, almost snow. Having consumed each other and all the firewood the night before, they made their way to the car and down to the country store for some smokes. Also on their list: a little cheese Danish and two bundles of *burn-the-captive-tourist* firewood; six pieces for four dollars? What a rip-off. Charlie's manhood was somehow challenged or maybe disrespected on some Cro-Magnon level. Being the hunter-gatherer and Alpha Male, buying wood from 'Your Burnt Industries' of Campo, California, made him wince.

Denice saw it. "Wipe that frown off your face, handsome. After last night, you're still my stud muffin."

Charlie stood there with the offending wood bundle and mumbled in his best Elvis, "Thank you. Thank you very much."

The pimply-faced kid at the counter smiled, "I'm feeling a lot of love here today."

"Good grief," Charlie said under his voice. Misinterpreted comedy is such a waste. But that was in essence the vibe that surrounded Charlie and Denice. They were partners, yet opposites. When Charlie and Denice returned to the cabin, Denice began the next thing on her "to-do list" for the day.

"Move up off the bed honey, I need to make it up."

Charlie didn't move a muscle. "Why are you doing the maid's job?"

"Because for the next 48 hours this is our bed. It's got to be cozy when we crawl in."

"I'm sure the maid needs the hours."

From inside the tiny bathroom Dee's voice, sounding like it came from inside a cave, said, "This, this right here is what I'm talking about." She entered from the bathroom carrying a pair of Charlie's underwear with her thumb and forefinger.

"You won't even pick up your dirty boxer briefs. You want a stranger to deal with your underwear for seven bucks an hour?"

"I leave a tip."

"Not the point. Now get. Off. The. Bed!"

"Okay, but I'm not leaving a tip if you're going to raise your voice. Hey, have you seen my smokes?"

But as lost as he seemed at times, it was just a case of a distracted mind. Charlie knew exactly what was going on. He knew what was required at any given moment. He was smooth and confident, and that made Denice feel safe. It boils down to absolute trust. It's hard to find that person in a world of self-centered egomaniacs in a beauty pageant culture.

That's why they made such an outstanding team, ignoring outside influences and never taking their eyes off the ball. Focus is everything in this business. It wasn't *Eye Of the Tiger*, but rather *Eye ON the Tiger*.

After a cheap breakfast and plenty of overpriced wood, they pulled out of the store and noticed a very old, very disheveled Latino woman. She was walking on the wrong side of Old Highway 8. She had on a blue housecoat, the kind your great grandma always wore on Thanksgiving. It was extremely cold and she was shivering, looking down at her feet with each careful step. But what was most disconcerting was the blood on her legs from knee to ankle.

Denice's reaction was immediate. "Oh my God. That poor woman's hurt, and why in the hell is she walking in this rain? Look at her legs. Charlie, stop!"

"Okay, babe. We're on it." Charlie pulled out onto the road and up to the side where the old woman was walking and turned on his flashers.

Denice rolled down her window, "Are you okay, ma'am?"

The woman did not answer.

Denice opened the door, jumped out, and blocked the woman's path. "*K-onda, niña*? Are you okay, Grandmother?"

The old woman's tears were immediate and torrential. The words came like automatic gunfire. Denice reached out to her and they embraced. The old woman sobbed and wailed before looking up and rattling off 1,000 rapid-fire words in Spanish.

Neither understood the other, nor needed to. The sound of suffering is universal. You didn't need to speak Spanish to know this person had been through hell.

"Get in." Denice motioned to the open door, but the woman just stood there, trying to decide if this was a good idea.

Charlie comforted her. "It's okay, *señora*," wishing he could say something to ease her fear. There's something else that's universal, and that's a smile. Charlie flashed his best Burt Reynolds, *Smokey and the Bandit* smile that he saved for just this kind of occasion. It worked like a dream. The old woman managed a bashful smile back, full of crooked teeth, which could barely be seen behind her thankful grin. No anger. No malice. Just relief at the thought that her nightmare might be over. Every wrinkle on her face went up towards her forehead just like a Cabbage Patch doll. The effect was startling.

"Come on ladies. Let's go before we get run over."

Denice helped the old woman into the backseat and closed the door. She then jumped in the front seat and said, "Let's go back to the cabin. We'll find Valentino and have him talk to her."

"Okay." Then looking back Charlie added, "Looks like she could use a warm fire and some rest."

"I can't believe she was out like that in this weather."

It was just a few short blocks back to the cabin. The three hustled inside, Charlie with an armload of wood. Once inside the cabin, the old woman reached into the front pocket of her dress and pulled out a soaking wet piece of paper. There was a smudged phone number on it. She said something in Spanish and pointed to the slip of paper.

"I think she wants us to call this number, it has a Los Angeles County prefix."

"Starting to get the picture here. I'll bet she couldn't keep up with some coyote."

There were many organizations and many coyotes. Most coyotes were brutal when it came to stragglers. Wiley would not have tried to run grandma here through the gauntlet. She wouldn't stand half a chance. Ramona would have classified her as a VIP and made other arrangements.

Denice dialed the number, "It's ringing."

Charlie and the woman were silent. Waiting.

"Hi. My name's Denice, my husband and I are calling from Campo, California. We found a woman who we believe is named Isabelle."

She was cut off by ecstatic voices in Spanish accents. "You found Grandmother? Thank you, Jesus. I can't believe it. Hey, Carlos, it's your mother. They found your mother."

A man's voice came on the line, and Denice put it on speaker. The three *amigos* clustered around the phone. In Spanish they spoke to her, "Mother, are you okay?"

"Yes, *mijo*, I'm not dead yet."

"Where are you?"

The grandmother replied, "I don't know, but I have been walking for two days. I found a road and this nice couple picked me up. They took me here."

"Where is here, Mother?"

"I don't know. But there is a fire in the fireplace and it's very warm."

"They can hear you," the grandmother replied.

In English, came a deep baritone voice, "My name is Carlos. Whom am I speaking with?"

"I'm Denice."

"Are you the police?"

"Not hardly, sir."

"My mother. Is she okay? She is, how do you say, very hardheaded."

Charlie said quietly to himself, "Duh, she's a woman."

"I think she's a sweetie and she's okay." Denice told the man, giving Charlie a stern look.

"She is a diabetic," Carlos informed them, "and has lymphoma. We've been trying to get her here to spend some time with her grandchildren before...um...She will need to eat, can you give her a banana, and maybe some orange juice."

"Today's your lucky day," exclaimed Charlie. "This is what we do for a living. We move people from here on the mountain to L.A. Mom goes as a VIP. And you know what? It's friggin' raining. That makes it a piece of cake. So hang in there, Carlos, we'll get Mom to you before the sun goes down. *Gar-ron-teed.*"

"Thank you so much, sir, we will pay whatever you ask."

"Right now it's not about the money. It's about your mom."

That's another universal truth: Motherly love and the emotion it invokes, like a son's need to protect and love her, regardless of the risks. There is no fire that burns hotter in a man's heart than that which concerns his mother. Wars have been waged around a slight to a mother's love, honor thy mother is a commandment from God. For some it is not easy to do. But for Charlie, a mother's love was the queen of his heart. Many times he saw divine intervention in the relationships with the women in his life. Charlie was passionate about certain things, and getting Isabelle home to her family now topped the list.

Denice asked Carlos for his address and promised to update their progress later that day. They ended the conversation with,

"Don't worry. She's in good hands. Call if you need to. But less is better. See you soon."

When she hung up the phone, Grandma smiled and closed her eyes, she then let the exhaustion envelop her. She snored quietly, and both thought it was the cutest sound they'd heard since their girls were babies.

Denice said quietly, "I'll go back to the store to get some juice and fill the gas tank. We'll put some blankets and a pillow in the backseat and she can sleep on the way to L.A."

This run was in the hands of God, as sure as the sun sets in the west. It was nearly snowing. The checkpoint was closed. Having fed granny, they loaded Izzie (as Charlie called her) into the car. She slept peacefully in the back. They drove straight to Monrovia, and found the address easily. Charlie called Carlos, about an hour ahead of their arrival. It was a Saturday afternoon and the driveway was packed with several cars, and more parked on the street.

When the Nissan pulled up, the old woman was sitting upright in the back. Kids came pouring out of the house, big and small. Everyone hugged and kissed Charlie and Denice, showering them with a true hero's welcome. On the patio and inside the house, there were balloons and a banner proclaiming, *Welcome Home* in Spanish, obviously painted by the children.

Charlie and Denice were offered Coronas all day long. There was *carne asada* and burgers smoking on the 55-gallon drum barbecue. The old folks played bocce ball. The youngest child came and climbed up on Grandma Izzie's lap, like the old lady was a jungle gym. Someone passed around a baseball cap, and it was brimming with one-hundred-dollar bills and fifty-dollar bills. When Izzie's son, Carlos, approached Charlie with the hat, Charlie refused the money.

"We will light a candle in your honor, Charlie. You and your wife are a blessing to this family," said Carlos, holding back tears.

When it was time to leave, the emotions ran even higher. It had been a wonderful day. A kind of validation, maybe balancing out all that illegal activity. Charlie and Denice struggled with that aspect. But any doubt about their current mission went out the window when Grandma Izzie held Denice's face in her tiny fragile hands, then kissing her forehead told her through Carlos' translation, "You are my angel, my saving grace. I'll see you in heaven." She then kissed Charlie gently on both cheeks, and said, "You are my knight in shining armor today, *señor*. Bless you and thank you."

As Izzie walked away, she was saying something in Spanish. Carlos pulled her back saying, "Mind your tongue, Mother." Carlos looked at Charlie, and said quietly, "She said if she was 40 years younger, she'd give your wife a run for her money."

Izzie had left the rear window down on the Maxima. As Charlie and Denice pulled out, a young boy about 10 or so, ran up and threw the hatful of money into the open rear window, and the bills scattered all over the rear seat. The young boy stuck out his tongue at Charlie, and blew him a raspberry. Then he ran back to his father, Carlos. As the boy clutched his daddy's leg, the two waved as Charlie and Denice drove away.

"You're a good man, Charlie Brown," said Denice, and the appreciative family disappeared from view.

"I'd rather you call me, Chuck."

LOVE IS NOT A SUICIDE PACT
Chapter 14

Charlie and Denise headed back to home base to check off things on Denice's to-do list, an arbitrary event that took place at random intervals.

Something inside her would all of the sudden start to itch, causing a tick on her right eyelid. At this point, she would just have to organize something quickly. When they were first married it was the living room furniture. Later, it was the girls' rooms or the Tupperware drawer.

Sometimes when the urge became overwhelming, Charlie would find her in his garage in the late hours of the night. Their garage was the Taj Mahal of overhaul, a place for the organizing of nuts and bolts. She categorized gaskets, lined up spray paint cans, and so on.

Charlie did not oppose this behavior, for fear that Denice might implode. Now that they mostly lived in hotel suites, mountain cabins and SUVs, it was all about the to-do list, car washes and laundromats. Love is all about understanding and compromise. Charlie would take her to the Beer & Bubbles coin-op laundry. Denice would give him clean underwear. That was another California first; drink yourself stupid while watching the dryer go round and round. Charlie always accompanied Denice to the laundromat.

First on the to-do list was to see their grandson Brandt and shower him with colorful, plastic toys, most of them with wheels. Second was a conversation with Renea (Brandt's mom) about having her help them run babies across the border. Third was to swing by Timmy One-Hit's house, and give big Mama Slumlord a butt-load of money. The rent is high and always due, not unlike with Captain Ugly Pants.

Charlie and Denice sat down to have a conversation with Nea-Nea. But then suddenly, on the TV blaring in the background, they heard Johnny Rotten's name (Larry's dim bulb brother-in-law). San Diego's Channel 39 News Alive cameras were focused on an intersection in Alpine. Police were involved in a standoff with two suspects in an AMC Pacer.

"Holy shit, Denice. Look, it's Johnny standing next to the car."

"That looks like Shelley on the passenger side," confirmed Denice. "Oh my God. He's got a gun. What's he doing?"

"Puttin' it in his freaking mouth!" shouted Charlie in disbelief.

"It seems this man is holding himself hostage," the anchor on TV reported.

Charlie said to Denice, "Can you do that? I mean, hold yourself hostage?"

The local newsman continued, "You saw it here first. Channel 39 News Alive at five. The suspect is pulling the trigger and...Oh, my! The gun has misfired and officers are moving in."

"Look!" Denice exclaimed. "Shelley's hitting the cop on the head. Oh my god. He hit her with his Billy Club" Denice and her daughter winced.

"What a dumb-ass," Nea-Nea concluded.

"Wow, laying there like that, she kinda looks like Larry." Charlie was laughing so hard, he thought he had wet his pants. The image of Johnny Rotten trying to smoke the business end of Charlie's old snub-nose was hilarious.

"I'm calling Larry," declared Charlie.

"The hell you are, Charlie DeVille," Denice interjected.

"Aw, come on, honey."

"This is not funny," she said, as she tried to hold back a smile.

"Bullshit. You can't even say that with a straight face."

"He's got a point, Mom," Nea chimed in. And then turned her attention back to the TV. "Trailer park comedy at its finest."

✠ ✠ ✠

Nea-Nea drove an IROC Camaro. Being as tall as her father, along with her need to carry around a bunch of baby crap, a small economy car just would not do it. Nea was a very attractive woman, with long brown hair that could be any shade between black and dark red, depending on her love interest, financial situation, or phase of the moon.

She was also a very spiritual woman, with a charming sense of good-conquers-evil. Physically, she was very strong and well-endowed with an ample bosom, just like her mother. That, of course, brought with it the challenge of fending off jerks, which certainly, she was up for. Try some bogus pickup line that included the word *tits*, and you would see how fast you were introduced to the floor. Nea-Nea did not hit like a girl.

Just ask Larry.

✠   ✠   ✠

Driving through the rural back streets of Jacumba with her mom and dad, looking for a car she'd loaned to a friend named Richard, Nea-Nea spotted a mobile home. It was a single-wide with a large piece of its skirt missing.

"Dad, stop the car."

"Why?" replied Charlie, screeching to a halt.

"What is that?" asked Renae, shielding her eyes from the sun. She got out and walked over to the mobile home, stood in the front yard, then bent down to look beneath the missing mobile home skirt. To her horror, she saw a group of people lying in various positions with only inches to spare. It was at least 95° in the shade.

A woman motioned to her mouth and whispered something in a raspy voice, but no sound came out.

Nea-Nea angrily ran back to the car. "We need water. Now." she commanded.

Charlie knew Larry used this mobile home to store his people, now that he didn't work for Ramona anymore. Denice looked at Charlie. This was a tricky situation.

If they could see these people, so could the rest of the neighborhood. It's one of the basic moral dilemmas of the business. Is the Border Patrol watching and baiting them? There's no way to know. Is it better to grab these poor people and try to run? Or do you leave them to possibly dehydrate and die. Or do you turn them in to the authorities and let the law take its course?

That's the conundrum.

"Take me to Larry's," said Nea-Nea angrily.

"Honey, not a good plan," Denice replied.

"Let's find your car first," added Charlie.

"Fuck the car."

Uh-oh, Charlie thought. There is the F-bomb, not a good sign. When Nea got a thorn in her paw, look out, *GAR-RON-TEED.* He turned to his oldest daughter and said, "Look, baby girl, I can fix this. Let me make a couple calls."

"I'm fixing it right fucking now, Daddy. Take me to Larry's."

When any of Charlie's girls, including his wife, called him Daddy or Papa, he turned to mush. He could not find *no* in his vocabulary anytime the request started or ended with, *Daddy.*

When they arrived at Larry's, his Mustang was in the driveway. As soon as he'd stopped the car, Nea was out and through the gate. Charlie thought to himself, *Dammit, here it comes.*

Nea pushed the doorbell and Larry answered. He opened the door wide, with a big smile. The pervert probably thought she was there to flash him. Nea drew back her closed fist, stood firmly on Larry's left foot, aimed for the back of his head, and punched him right in the face. Daddy smiled. He taught her the foot thing. Denice just put her head in her hands.

Captain Ugly Pants dropped like a dirt clod. His head bounced once on the linoleum. He made a kind of gurgling noise right before his eyes rolled up into his skull. Nea bent down, grabbed the front of his shirt, and started a one-way conversation, "You *will* get those people out from under that single-wide. You *will* feed them and bring them water."

Larry opened one eye and looked up from his prone position in the entryway. "Bring them water NOW," she hissed through clenched teeth. "And they had better be in L.A. by morning, asshole."

Larry blinked his one good eye, which Nea took as a *yes*. She moved his arm out of the way with her foot as she reached inside the entryway, grabbed the doorknob, and closed the door.

Returning to the car she wore a smile of satisfaction for a job well done. Nea jumped in back of the Maxima and sweetly said, "Mom? Dad? Let's go find my car."

✠   ✠   ✠

A guy named Richard Elrod, now known as "Dick Rod," since he'd not returned Nea's car nor her calls, had borrowed Nea's car. Had Dick Rod been able to see Larry at the moment, he probably would've been waxing the car right now in her driveway.

Dick Rod and Captain Ugly Pants were now partners. They were the exact opposite of cool in Nea's mind. More like dumb and dumber. But it was about to get worse. Unbeknownst to the DeVille family, the reason Dick Rod had Nea's car was because he was modifying his van to run people. Not for Ramona, but for her competition.

However, that competition didn't include the same quality of service, or professional personnel. Some of these smugglers combined their trades. In other words, they'd offer a free ride to L.A. if you'd carry a backpack full of coke.

The backpack seemed to always arrive in San Diego. That was the easy part. However, the unsuspecting villager didn't always make it to the Promised Land. These smugglers were ruthless and barbaric at times, so Larry and Dick Rod fit right in. Larry had stashed the group under the house and had taken the backpacks, while Dick Rod dropped them off at Duffle Bag Man's house, near the spa.

Nea-Nea's car was presently nextdoor at Wanda's house. Wanda was a neighbor of Larry's and a friend with benefits to Dick.

Dick was 5'10" with blonde hair and blue eyes. He was handsome in a Nordic sort of way. Not quite a Viking, but maybe an inbred Norseman with a little Viking blood as a result of some downhome raping and pillaging. He had a powerfully built upper torso, but he had very un-sexy bird legs. Dick always donned faded jeans and too-tight tee shirts.

To say Nea had a bad *picker*, as Charlie called it, was an understatement. If she thought a guy was cute, he probably had a wart on his penis. If he was close to the Lord, chances are he read "Mein Kampf" in his spare time and probably had a swastika tattoo somewhere. Charlie and Denice constantly worried about this unexplainable phenomenon, so it was not a surprise she had gone on a date with Richard, and allowed him to borrow her car under false pretenses. She knew nothing about him, except that his parents lived in Jacumba and seemed to be nice.

Dick Rod was not so nice.

When the family found Nea's IROC at Wanda's, Nea was surprisingly calm. She kissed her mom on the cheek as she exited the car, turned and poked her head inside and said, "Love you guys."

Denice said back, "Love you too, sweetie."

Concerned, Charlie asked his daughter, "You all right, honey?"

"I'm good, Dad. Don't trip."

She had just knocked out a 230-pound grown man and located her stolen car. *Don't trip* just didn't cut it as far as reassurance. That was why they did not just drop her off and split. They turned the corner, stopped and made a U-turn.

As Nea's watchful parents hung back, to her credit Nea did not even go to the door. She just jumped in her car and smoked the tires to the rims, right in front of the house. Charlie looked at Denice and said, "So I guess there won't be a second date?"

"Ah, no. Not likely, I'm proud of her, though."

"Right. Me, too. She knocked him smooth out. Even remembered the toe thing I showed her."

"Jesus, Charlie, that's not what I'm talking about. She chose not to confront him. She's making better choices," explained Denice.

"Hmm. Maybe. Or maybe her hand hurt," reasoned Charlie.

"What in the hell does that have to do with choices, Charlie?"

"Well, she's not real good with her left hand, and there's two of them. She probably chose to wait until the swelling in her right hand went down."

"Are you freakin' kidding me, Charlie DeVille?"

"God, you look sexy right now. Let me kiss you, sugar lips. I want you so bad right now. Take off your pants, woman."

"Charlie, you are so full of shit."

"Yes. No last name. Almost there."

"You are the problem with these girls, you're never serious. Always with the jokes."

"Your brown eyes are so sexy with a flash of anger. Please. Take your pants off."

"No," defied Denice. She looked out the window, so Charlie couldn't see her that her will was weakening. *Damn you, Charlie DeVille! You really know how to charm the pants off a woman!*

"My Little Lamby-Chop...Come on. Pleeeez?"

Well, that did it, the pants came off. Maybe not in the car. But for sure in the next 20 minutes, as the cabin was only 10 minutes away. Zero to hero in seconds flat.

Humor. The ultimate anger management tool.

WANDA WORLD
Chapter 15

Wanda was a whore, a smuggler, a drug dealer, and a pain in the ass. Especially to her husband, who lived and worked in Mexico. Some folks say, *Dealing with Wanda is like jacking off with sandpaper.*

Her M.O. was to hide people in bushes, in other people's sheds and yards, at Larry's place, anywhere but her house. She would do anything or anyone for money. Cash was king in Wanda's world, and her give-a-shit switch was never engaged.

Jacumba is like any other small town USA, where gossip abounds. But unlike other places, Jacumba's gossip does not mutate. The basic information stays the same, no matter how many times the story is told. This comes from the importance of the gossip: Who's working for whom, who has people, guns or drugs. *The Network.* Everyone depends on the Network. It's completely underground, the same today as it was 100 years ago.

In the holiday months everyone in the Cortez Cartel goes home to Mexico City. But that does not stop others who are not so organized. That means lots of opportunity for wide-open commerce, using the rumor mill to find people, snatching them with or without the knowledge of the broker. Once a coyote releases interest in the immigrants, if they are not in the protective custody of a runner or a broker, this *snatch* calls their family. He makes the deal, does the run and collects the cash. Life's a Cabaret. Let's party.

Charlie and Denice loved the party.

They were on the way to Barona Casino from Enterprise Car Rental. They stopped at home base to remove and store the back seats. They disguised the back of the SUV as a camping area, a place for them to sleep on the way to L.A. Pulling into the valet at Barona, Charlie showed his platinum card.

"Good afternoon, Mr. and Mrs. DeVille."

The young valet did not need the card to know Charlie and Denice. He parked them in VIP, right in front. Right next to BMWs, Jaguars, and the occasional Bentley. Charlie and Denice went directly to the concierge at VIP and acquired a complimentary suite. Then on to the platinum cashier and bought $1,000 in twenty-dollar bills, with the Blazing Sevens in mind.

"What's the horseshoe's status?"

"It tickles right now."

Charlie was vexed, he didn't know if he should rush her to the Blazin' Seven carousel or to the room. So he did the only thing that came to mind. He squeezed her ass with his right hand and blew in her ear.

"Forget it, Charlie, not now."

Decision made. He gently guided her to the Progressive Sevens. And a good decision it was. It took less than 10 minutes of Charlie running buckets of gold coins to the cashier cage before she hit.

"Look, baby. Three flamers."

Charlie looked up at the progressive amount that's on top of every machine on the carousel; $1,887.

"Atta girl, baby. My little jackpot queen. Only took you six to do it. We're way ahead."

"As soon as the cashier pays me, let's go up to the room. I need a shower.

"Me, too," said Charlie.

"And room service."

"Me, too."

"And a massage."

"Me, too."

"From you," Denice clarified.

"Oh. Oh, yeah. I'm there for you, baby." Charlie reassured. He laced his fingers together and turned his palms out, cracking his knuckles like a boxer. "I got this."

Denice snuggled up beside her man. "You sure do, handsome."

✠　✠　✠

The next morning, they woke to the sound of the hotel phone with the wake-up call. After a breakfast of Denver omelets with sourdough toast and mocha coffees, they rose to greet the day. For most people, the day was almost over at 3:45 in the afternoon. Check-out is at it 11:00 a.m., unless you're VIP platinum, in which case check-out is when you leave. You leave in your car, with your luggage, and usually having lost all your money. Charlie and Denice left in their car with their luggage, but to their credit they made their exit with an extra thousand in cash.

By the time they reached the mountain it was almost dark. They knew in advance that Wanda had stashed two Mexican sisters in a bush on the outer edge of the town proper. Locating them turned out to be easy. Turns out the girls were afraid of the dark, so when the occasional car would go by, they would step out of the bushes.

"I think that's them."

"Gee, I wonder," Charlie quipped. "Ya think? They're covered in mud." Charlie pulled up next to them. He stopped and they jumped right in. No "hello," no "Are you a rapist?" No fear. They just jumped into the van. Who knows how long they had been there, it must have been a while.

Denice questioned them, "Hello, do you speak English?"

Nothing. Not even a peep.

Charlie looked over his shoulder and said, "Wanda?"

The girls nodded their heads.

"You want to see Wanda?"

They both shook their heads no. They looked over at the van door like they were going to bolt straight out of it.

Denice said, "Peg-Legs' house is two blocks up and left. Let's go by and see if he's home."

"I don't know, babe."

"He speaks Spanish. The checkpoint's open anyway. At least they can clean up."

"Okay" Charlie agreed reluctantly "I need to call Elwood and get things queued up to run."

"The Maxima is at the Acorn, maybe he could bring up the Ryder truck and park it in the truck parking. That way we can use it later?"

"Sounds like a plan, Pumkin, hope he answers his phone."

"Look. Peg-Legs is home. His front door is open."

At the sound of the van pulling in the driveway, Peg-Legs came out of the house, looking like Festis of *Gunsmoke*, with a straggly brown beard and longish hair. He had a pock-marked face that scared small children. His legs bowed outwards. He moseyed over to the passenger window, "Wa-wa what's up g-g-guys?"

"Hey, Bobby. How are ya, hon?" Denice asked him. She didn't call him Peg-Legs to his face.

"Bu-b-b-broke."

"Well. Maybe we can fix that. We need to store these two ladies here. Can you find out where they are going and make a deal?"

"DAMMIT-dammit-Wanda's??"

"Yup."

"F-f-Figures. C-c-come on in."

Have you ever heard someone stutter in Spanish? It's damn hilarious. If you don't understand the language, it's even funnier. He sounded like a cockatiel with Tourette Syndrome. You needed time and patience to have a conversation with Bobby Peg Legs.

Denice always did the talking because Charlie could not keep his catalog of jokes to himself, and it's not acceptable to make fun of the handicapped. Denice would not buy Charlie's sophomoric logic, and neither would Nea-Nea or any other female, for that matter. Apparently, making fun of the mentally or physically challenged is a guy thing.

"I wonder. Did he stutter before they broke his legs?"

"Still not cool, Charlie DeVille."

"Sorry."

Bobby Peg-Legs made the call and somehow he stuttered through the deal: Three thousand dollars for both. That was a steal, since probably no money had exchanged hands yet. Most deals were C.O.D., but since they had been snatched, it's whatever the market will bear. So Denice gave Bobby Peg-Legs a hundred-dollar bill for food and storage.

"We will be back tomorrow, hon," she promised.

"K-k-kay, guys."

Charlie backed out of the driveway. It was dark now and spooky. As shadows moved between the houses, and the ink-black desert swallowed up the highway ahead.

"Back to the room?" Charlie asked his wife.

"Okay."

"Need to call Elwood, let him know to be ready to roll. We need to pick up the Maxima."

Denice got the phone number out of her purse and dialed Elwood's number.

Elwood answered, "Yo. Boss."

"What ya doin', Elwood?" asked Denice.

"Shaving my cat." Elwood grooms his cat so that it looks like a poodle.

"That is so mean, Woody," Denice replied, sympathetic to the cat.

"Naw. She digs it," Elwood responded in all seriousness.

"I really doubt that, hon."

"Hey, did you know that wherever the fur changes color, so does the skin? Puter looks like a ice-cream sandwich." Elwood thought his cat could count, because it tapped its paw on the floor. So he called her Puter, short for *Computer*. But in reality the cat's foot-tapping was probably just its spastic response to being shaved. Crazy.

Denice said to Elwood, "Stop shaving your Puter and get ready to run."

"Yes, ma'am."

"Now."

"Yes, ma'am."

Denice looked over at her husband and said softly, "Poor Puter."

✠　✠　✠

Words of Wisdom by Charlie's Dad: *"Son, wisdom is what comes from making a shit-load of mistakes. Everyone makes them. However, if you make the same one twice you're stupid."*

Don't be stupid. Although it is hard to keep fur clean when your puppy plays in the mud.

The sisters got to Los Angeles safe and sound, via the long way down the backside of the mountain. Elwood did a stellar job of running point to the checkpoint. He was coming from the old Desert Inn and Travel Lodge, where he had registered under *Dean Martin, Tropicana Hotel, Las Vegas, Nevada.* License plate number, *PSY LUVR.*

Charlie and Denice were on the way to Jacumba to pay Bobby Peg-Legs his cut. Being it was a moonless and cold mid-December night, the air was clear and crisp, which can make the night all that darker. Cruising slowly through this haunted murkiness, they came upon La Posta Road, located in the little town of La Posta.

La Posta Road runs parallel to old Highway 8, and is a frequented detour for runners. The town was fashioned in the style of the Alamo: white stucco dwellings, two-stories mostly. It's one and only old hotel sported a hitching post out front, a second-story, and a Promenade-type walkway. Throw in some old rocking chairs and it looked like something from a John Wayne movie.

As they passed the hotel, Denice turned to Charlie, "Did you see that light?"

Charlie rarely missed anything these days. "Sure the hell did. What was that?"

"It looked like a ghost."

Through the window, the bluish hue inside the room left a residual imprint on the inside of their eyelids.

"Turn around baby."

"Already doing it." Charlie made a U-turn. They slowly drove by the hotel again. "Okay. It looked like it came from the second window from the left."

As they passed by a second time, the mysterious white light left a blue glow in all four windows. They were nervous and on edge anyway, just by being on the mountain after dark. That, mixed with all the stories and legends, makes the mind wander.

Denice was spooked. "That was a ghost, Charlie. Had to be."

"Holy crap. No. Come on. It can't be," Charlie replied.

They made a U-turn again. The town was absolutely pitch-black. Going past the hotel, the same thing happened.

Charlie pulled the van over. "I'm checking it out."

"You're not leaving me alone here."

"Come on then. Stay close."

They slowly climbed the stairway on the side of the building. Then they rose to the veranda, very slowly and very quietly. Charlie cautiously looked around the sill of the second window to the left, when...*FLASH*. The light was so bright, it left a huge dot in front of his vision, around that dot, was a tripod with a motion activated 35mm Nikon.

"Shit! We gotta go!" Charlie and Denice practically jumped off the veranda and into their car. They squealed away, leaving the single eye of the camera to record history.

In this business, there are no experts, just varying degrees of ignorance. Don't be ignorant. Don't give the Border Patrol a face shot to match the vehicle license number.

That's just common sense.

✠ ✠ ✠

If that was not enough excitement for one night, just before the Kitchen Creek Road turn off, Charlie and Denice were pulled over by Barney Fife, of the California Highway Patrol. There is just no other way to describe this law enforcement officer. Bottom line? He was a dick in a uniform. He wore a tie around his neck to keep his uncircumcised foreskin from flying up and covering his face. This penis with feet was actually wearing his mirror aviator sunglasses at night.

He sauntered up to Denice's window, proving that he was at least smart enough not to confront Charlie first. He didn't look like he had a sense of humor.

"License and registration please."

Charlie and Denice just sat there. You could not tell who he was talking to with the mirrored glasses. He slid them on his head with a two-finger gesture, reminiscent of Poncharello from the 1970's TV show *C.H.I.P.S.*, only this guy was white. He also had missing teeth in a rather large head. His beady little eyes burned into Charlie.

"Now, sir, identification and registration, *please*."

"Zieg heil," replied Charlie in his best German accent.

"Oh, a funnyman."

"You are what you eat. And this woman next to me is funny as hell," said Charlie, as he handed the officer his license and registration. Denice shot Charlie a *Not now!* look.

The guy glanced at Charlie's documents. "Mr. DeVille, cut the crap. This here mountain is buzzing with assholes like you smuggling illegals. Where are your rear seats?"

"I don't appreciate the inference, officer. My wife and I were just having a dalliance in the woods. Surely you understand."

Barney Fife was trying to figure out what dalliance meant. "You need to rent a van for that?"

"Yes," replied Charlie straight-faced.

"Really?"

"Yes."

"Well, Mr. Smarty Pants, I'm calling the rental company to advise them that you are smuggling aliens in their equipment."

Charlie's mind almost blew a breaker. While Barney dialed his cell, Charlie quietly said to his wife, "First off, my name is not, and never will be, Smarty Pants. Second, what kind of grown man uses the term Smarty Pants? Third, it's 9:00 p.m., the rental place is closed. And there is not one alien in the back. And fourth, this is not equipment; it's a family van. Do you see a backhoe attachment anywhere on this? That son-of-a-bitch."

Always the voice of reason, Denice hushed her hubby. "Settle down, honey. Your face is all red. I can tell even in the dark. You're just getting worked up for nothing."

"Nothing? You see that black thing on the right side, hanging off his belt? Honey, that's a gun."

"So? There's nothing he can do." She looked at the buffoon of a cop. "Don't they have a limit on how big your head can be to issue a fire arm?"

"Don't think so, lamb chop. Look at him."

Barney spoke into his phone leaving a voicemail. "This is Officer Blah Blah of the California Highway Patrol. I have a Mr. and Mrs. Charlie DeVille here in one of your rentals. They've removed the rear seats. I firmly believe they are using said van to smuggle illegal aliens. Be advised."

After he ended his call he returned to the passenger window of the van. At which time Denice dryly said, "Thank you, officer. You've saved me the embarrassment of telling them I was fucking my husband's socks off back there."

Charlie was taken aback. At this moment he was as proud of his wife as he'd ever been. She had dropped the F-bomb. And right on target, too. Deadpanned and funny as hell. Charlie was trying hard not to laugh. Officer Barney was offended. Denice was stone-faced.

"Officer, may we go now?" Charlie asked firmly. "It seems I have an erection."

"Get the hell out of here," commanded the cop, not knowing what else to say.

Charlie put the car in gear and off they sped.

As they left the patrolman in the dust, Denice asked Charlie, "You really got an, um. You know."

"For you? Always."

"Good. Because you know I never lie to the police."

CLINT EASTWOOD AND THE TALLEST MEXICAN IN THE WORLD
Chapter 17

Elwood's family lived in Panama City, Florida. It's sometimes called "The Redneck Riviera," and perhaps is the only place that parties as hard as Southern California. It is a big spring break destination for the East Coast college kids.

In the South's Gulf Coast, they call California the Left Coast, but, if you're facing Cancun or Mazatlan, it's always the Right Coast. We've got the waves (they don't even know what those are on the East Coast). Cali's got the girls, the fast cars, the sunshine, and roller blades.

California is the starting line of the fast lane. Cool starts here, smuggling only ends around Christmas, which is why Woody was heading to Tucker Town, home of the Tucker Clan.

With things having slowed down some, and with Charlie and Denice's Family Trust a little healthier these days, they had time to find and buy a small beige Toyota pickup truck. It had a fiberglass shell without side windows. It was very non-distinct, just an everyday truck that no one would notice, which is just how they liked it.

Charlie took it to home base and installed over-loader rear springs and air shocks. Also he put in a CB radio and a butyl rubber pad in the truck bed, reasoning that he'd lay people down comfortably, covering them with a blanket. This was necessary because the camper shell's rear access door had a tinted window.

With Elwood on vacation, they returned the Ryder truck, minus the pool furniture, and loaned the Maxima to Nea-Nea.

The mountaintop is a small area, and it's a tight-knit community. The Border Patrol are everywhere, so it's imperative you change vehicles often. Rentals are an option, but nothing blends in like an 80s-era pickup truck on the reservation.

Knowing that Bobby Peg Legs *shopped* the bushes near his house everyday at dusk, he always snatched a few travelers that he could outsource to people with wheels. This was a great setup for Bobby, in that neither he nor his brother had a car.

Occasionally, Charlie and Denice were happy to pick up an extra run from Bobby Peg Legs when things were slow. This was one of those times. They prepared for this run by renting a small, powerless economy car at nineteen dollars per day. Denice would take Elwood's place riding point in the rented car, while Charlie transported their clients in his truck.

The plan was to go down the backside of the mountain, veering left through Borrego Springs. Then up and over the Wells Mountain, past the airport, and over the desert to Blythe. There the road comes out right past the Border Patrol checkpoint. They then would turn left towards the Salton Sea. That place smells like a million armpits. It's hard to even breathe the air. The inland sea was dying from the run-off of nitrates used by farmers to fertilize their crops. Once a thriving ecosystem, home to millions of Tutwava fish, now all that was gone. Not one single fish survived the ruination.

Charlie and Denice were confident in their plan. But shit can always go awry. At Bobby's they did not have the advantage of Ramona's network. So they watched out the back sliding glass doors, until the two Border Patrol Broncos had left their positions on the mountain behind Bobby's house. Apparently there was an old nudist colony somewhere up in those hills – old meaning it was frequented by the retirement set. Valentino had been there. He said it was like Girls Gone Wild, senior edition.

As soon as *the eyes* retreated for their briefing, Charlie and Bobby loaded four men into the back of the truck, and then covered them with a blanket.

Followed by Denice in the gutless rental, they headed down the backside of the mountain, heading east on Highway 8. But at the bottom of the grade, where you turn left towards Wells, they found the road closed. This forced them to continue to the Indio exit. At the end of this two-mile road, it dead-ends into Highway Business Loop/Main Street.

If you turn right, you find yourself at the Desert Travel Lodge, a favorite accommodation for the likes of James Dean and Dean Martin. Turn left, and you end up at the largest and most technically advanced checkpoint, a mile and a half towards the Salton Sea. The road then continued on to Palm Springs.

Anyone in the game would tell you, your chances are almost zero running illegals through that checkpoint; they were almost never closed.

Pulling up to the stop sign with Denice right behind him, Charlie flipped his turn signal to execute a right-hand turn. However, some genius at Toyota thought it'd be a good idea to include the bright-light toggle on that same turn-lever.

And that's why Charlie flashed his bright lights at one Officer Rodriguez as he was doing his nightly patrol.

Shit.

Being a studious officer, as well as a sergeant of the Indio, California, Police Department, Officer Rodriguez flipped a U-turn and got right behind Charlie.

"You got company, babe."

Charlie left the radio in his lap, but keyed the mic.

"Great. He's red-lighting me. Perfect."

Charlie activated his right signal again, and saw he had his bright lights on. BRILLIANT! He pulled to the curb, and made sure to keep his hands on the wheel. In California, when being pulled over, you *always* leave your hands where the police can see them, unless you want a close-up view of the officer's firearm.

Officer Rodriguez came to the window with his flashlight.

"License and registration, please."

Denice passed slowly, and parked at a small pharmacy where she could watch the exchange unnoticed.

Officer Rodriguez wasn't a bad guy. He was a competent, confident officer. He considered police work his job, not his calling or his identity as a man. Some cops believe they were ordained by God himself to *protect and serve*.

"Are you having some kind of malfunction with your bright lights, sir?" Officer Rodriguez asked Charlie.

"Yeah, Asian engineering. What are ya gonna do?"

"Excuse me?" the officer asked, obviously tracking Charlie's racial slur.

"Look at this, officer," pointing to the offending handle, as if it was the truck's fault.

"Okay. One moment, sir."

Officer Rodriguez went back to his cruiser to call in Charlie's license for warrants and wants. They can do this with a microphone that is always attached to their left shoulder. But most cops will return to their car and point their spotlight at your side mirror. Then they'll wait for you to do something stupid. Knowing this, Charlie sat there with his hands dutifully on the wheel.

Unfortunately, as Officer Rodriguez walked back to the driver-side of the truck with his flashlight blazing, one of the men in the back moved. That caused all of them to adjust their position.

The whole truck rocked.

Officer Rodriguez shined his light in through the back window.

"Mr. DeVille, please exit the vehicle. Slowly."

Charlie complied.

"Join me at the rear of the vehicle."

Again, Charlie did what he was told.

"What the fuck is going on here, Mr. DeVille?"

"They're, um...sleeping."

"I can see that, sir." Officer Rodriguez got right in Charlie's face and said quietly, "Those are my people back there, Mr. DeVille."

For the first time Charlie took a good look at Officer Rodriguez and decided he was the tallest Mexican-American he'd ever seen.

"I'm not going to insult your intelligence by telling you some lame-ass story. It is what it is, sir."

Officer Rodriguez paused and took a breath. "You've put me in a goddamn hard place. I can't just turn my head here. You're pissing me off. You're pissing me off really bad right now, Mr. DeVille."

"Sorry, sir. I'm a little angry at myself right now for buying a piece of shit vehicle with a badly engineered fucked-up turn signal lever."

Officer Rodriguez was at a crossroads. And Charlie had put him there. Both were doing their job. Yet Charlie was breaking the law. Still...if one of Rodriguez's relatives had not broken the law years ago, his own father would never have come to Cathedral City, California. And Officer Rodriguez would not be a sergeant in the Indio Police Department today.

"God dammit, DeVille. You put me in a bad position. Those are my people. Shit!"

Across the street Denice could see the officer with his flashlight pointed in the back. She knew what was coming next. What she did not know was the turn their conversation was about to take.

"Look, DeVille. Here's what I'm gonna do. I have to call the BP, I can't just let you go. I've sworn to uphold the law. Have you ever been arrested by the BP before?"

"No, sir."

"Okay. You'll walk tonight. These people get a ride back. You really are pissing me off right now."

"I am sorry, sir."

What else can a man say? It never occurred to Charlie that *some* of his enemy might actually be on his side, and that in the arrest phase of a routine traffic stop, this cop had deep, deep conflicts.

"Okay, Mr. DeVille, I want you to get those people out of your truck."

Charlie opened the rear camper door and dropped the tailgate down. The four men were frozen in place. They feigned sleep until Rodriguez said something in Spanish, and the men sheepishly disembarked and stood milling around under the palm trees.

Charlie looked at them and shrugged his shoulders, palms up. They smiled back, as if to say, *Nice try.*

"Okay, Mr. DeVille, I want you to drive your truck down two blocks, then turn right. Go down one block, park the truck. Then come back. *Walk back.* You don't want to know what will happen if you don't come back. Do you understand?"

"Yes, sir, I think so."

"I'm not going to impound your vehicle, or hand it to the BP, that way you won't lose your truck. Got it?"

"Thank you, sir."

"Do you think that the young lady in the white car will wait for you?"

"Holy shit. You don't miss much, do you?"

"She hasn't stopped watching. And no, Mr. DeVille, I don't miss much."

Charlie thought, *atta girl* as he walked back from parking the truck. Never leave your wing-man.

Officer Rodriguez pointed to the front of his cruiser. "Follow me," he commanded.

Charlie obeyed, and away from the ears of Charlie's clients the patrolman completely changed his tune. "Okay, Charlie, I work 3:00 p.m. to 11:00 p.m. Wednesday through Sunday. Adjust your schedule accordingly. If you put me in this position again," he said pointing to the open window of his cruiser, "I'll drop my badge and gun on the front seat and beat the brakes off you."

Charlie looked at Officer Rodriguez's ham hock fists, then followed his beefy arms to some very pissed off eyes – which were dark, steady, and drop dead serious.

"I hear you loud and clear, sir," said Charlie with the upmost respect. "Loud and clear."

✠   ✠   ✠

Nearly an hour later, a young, pimply-faced kid in a Border Patrol uniform arrived. This was obviously the boy who was picked on and bullied every moment of his pitiful life. He surely had a pair of squeaky, non-distended testicles, and a voice that could etch glass.

"Officer Rodriguez, do you have any zip ties? I don't have enough handcuffs," the child-officer asked. He had the body of a little girl, and the mind of a kid who burns bugs. Even from where he was standing Charlie could tell this kid's breath smelled like he'd been snacking on cat turds.

"They've been standing here for 45 minutes waiting for you," replied Officer Rodriguez. "I doubt they're going to run."

"Procedure, officer."

"Right. Nope, sorry fresh out."

"Dammit." The kid pointed at Charlie, "You, turn around, scum bag."

Charlie looked at Rodriguez and inclined his head toward the dork. "Clint Eastwood, he's not."

Officer Rodriguez discretely grinned for the first time all evening. It was the kind of smirk that sparks an infectious, barroom giggle. The four Mexican guys started to chuckle. Charlie loves a good laugh, so he started to crack up. Soon everyone, except the kid, was laughing out loud.

"Think you're funny, do ya? *Punk?*" yelled the young officer to Charlie. "You're in a world of hurt."

Charlie audibly farted, and then he added, "Nope. Not anymore, kid." That was probably not the smoothest nor best course of action.

"You won't be laughing in lockup, asshole," Kid-Cop snapped.

At this point, Charlie decided it was time to listen and cut the clowning. Denice watched as they loaded into the white and green BP van. The kid jumped in the driver's seat and pulled away.

Officer Rodriguez turned off his flashing blue and red light bar, and headed towards Denice. He waved as he went by, and smiled.

Denice was stunned. Scared. And a little lost for a second. Her mind had begun the task of her to-do lists. This was always good for her head when she was stressed. It helped her to categorize and compartmentalize her thinking process, and not pee her pants.

First? Get a motel room.

Second? Charge the cell phone.

Third? Call Nea-Nea.

Fourth? What's up with the truck? Gotta check. Make sure it's locked. Make sure the keys aren't in it. Have a pee, and so on.

✠ ✠ ✠

After arriving at the checkpoint, Charlie was manhandled into a small room. It was ten by ten, one of three holding cells in the main control room of Check Point Alpha. This was the most advanced checkpoint in Homeland Security's arsenal of *Monitoring Mexican Movement*, the three Ms of Border Patrol surveillance.

And the fruit – don't forget the fruit.

As Charlie looked out the small window in the middle door of his cell, he could see two men at four computer video screens, two of which were the dark screen illumination of night vision cameras set up in the desert. The other two were a combination of microwave beam and pressure sensor pads buried under the sand that alerted them to movement around the area. Mostly, it was coyotes walking people and drugs around the checkpoint. Charlie was astounded at the technology and watched every movement, listened to every word, though they were slightly muffled through the closed door.

"Six degrees left, camera nine," one of the men ordered.

"Okay. Scan there, 100 yards and to your left," came the reply over the radio from a disembodied voice.

"Roger," said the guy at the camera controls. "Three moving to the right. I count nine."

"Ten-four. Nine in line," confirmed the voice on the radio.

"Slow up. Split up. They're thirty yards straight ahead of your twenty," advised Camera Guy.

"They stop moving?"

"Ten-four. Looks like the leaders are listening."

Guns drawn, the officers moved forward. The sound of an electronic beep indicated that another microwave beam had been broken, and the operator looked over at a different screen.

Suddenly another officer opened the cell door, and ushered two more people in with Charlie.

"Busy night, I guess," said the new guy.

"You ain't seen nothing yet," said Charlie, gesturing toward the control room. Charlie continued to watch the video game of cat-and-mouse play out, and the cat always seemed to win. As the night progressed, the cells filled to maximum capacity.

Teenybopper cop "Eastwood" unlocked the cell door, then he pointed at Charlie, "You, come here." Charlie followed him out to the van. "This is your lucky day."

"Gotta a dog named Lucky," Charlie said.

"I don't give a shit about your dog. We're busy. Too busy for the likes of you. Get in the van."

Charlie got in the passenger side, and the kid pulled out and headed towards Indio. As soon as he was out of sight of the checkpoint, he pulled the van over to the side of the highway.

"Get out, scumbag."

"Here?"

"Here, and I don't ever want to see your face again."

Charlie pointed his finger at the kid and pulled the proverbial trigger. "Right back at ya, Eastwood."

"Fuck you."

"Sorry, pal. Married." Charlie gleefully hopped out of the van and waved at the kid, who then did an angry U-turn, nearly rolling the van over.

Charlie got a pass. No fingerprints. No record of the arrest. No credit on the kid's performance evaluation. But Charlie was sure the young BP officer would tell his mom all about it anyway when he got home.

Charlie walked back to the truck and reached through the rear-sliding window. He found the walkie-talkie. "How about it sweet cheeks, you out there?"

"Oh my God, honey, are you okay?" asked Denice in a panic.

"My feet hurt."

"What?"

"Punk made me walk back, like 40 miles." It was actually only around two.

"Poor baby."

"Yeah, where are you?"

"Kings Inn, next to the CVS pharmacy. Room number 102."

"Be there in a minute," said Charlie wearily.

"You want a ride?" asked Denice, even though she knew he had the truck.

"Naw, I can see it from here."

"Hurry. I miss you."

"Miss you too."

When Charlie arrived at the motel room and wrapped his arms around his wife, the world came back into focus. The events of the last eight hours had left him shaken. A close call for sure, but as he filled Denice in about what he'd observed at the checkpoint, his mind began absorbing it as a learning experience.

Now he knew exactly where *the cat* was.

SHE'LL BE COMIN' ROUND THE MOUNTAIN
Chapter 18

In California, where more baby showers are given for new 'Beemers' than actual babies, women control seventy percent of the cash and one hundred percent of the pussy. Guess who's running things, *really* running things?

Charlie and Denice headed back to Barona Casino, where they were put on the fourth floor, poolside. Denice did a little shopping at the gift store, but could not find what she needed. Charlie was back up at the room and dug out his trunks and her bikini.

"Let's go for a swim before dinner, babe. Pool looked awesome on the way in."

"So did the Jacuzzi, I could use a soak."

One of the perks of California living is a temperature of seventy-four degrees in December at sunset. It favors you with beautiful orange and purple skies that change like a kaleidoscope.

"Red skies at night sailors delight," not to mention Mimosas poolside on a warm California evening. The stress of the day sheds like snakeskin.

Later, up in the room, Charlie waited for Denice to finish dressing for dinner, when the company phone rang.

Charlie answered, "Helloooooooo?"

"Hey, funny man. Where's your wife?" asked Ramona from the other end of the phone.

"Locked in the closet."

"Doing what?" asked Ramona, playing right along with Charlie's quirky sense of humor.

"Mixing. Matching. Pissing me off."

"You mean she's trying to find something to wear?"

"Yeah. Hold on," said Charlie, realizing this could go on forever. He hollered to Denice, "Honey. Ramona's on the phone for you."

"Okay. Be right there," answered Denice from the depths of the closet.

"Charlie, can you and your wife meet Julio and me at the Viejas tomorrow?" Ramona asked before Denice could get to the phone.

"Sure. Here's Dee."

Denice took the phone and greeted Ramona. "Hey, girlfriend, how's things?"

"Good. Bring your old man for breakfast tomorrow at 9:00 a.m., he knows the place."

"Okay, hon."

"See you," Ramona said, as she hung up the phone.

Afterward Denice asked Charlie, "What do you think that's about?"

"Probably about kids," answered Charlie. "Kinda scary, don't you think? Driving kids across the border."

"Let's hear her out."

The meeting the following day took place at Viejas, next to a massive crackling fire. In January, the temperatures plunge all the way down to a frigid fifty degrees, and for the natives of San Diego, that's freezing.

Ramona started the conversation with, "Meet Julio in Tijuana, on Revolution Avenue, in a small cantina. Here's the address," Ramona handed Denice a slip of paper and then motioned toward Charlie. "The first meeting you can bring the Great White Hope here, but not after that. Have you talked to your daughter yet?"

"No. Not yet," replied Denice. "I need to have a conversation about parental guidance with this guy first." She nodded toward Charlie. "You know what I mean?"

"I understand," Ramona confirmed. "While you're discussing this, I want you to consider a few realities."

"Okay. We're listening."

"The parents of these children are most likely already here. You will be reuniting broken families. Also, infants under two do not need IDs. And they are not in question if the parent or parents have a drivers license or American citizenship. If your daughter or daughters have their own children with them, the risks are almost zero.

Denice looked at Charlie, and Charlie shrugged. Denice asked Ramona, "Would Nea have to meet anyone on this side if Julio's going to be in Mexico?"

"We can work it out many different ways. She can meet you across the border. Trade cars with you. And you can make the trip to L.A. If that's the case, we've been using a safe house in Chula Vista. But if you can, work a scenario to effect delivery to me in L.A. So much the better."

"Okay. Let my husband and I run this past Nea," replied Denice. "We'll call you the day after tomorrow, at the latest."

"Fair enough. I've got one more request. We've got a VIP in Jacumba. She's at a friend of Edgar's. We need to move her. But it's dangerous."

"Why?"

"She's Chinese."

"So?"

"Communist, Chinese."

"Oh."

"She is a favor for a friend of the big boss. That's all I can tell you. That's all you need to know."

"Why is it more dangerous?"

"Homeland Security frowns on it because so many borders are breached, bringing Chinese here. That's why it pays $2,500," Ramona said.

"For one person?" asked Charlie.

"That's right."

"Consider it done," answered Charlie, undeterred. "I've got an idea."

Ramona provided an address and phone number for Edgar's friend. They agreed to talk in 48 hours about the infants.

✠   ✠   ✠

Charlie and Denice rented a cabin at Live Oak Springs and invited Nea and her infant son, Brandt, up to spend a few days. They walked in the woods chasing squirrels, and soaked in the Jacuzzi. Lily thought Denice's grandson was the cutest thing on the planet.

Nea had arrived in a red Ford Tempo, a four-door with plenty of room for the immense amount of baby paraphernalia that she swore was necessary. The leaf does not fall far from the tree.

Night fell on Live Oak. At 4,000 feet above sea level, the clear mountain air was freezing. Charlie lit a fire in the cast iron stove. Nea fed the baby while Denice cleaned up the supper mess. When Brandt was asleep, with the three of them enjoying the warmth of the fire, Charlie and Denice explained Ramona's request and the plan with their daughter. Nea was an adult, and Charlie and Denice laid out the details without bias, and let Nea make this decision herself.

"So what do you think?" Denice asked.

"I think I haven't received a lick of child support, lately."

"Have you talked to Randy about it?" Charlie interjected.

Nea snorted, "Yeah. Twelve feet of snow in Illinois, no work anywhere."

Charlie sighed sympathetically. "It's completely up to you, hon."

"I'll think about it," promised Nea-Nea. And then she smiled. "But I'm up for the Asian girl."

"Charlie and I were thinking," said Denice. "You, Brandt and I would go through in broad daylight, with Charlie behind us."

"She does not speak any English," Charlie reminded everyone. "So I was thinking we'd teach her to say, 'I'm a student at San Diego State University.'"

"Just in case they ask," added Denice. "But who knows, if they're busy, they may just wave us through."

✠   ✠   ✠

The next day the entire family found themselves in line at the checkpoint with the Asian girl in the backseat. The sun was shining, the traffic not too heavy. They had the windows of the Tempo down, and Charlie could hear Brandt's cassette of Sesame Street's *She'll Be Coming Around The Mountain When She Comes* blaring out of the stereo. All three girls were singing, and Brandt was waving his arms in his car seat and thoroughly enjoying Ernie's rendition of the old folk song.

Charlie also had his window rolled down. The first thing you do when approaching a checkpoint is roll your window down.

There was a second of panic when he saw the agent bring his face to the right rear driver's window, and asked, "Are you a U.S. citizen?"

"I go to San Diego State University," replied the Chinese girl in broken English.

The agent pulled away. He glanced at Denice's cleavage, then at Renea's cleavage, and had a bit of a man moment. After that he waved them through.

BADA BING.

You gotta love it when a plan comes together.

Charlie keyed his walkie-talkie, "She'll be comin' around the mountain, she'll be comin' around the mountain, she'll be comin' around the mountain when she comes," he sang into it.

They continued on to Bellflower, where they pulled into a Carl's Jr., next to a silver van.

"Excellent job, my friends," cheered Julio.

Nea sat in the passenger seat. Julio did not get out of the van. Charlie opened the passenger side, and helped the tiny "college student" out of his vehicle and into Julio's van. Julio handed Charlie the wad of bills, examining Renea's ride. "The red car is perfect. For Mexico."

"All right, I'll call Ramona tonight. I'm sure it's a go. But you know women. Option to change their minds, and all that."

"Right up till go time. After that, there's no changing their minds," reminded Julio.

"Gotcha. *Hasta, luego.*"

Charlie went to the window of the Tempo and handed Nea ten Benjamin Franklins.

"Good job, honey." He put five in his pocket, and handed ten to Denice with a smile. "Nicely done, Pumkin."

"Thanks, baby."

"Jump in the Toyota, let's stop by Pechanga on the way back."

They said their goodbyes, and planned to meet back at the cabin later that evening. Barring no big jackpots.

✠　✠　✠

The phone rang and it sounded like a fire alarm in the small cabin. Denice rolled over and looked at the clock. It was

4:00 a.m. Had she not known it was Ramona, she wouldn't have answered it.

"Hey, girl," slurred Denice groggily.

"Good morning," replied Ramona on the other end of the phone.

"Four a.m. is not morning. It's the middle of the night," corrected Denice through closed eyes.

"Are we a go? Should I send Julio?"

"Yes."

"Is 2:00 p.m. okay?"

"Okay."

"Be safe."

"You too." Denice hung up by dropping the phone onto the floor next to the nightstand.

✠ ✠ ✠

They all decided to give it a try that evening. All they needed was another car seat, and then when the time came they could be in Tijuana in less than two hours. On this first run, Charlie would babysit. Nea had a car-seat for Brandt. But they needed an infant seat also. Just in case.

FLYING BLIND
Chapter 19

Flying blind. In our business, it means running the checkpoint backwards, no lights, in the middle of the night. Only fools take this kind a chance, and Dick Rod was one of those fools.

Dick had his girlfriend *de jour* load seven Mexican Nationals into his newly modified van from Larry's garage. He headed north on Old Highway 8. It was 1:00 a.m. Only a sliver of a moon was visible. Quiet and cold, the glow of bright lights of the checkpoint flickered to the west. Interstate 8 has two lanes in each direction, west and east. The I-8 business loop intersects with the interstate before and after Jacumba. The onramp westbound goes under I-8, enters the highway, and then the BP checkpoint.

Dick Rod shut off his lights and entered the emergency lane of the eastbound oncoming traffic.

The eastbound and westbound lanes of the grade were separated by 15 to 20 feet of median and were at different elevations. At the Kitchen Creek checkpoint, the eastbound lanes were barely visible because the eastbound lanes were close to 20 feet lower than the westbound lanes. (These were the ones monitored by Border Patrol.)

At 1:00 a.m., you'd be surprised at the amount of traffic traveling east. Imperial Valley is the salad bowl of the United States. Big rigs roll both directions at all hours.

Big Papa's Kenworth was no exception. Running empty, back to Indio for another load of alfalfa. He was pulling the grade at 50 mph, to mile marker 17, five miles from the crest. He called his wife, "Hey, baby."

"Hi, honey. When will you be home?"

"Two hours down, two hours back. I'll be home for breakfast."

"Hurry. Miss you."

"Miss ya too, Mama Bear." Big Papa downshifted.

Dick Rod lowered his accelerator and swerved into the inside emergency lane.

"What the fuck are you doing, Rich?" asked the girlfriend.

"Don't trip babe. I'm running blind."

"God dammit, Richard. Let me out."

The people in the back were clueless to the impending disaster, as they were under a plywood sub-floor, built into the van for smuggling purposes. Two miles ahead loomed the glow of lights, illuminating the lanes into the checkpoint. The Border Patrol never seemed to look at the dark eastbound lanes, and even if they did, they probably would not see the dark blue van with no lights. The van with a death wish, cooking over 70 miles an hour in the wrong direction.

Big Papa spilled his coffee trying to fill a cup with his thermos. He shifted gears. Now going at 52 miles per hour at mile marker 19.

The passenger realized that Dick Rod just didn't give a damn. She sat back in her seat and said a silent prayer. Lights were growing brighter and brighter ahead.

The big Kenworth double flatbed trailer reached mile marker 20 at the top of the grade. There was a U-Haul rental truck doing 45 miles per hour coming in the slow lane. Big Papa hit his blinker and veered into the fast lane.

Dick Rod reached the top of the grade just past the checkpoint, and raised his hands in triumph. He let out a rebel yell, oblivious to the carnage ahead of them.

Big Papa looked down to check his speed. A wind gust from the high desert moved the rig two feet to his left, and he tried to correct it, but tandem trailers take a slow hand and much finesse. Big Papa never had a chance.

Dick Rod didn't know what finesse was. He turned on his lights just in time to see the Kenworth logo of Big Papa's truck bearing down on him.

Dick's van and all its occupants were crushed in a millisecond. What was left of the custom van was pushed almost a half-mile back, down the way it came.

Big Papa's truck did a jack-knife, and eventually came to a stop just past Kitchen Creek. Papa's leg was badly broken and his head was spinning.

This tragedy was the by-product of selfish greed. Crazy, drug-induced thinking that lead to chaos, that lead to nine more lost souls that died horrible deaths and emerged to wander the desert; to add to the misery; to haunt people like Larry, who would turn a blind eye to the Dick Rods of the world.

It's like Charlie's dad says, "There's a right way, and a wrong way. Get it right, son."

Well, guess what, Dick Rod? Natural selection says, *You LOSE, son.* This world is better off without your DNA.

Word travels like wildfire with a tragedy like this, and further justifies more compassionate operations like Ramona's.

Charlie and Denice had an especially hard time dealing with the deaths. Sitting in the little cabin, the profound feelings overshadowed the success their daughter Nea had, bringing a baby to the waiting arms of its mother in Chula Vista. The mood was solemn.

Charlie was angry. "That son-of-a-bitch."

"Those poor people," Denice exclaimed.

Nea added, "I can't believe this. How could anyone think that was a good idea?"

Charlie said, "He planned it. He'd done it before. And he'd done it in a car. Larry told me about it."

"Oh, really? Captain Ugly Pants? He'd better hope I don't see him," added Denice.

"I'm sure he's long gone off the mountain by now. He's probably scared shitless," Charlie told them.

✠　✠　✠

There are things that change a person's circumstances. Events that sway the balance, Charlie thought. He was certainly changed by this turn of unfortunate events. Like soft iron becomes hard steel in a white-hot furnace. It's melted, blended, and poured back into a mold life has built for you. Now, you're harder, denser.

Now you're an emotional alloy.

STRICTLY BUSINESS
Chapter 20

Rudolfo was an American citizen whose roots were in Argentina. He considered himself a consummate Latin lover, the *Rico Suave* of Southern California. He was tall with plenty of hair – much on his head, more on his chest. He rolled up his sleeves on his tight T-shirts and thought, *This mangy look suits me.* He squeezed into Sergio Valente designer jeans and asked the ladies, "Do these jeans make my butt look big?"

Yes, Rudolfo. Yes, they do. They also make you look gay. Very gay. Come on, Rudolfo. If you think you're a ladies' man and your butt is in designer jeans, you're confused and need some guidance.

Nea was the target of Rudolfo's affection since the day they ran their first infant.

"Do you like the thought of being my wife?" he asked Nea.

"Shut up, Rudolfo. You're creeping me out," responded Nea-Nea flatly.

"We would make beautiful babies together."

"Make them yourself. Count me out."

"What are you sayin', my love?"

"First off Rudolfo, I'm not your love," corrected Nea, full of disgust. "Second, this is strictly a business arrangement. I don't even know you."

"Ah. But if you did, you could never resist my charm. Admit it."

"Your charm smells strangely like cilantro and musk. Yuck."

"You don't like Calvin Klein?"

"Musk is what hunters use – along with deer urine. To attract dumb-ass animals."

"Precisely," Rudolfo leered. He assumed he had just made a stunning point in his favor.

✠ ✠ ✠

Rudolfo drove, while Nea was in the passenger seat with the baby in back, sleeping soundly in his car seat. Rudolfo played with his fake wedding ring as they waited at the international border.

A small child came up to Nea's window, *"Chiclets? Chiclets?"*

Nea rolled down her window, handed the young boy a dollar, and received a handful of old, stale candy. When she turned her attention back into the car, she noticed Rudolfo ogling at her.

"Rudolfo, if you don't stop coming on to me I'm going to tell Julio you're gay."

"What? You would not dare!"

"Try me."

"You are so mean, *Chiquita*."

"Don't call me that. I'm not a fucking banana. And I'm certainly not your *Chiquita*. Just do your job and don't talk to me."

They pulled forward up to the booth and showed their California drivers licenses to the Border Patrol officers.

"What was your purpose for visiting Mexico?"

"Shopping," Nea-Nea told him.

The officer asked her, "Do you have anything to declare?"

"No, sir. Just some clothes and a good meal." She was pointing to the bags next to the car seat with the sleeping baby sucking on his pacifier.

"Move along then."

Rudolfo collected the IDs and said, "Thank you, sir," and received no response from the agent. The agents at the international border are all business and do not engage in any chit chat.

Nea dropped off Rudolfo and the baby in Chula Vista, and then collected her money. She headed straight to the cabin for a long shower.

Running can be a sweaty business. Nerves can cause all kinds of physical trauma. Plus, being cramped in a small space with a horny, sexually-confused Latin man adds to the misery.

✠   ✠   ✠

Charlie looked at Denice, "Turn it up. Turn it UP." *Papa's going to let you try again. Momma's gonna love you till the end.* Lyrics from a song by The Uninvited rang out from the big Ford Excursion's sound system. The song *Black Sheep* was one of their all-time favorites.

Charlie and Denice had probably logged a half million miles together. As a family with the girls, and as semi-retired *Good Sam* club members, pulling the Love Bus here, there and everywhere.

Now they were playing the *running* game. The ride home after a profitable run was a joyful occasion. Cruising together, they listened to The Uninvited blissfully blaring on the car stereo.

Charlie had two younger brothers in the alternative rock band, The Uninvited – which was based in Los Angeles. When not on tour, The Uninvited played all the cool clubs on Sunset Boulevard. And when Charlie and Denice were in L.A. you could always find them dancing the night away at the Cowboy Club or the Rainbow Inn, two clubs in which the Uninvited played regularly. The memories of the music took them back to crazy times, the frivolity of their youth, when one has no concept of mortality...or responsibility.

It's funny how a melody can bring back a remembrance. Something you can share. A musical combination to the padlock on a time capsule that starts a conversation of *Do you remember when?* Their love and trust was earned through years of having each other's back. And not just when it's convenient, or when times are good. But when it's *inconvenient*. When it hurts, when you're sick, but she's sicker. So you do the dishes. You drive the kids to school. You go to work and then you come home with a smile.

The truly good times were ones like those: dreaming together. Struggling together. Conquering together. Then, sharing the victory.

"Is Elwood gonna meet us up at Barona?" Charlie asked.

"He's gonna call us when he lands. Nea will pick him up in the Maxima," replied Denice. She was in charge of keeping track of such things.

"Okay. Let's get him a room with us at Barona. He'll be ready to roll when we are."

Elwood valet parked the Maxima, and then called his higher-ups.

Charlie answered. "Wood man, how's it hanging?"

"Low and to the left."

"How was your trip?"

"Good, dude. Spent most my time loitering at the shotgun shack. Weezen the juice with Pops and my cousins."

"Weezen your what?"

"Juice man, ya know? White lightning."

"Oh. Right."

"Where you at?" Elwood asked Charlie.

"VIP, baby. Jackpot party at Barona."

"Be right there."

☩   ☩   ☩

Elwood entered the casino and quickly found his bosses. Denice and Charlie stood up as he came around to their slot machine. Charlie's shirt read "Head South," with an arrow pointing to his, well, let's just say *belt buckle*.

Elwood glanced casually downward and said, "Cool shirt. Can I have it?"

Charlie smiled, "Not until you can live up to it."

Woody laughed and then kissed his other boss, the prettier of the two, on her cheek. "Looking good, Mrs. DeVille."

"Thanks, Elwood. Did you have a good time?"

"Yes, ma'am, I did."

Denice wore a tight, charcoal black top that laced over her shoulders, down her arms, and across her ample chest. Or, as Charlie called them, *The Girls*.

"Hey, Woody. Want a drink?" asked Denice.

"Naw. Still hung over."

"Ya wanna play?" Charlie pointed at a machine.

Woody moaned, "Naw. I just wanna take a nap."

"Okay, little brother. Here's your key. You're on the same floor as us. We'll try to keep it quiet."

"Thanks. Hey. Nae told me about the Dick Rod thing. Holy shit."

"World's a better place without him. I feel sorry for the people who were shut in the subfloor, though. Jesus."

"No doubt. What does Ramona say about it?"

"Julio's looking for Larry."

"Uh-oh. Man, that ain't good for Ugly Pants."

Denice broke into their conversation with a decent southern accent, "Don't you fret none, ya hear? Big Daddy's here. I'll never have you flying blind, child."

Elwood, looking shocked, said, "You ever live in the South, Dee?"

"No, hon, just funnin' with y'all."

"Okay, Woody. Well, we've got to go now. That was sexy as hell, and she needs to, um...practice that southern accent, uh...up in our room. So, um, beat it."

"Why mist-ah Dah-ville. Don't be rude!" mocked Denice.

"Fuck that. Later Woody. Come on baby, cash out. Let's roll."

✠ ✠ ✠

Fast forward, past a couple of hours of pornographic *Gone with the Wind* meets grits and girls raised in the south, Charlie and Denise lay there smoking, and not just cigarettes.

"Frankly my dear… I DO GIVE A DAMN," declared Charlie with a satisfied grin on his face.

✠ ✠ ✠

Charlie, Denice, and Elwood were dining at Kenny Rogers' favorite steakhouse, in the VIP section of the Barona Casino.

The three amigos had ordered the same; the special of the day, rib eye wrapped in bacon, pan-fried asparagus with hollandaise sauce, and cheese potatoes and chives. Charlie ordered a bottle of a hearty Malbec with their dinner, and a silky excellent Sonoma pinot noir for afterwards. Topped off by a cheesecake with chocolate rum sauce for dessert.

Forking up small bites of the decadent desert, they talked a little business.

"So I hear Rudolfo is falling for your daughter," said Elwood with a chuckle.

"Oh, he'll literally be falling all right, if he doesn't cool his jets," Charlie replied.

Denice opined, "He doesn't stand a chance; we're moving her up to Live Oak Springs."

"Really?"

"Yeah. Ron and Lily have a single-wide that's going to be available soon. It's nice. Charlie is going to put in new carpet and new kitchen counters. It's got a new heater. It's perfect for her and my little cutie pie."

Charlie lit Denice's smoke and offered one to Elwood, who shook his head. "I didn't like her living alone in the El Cajon valley. She can take care of herself but… you know," said Charlie, ever the overly protective dad.

"Y'all need help moving her?" ask Elwwod.

"When the time comes? Yeah."

"Cool. So anybody seen Larry?"

"Nope," Denice replied. "He's off the radar. His sister hasn't seen him since Johnny tried to smoke his handgun."

"That was some funny shit."

Charlie took a sip of his wine, "Got that right. Did you know he drove a Pacer? A freakin' AMC Pacer, for chrissake?"

Just then Denice's phone rang. She fumbled in her purse for six or seven rings. "Dammit."

Charlie looked at Elwood, "Don't say a word, dude, just don't."

Denice looked at the missed call, "Hey, baby. That's Ramona's number."

"Okay. You go up to the room and call her back. I'll settle up and meet you there."

Back in their room Denice filled Charlie in on her conversation with Ramona. They laid out their plan. Down the backside of the mountain to the Imperial Valley checkpoints. There was some odd construction going on at the off-ramp near the Kitchen Creek checkpoint, so it was way too hot to go west.

That left them all evening to play. Charlie went to the electronic room safe and pulled out eight one-hundred-dollar bills. He handed Denice $400.

"How's the horseshoe, baby? You feeling lucky?"

"I got you covered, handsome. I'm always lucky."

"I'm getting a little chubby right now."

"Save it for later. I'm way too full from dinner."

"Rain-check for Mr. Happy, right on."

✠   ✠   ✠

Playing the double diamond dollar machines, they sat next to each other. Elwood played quarters on some space alien cartooney machine, giggling like a moron. But it kept him busy.

Elwood wasn't much of a gambler like Charlie and Denice. Mostly he just looked for girls to impress, but instead they became instantly turned off by his bad Elvis impression.

Charlie and Denice were dropping dollars in the double diamond machines, waiting for the Progressive Blazing Seven's magic moment, when Denice's machine suddenly lit up and blared that familiar *DING DING DING* of a fat jackpot.

"Red seven! Double diamond! Double diamond!" Charlie shouted excitedly to his wife.

"That's 800! Double that, and double that!"

"What? That's $3,200. I can't wait to kiss you right on the horseshoe," said Charlie, knowing that going back to the room a winner made his wife extremely horny.

The cashier runner came back with 32 one-hundred-dollar bills, and Denice gave her one as a tip. The casino staff took Charlie and Denice's picture and they heard the jackpot announced over the PA system. The photographer handed them a Polaroid of their smiling faces next to the machine. Denice stuck it in her purse.

"Hey, good lookin', let's run $2,000 up to the safe," suggested Charlie. "And then I'm gonna give you a tongue bath. You've been such a good girl."

"Only if you order strawberry cheesecake from room service," said Denice conditionally.

"You gonna eat it, or wear it?"

She whispered seductively in his ear. "Both."

"Sweet!"

✠   ✠   ✠

Elwood knew what time it was. He went up to his room to get some sleep in preparation for the upcoming run. He would need it, as this was going to be the run from hell.

PASTOR CHARLIE DEVILLE
Chapter 21

Charlie pulled the K-5 Blazer into Nea's driveway. He saw Denice playing in the side yard with her grandson. Noticing Charlie pull in she stood up, dusted off her knees, walked over to the truck and jumped in the passenger seat to enjoy some air conditioning before Charlie shut the motor off.

Charlie reached behind him and into the back and pulled out two magnetic signs that were face down on the back seat. He told Denice, "I had a stellar idea on the way to rent the Ford Excursion."

Flipping over the signs Denice read aloud: *Church of the Holy Redeemer, Indio, California, Pastor Charlie DeVille.*

With excitement in his voice and exuberance in his gestures, Charlie ran down the game plan, "This is genius. Slap these babies on the truck doors. I'll wear a tie, you put on your Sunday best." Charlie winked and smiled, turned to face Denice. "We put ten people sittin' up, seat belts on and drive straight through the check point Sunday mornings. Is that not freakin' brilliant or what?"

Denice's smile fell off her face and was replaced by shock and then anger. It flashed in her dark eyes. Slowly and quietly she said, "That's the dumbest shit I've ever heard."

"What the hell does that mean?" Charlie barked.

Her voice rose, as did the flush on her neck, "It means you're jeopardizing our eternity."

Charlie raised his voice to match, "What's that? More of your anal retentive Catholic guilt raising its ugly head?"

"No asshole, you've crossed the line here. Not with God, with me."

"Ahh, Jesus Christ!" Charlie said, throwing his hands up in disgust.

Denice made a fist, knocked it on the side of her husbands cranium and said, "I want to talk to the compassionate loving Charlie I know is in there, so you dig down deep, find him and bring his ass out here to communicate face to face with his wife!"

Silence.

Denice continued, "It's not all fun and games. How are you going to stand at *The Gate* and make your case to the creator? You've got to draw the line somewhere," she summarized, pointing at the vinyl magnetic signs in his lap.

"Dammit Dee, it's a job. It's a dangerous occupation. We need an edge and I don't need this kind of shit from you!"

Denice, shaking her head, summed it up like this, "You pray to God for success, you do not use God to trick your adversary."

Stone cold silence. But Charlie's body language cried out *Bullshit!*

Denice lowered her voice and brought the attitude down a notch, tapping his chest with a polished index finger. "You wear God on your heart like armor to protect the inside, not the outside."

Charlie wiggled uncomfortably in his seat, but still said nothing. So Denice dropped a bomb, "If you don't want to draw a line, I'll draw it for you. I'll turn my back on this smuggling crap and you can fly solo."

Charlie was completely dumbfounded. His first reaction was incredulity. *How could she? The bitch.* Then, astonished that it had come to this, her comments left him bewildered and pissed.

Denice defused some of the anger by appealing to his intelligence, "Think Charlie. You know there's more out there than just this," pointing out the window. "You pray to God for victory, you don't use him as a disguise. Deception is Satan's tool."

Charlie's mouth was a straight and severe line, his lips barely moving, "The last thing I want to be is a tool, honey. You know that."

Using Charlie's father's advice Denice said, "Then straighten up and fly right."

Charlie sat still silent, as understanding dawned on him like water drawn from a well. The best thing he could do was to think this thing through: *This is important. My next move will have a huge impact on how she perceives* us, *our relationship. Gotta get this right. She won't want just an apology, she will want conviction. I know this woman, she needs me to understand how important her faith is, and if I respect that…well, that there's real estate I can't just trample on.*

More silence.

No jokes, no compromise, no ego-driven man crap.

As it turns out, it was as easy as rolling up the signs, rolling down the window, tossing them next to the trash cans and saying, "I'm a dork. I didn't see it. I'll try not to sabotage our eternity. I'm sorry, Pumkin."

And because Charlie had priors for being a clown in important situations, Denice held his eyes for a moment longer than necessary, searching. However, she found nothing but truth and maybe some remorse. She took his face in both hands, kissed him on the forehead and softly said, "Thank you."

"Still pissed?" asked Charlie.

"Yes, handsome. Yes I am."

FASTER THAN A
SPEEDING HELICOPTER
Chapter 22

"Okay, Elwood. Here's the plan. Denice and I will go down to Jacumba and pick them up. Then we'll head back towards the Acorn. You wait there. Denice and I will page you. Five minutes before going by, we'll go east on Highway 8. You catch up. I doubt they'll follow us even if they see us. Knowing the checkpoint is open, if we, you know, *grow a tail* going down the grade, you know what to do."

Elwood nodded.

Charlie and Denice jumped in the rented Ford Excursion. This may be the biggest SUV ever made. So big the Governor wanted to apply an extra gift tax to it, given the crappy gas mileage and all.

"This thing reminds me of a bus," Denice quipped.

"Yeah, I hear ya. It just cost me one hundred dollars to fill it up."

✠ ✠ ✠

Elwood followed them from Rancho Country Estates, up the grade and onto Old Highway 8. He hit the walkie-talkie, "Eyes up, boss. See you soon."

"Ten-four."

They came into Jacumba around 4:00 p.m. and pulled their big SUV up behind the post office. They then cut through the dilapidated parking lot to Edgar's cousin's house.

The cousins were sitting in lawn chairs and drinking Coronas, watching their kids play soccer in the dirt.

"Got seven. But two of them are girls. You know the boss, she don't want Wiley hiding girls up in the rocks."

"Taking them to Julio?" Charlie inquired.

"Nope. Straight to the boss."

"Got an address?"

"Century City Mall. Call when you're on the 10. You are going that direction, *esé?*"

"Planned on it, *vato*," Charlie's responded.

Charlie took no shit from these clowns. He and Denice were the most respected drivers on the circuit, bar none. If these Bozos were jealous, tough shit. If they had a problem with Whitie, they'd have to deal with it. One phone call to Ramona, and Edgar would come down off the high desert and beat them senseless. Storage was everywhere and not a concern. Running the gauntlet with smooth precision was a talent, almost an art.

Driving a lawn chair, drunk, took no talent at all.

One of the young men started to rise up out of his chair. Charlie reached into his pocket and pulled his phone out.

"Shall I call your daddy? Tell Julio you're playing tough guy with my wife standing right fucking here?"

"No, man. No problem here."

"Sit down, *puto*," one *vato* said to the younger man with the baggy pants and Reeboks. "Look, *señor*," he continued, turning his attention toward Charlie. "It's almost dark. You take a walk with your beautiful *señorita* here. Maybe 30 minutes. They'll be loaded and laying down in that big white truck over there. How's that for service, *señor?*"

Charlie pulled a one-hundred-dollar bill out of his front pocket and handed it to the man, "Perfect."

"We're on the same side, *señor.*"

He looked at the young gangster, flashed a smile and said something in Spanish. Probably called him a dumb-ass, showin' off the bill.

Charlie said, "Thank you, *señor.* And we are on the same team. My wife and I pay for good service. Good business is good for everybody."

Charlie pulled out another one-hundred-dollar bill, handed it to the kid with the saggy pants nodding his head toward the man. "Make our job easy. Make your life easy."

The young man put down the tough guy expression, grabbed the bill with his left hand, and stuck his closed fist out. He and Charlie bumped knuckles. The youngster smiled and said, "Good luck on your run."

✠ ✠ ✠

Charlie and Denice started strolling toward Larry's. Going past Elrod's parents' house, you could sense the loss. The ghosts. His ghost, already present. A chill ran down Charlie's spine. He produced a Pall Mall as Denice thought the same thing.

They stopped just past the house, *flip-click-flame*, lighting their smokes. They continued on to Larry's place. That presence was there, also. No words were said. Like a dark omen, a chill in the air, a stain on the Cosmos. Like pain from a wound you can't see. They held hands all the way back, quietly smoking.

✠   ✠   ✠

The exit from Jacumba with their human cargo was smooth as glass. Just before Live Oak Springs, they paged Elwood, who rang back immediately. "Let's roll."

"On it."

Elwood passed them at the Desert View/Rock Tower exit. He scanned the terrain back and forth behind boulders and frontage exits. He was good, very good at his job. And he had a bad feeling.

"Mad Max to Boss Man."

Denice answered, "What ya got, Mad Max?"

Charlie looked at Denice, "I'm rubbing off on the boy. Mad Max, that's good."

"Boss Lady," Elwood continued, "I've got the heebie jeebies. Something don't feel right."

"Okay, sweetie. We'll stop at the Springs Motel."

"Ten-four."

Denice turned around as they came off the grade. She told her passengers, "Everybody down, please."

The five men and two women had not uttered a sound the entire trip. It was always the same. But when Denice spoke they always did what they were told.

So everyone hit the floor.

"It's okay. It's okay," Denice tried to assure them. "We're just pulling over for a minute."

A woman translated and they all exhaled.

They stopped at a Denny's across from a Union 76 gas station.

"We should motel up," Woody said, "and let me run through to the airport. Something ain't right, you notice not one BP on the road. None up on the hill, either."

"Now that you mention it," Denice concurred. "Woody's right. Better safe than sorry. Let's check in at the Well Springs Motel."

Denice registered under her own name, having to show her ID. But under license plate, she wrote BTUWN 2. The Indian woman with the dot on her forehead couldn't care less.

The little eight-room, single-story motel was vacant, except for one room. The shabby exterior was just a front for a shot-out interior, with green linoleum peeling in the bathroom, and a 1970s-era, matted beige shag rug. It looked like it had mange. The only plus was the brand new air conditioner rattling in the window. Once all nine passengers were crowded into the cramped space with two double beds, they turned the AC on high, and Elwood went for food. Once again, they had loaded Mad Max with bags of cement.

Looking out the curtain, Charlie said to Denice, "That boy looks like he's got a load."

"It doesn't make sense to run until daylight. Can't see in the dark so, what's the use of a point man?"

"All right, I agree."

Charlie turned to the oldest female, "You speak English?"

"*Sí, señor.*"

"We stay here tonight. You want a shower? Go ahead. When little brother gets back with food, my wife and I will leave for a few hours."

Denice added, "Don't worry, everything will be fine. We just need daylight."

"*Si, señora.*"

Elwood returned with bags of microwave burritos, potato chips, six packs of Coke, and cans of jalapeno peppers.

With no can opener.

"What the hell, Elwood? How are they supposed to break into those cans?"

Elwood said, "It's a fucking desert out there, man. In case you haven't noticed. I'm not driving 40 miles to Indio for fast food."

"Chill, man. I was just wondering how the hell do I open these here jalapenos?"

✠   ✠   ✠

Charlie and Denice went to Denny's for their favorite meals. Charlie's was the All-American Grand Slam, and Denice's was the country-fried steak and eggs. They had spent many an evening on the road. At Denny's they would stop to drink coffee and talk. On this particular visit they took a moment to catch up with Ramona by phone.

"We're running late, Ramona," said Charlie.

"Is everything good?" ask Ramona concerned.

"Yeah, except our motel room."

"You still, at the resort?"

"No, we're still a ways away."

"Morning then," Ramona confirmed.

"Lord willing and the river don't rise."

"Call me."

"Will do."

✠ ✠ ✠

Back at the room Elwood was presently falling madly in love with a beautiful young Latin girl named Esperanza. She spoke just enough English to sound exotic, and her big almond eyes spoke louder than her soft voice. Elwood was entranced. Not 15 minutes ago her hair had been full of brambles and almost completely matted on one side of her head. Now she was all showered and clean.

Elwood pointed to his chest and shouted, "My name is Elwood."

"I am as Esperanza. And I can hear just fine, Señor Elwood."

Elwood blushed. "Sorry," he replied in a normal tone. "It's just that you're so pretty and I don't speak Spanish and..." He trailed off. He shook his head in disgust. All the cool had left. All the witty words and sharp repartee was replaced with a stutter and a dumb-ass puppy love stare. Now would be a perfect time to raise the bar and not pick your nose or scratch your crotch. Elwood was about to do so, subconsciously when he heard the key in the door. Charlie and Denice walked in.

Charlie noticed the faraway look on Elwood's face. "Close your mouth, Woody. Jesus, you okay?"

"Yeah, Boss. I'm good."

The room smelled like a weird mixture of soap, wet hair and high desert bushes. Charlie looked around and was surprised to see that most were asleep. One man obviously had a sinus condition, and sounded like a pig rooting for truffles. Denice started arranging the bed nearest the bathroom, pulling off the comforter. She covered three men on the floor, then looked over at Woody, who was intently staring at Esperanza, climbing onto the other bed. Denice looked at Charlie and whispered, "Love is in the air."

"So are my funky armpits, I'm getting in a shower."

"Me, too."

"Sweet. Love is in the shower."

☩ ☩ ☩

Morning came, and the room looked like a bomb had gone off inside. The sun tried to squeeze through the heavy green curtains when Denice looked at her phone for the time. It was 6:30 a.m.

Elwood was awake, lying on the floor between the beds, and both girls were on the one bed. He awkwardly stared straight at the ceiling. Denice spoke softly, "Elwood, run the road to the base of Wells Mountain. Then hurry back."

"Okay, Mrs. DeVille,"

"My name is Dee-Dee to my friends."

"Yes, ma'am, Dee-Dee, ma'am."

Elwood was enthralled with the sleeping form of the young woman. Suiting up his mental armor, his mission was to rescue and return this damsel. He loved that idea.

Charlie noticed that starry look in Elwood's eyes. "Woody? Dammit, snap out of it," Charlie told him. "Plenty of time for that shit later. I'll get her phone number for you. Right now, you've got work to do. Did you hear what the boss lady said? We're not paying you to undress the girls with your eyeballs. Now go do your job."

"Yes, sir."

Woody grabbed his keys off the table and he was out the door.

✠   ✠   ✠

The group was anxious, and totally dependent on these white people. They seemed nice enough. Not crazy, like all the stories people told back home about white people. And the huge white truck with the leather seats was like a limousine. The two youngest men from a village near Matamoros had never seen one, much less rode in one.

The oldest man, in his 30s, looked at Esperanza, and said softly in Spanish, "The young man has fallen for you."

"That is not my fault, *Señor* Garcia."

"I hope he does not lose focus."

There was little she could say, she just sat there holding hands with the other young woman, who was wild-eyed with fear, and had been since Hotel Mexico. She had not spoken one word.

Elwood returned less than 40 minutes later. "Clear, as far as I can tell."

Charlie said to him, "Okay, let's move the people into the truck. Denice, go check us out. Have a conversation with Miss Congeniality while we load." He shifted positions, and said to Elwood, "As soon as we're done, you turn left out of here. Go to the Union 76 and get gas. As soon as you see us roll out, come on with it."

Elwood said, "Good plan, boss. That Indian lady looked at me like I was Satan, or some bad yogurt."

"Yeah, she's nosy. Don't want any anonymous tips to the BP. Make sure your Radio's on channel 14 and your batteries are good. Phone too."

Elwood nodded his head. He looked at Esperanza and said, "Okay, ladies first. Same deal. Down on the floor."

The exit was successful. Denice did a good job of distraction, the art of illusion and seclusion. Half a mile outside the motel parking lot, Mad Max was flying past the big Ford Excursion.

Scanning left and right, taking in both sides of the road, Elwood was on his game. The road rose and fell with the topography of the desert terrain. Acacia bushes were seven to eight feet high, bordering each side of the road. Jagged rock jutted up and out of the earth on the westbound side. A good point man runs between three quarters to one mile ahead at about five miles an hour faster. He slows down occasionally to maintain distance. The *load* vehicle always does the speed limit or the flow of traffic.

As Elwood came over the rise, one mile from the beginning of Wells grade, there were two Border Patrol units, each facing the opposite lane of oncoming traffic. Their windows were down, and they were talking across the narrow two-lane highway. Elwood immediately went into action on the radio in his lap. He keyed the button, "One on each side. Flip it."

Charlie pulled towards the side, preparing for a U-turn. Elwood's mind was taking in everything. He thought of Esperanza. He couldn't let her down. He flipped a U-turn, an eighth of a mile past the two officers. They had stared him down on the way past. Elwood sped up to 65 miles per hour, his foot to the floor.

One officer said to his partner, "Here he comes again, Jerry."

Jerry was preparing to pull out behind Elwood, but just then Elwood pulled to the right and side-swiped Jerry's cruiser, tearing off his front fender and a chunk off his driver's-side tire.

"I'm coming back toward you, Boss. Don't flip. Don't flip. Punch it."

Charlie slowly pulled back onto the roadway.

Jerry's cruiser was out of commission. Jerry picked up the Motorola, as his fellow officer flipped a two point U-turn, and sped after Mad Max. Elwood reached 80 mph, up and over the next rise, then slammed on his brakes. Stopping dead square in the middle of the road, he jumped out of the car. Not one second later, the cruiser with lights and sirens blaring flew over the rise.

The officer did not see the Maxima till the last second. He veered to the right at the last possible moment. It was his only choice, as Charlie's big white SUV was coming in the opposite lane. His passenger-side wheel hit the sand and gravel shoulder, flinging his cruiser out into the desert at 70 miles per hour. The vehicle flipped, and the officer's head hit the wheel. Everything went dark.

Jerry called in the helicopter unit. Elwood ran back to the car. Charlie and Denice passed Jerry's cruiser and gawked at the wreckage. Jerry was too preoccupied to acknowledge them driving by.

"Holy shit! God almighty!" Denice exclaimed.

She and Charlie both saw the cruiser in a slow motion, kind of an altered reality. It was upside down, and lost in the Acacia trees.

Flying past in the opposite direction, Woody hit the walkie-talkie, "Gotta go, Boss."

"You okay, Wood Man?"

"Yeah. Car's toast, though."

Elwood's Maxima was bashed in from its passenger headlight to rear door. Smoke poured out from under its hood. Antifreeze sprayed on the windshield and the wipers were only making the visibility worse. Woody had to look out the side window as he drove.

"Haul balls, Elwood," commanded Charlie into the walkie-talkie. "Ditch that piece of shit, just like we talked about, motherfucker. Go!"

Charlie and Denice had just passed Jerry, and were trying to decide if they should stop. But Jerry looked okay. Plus, he was a cop. So...you know...

Jerry was mad as hell, and the cruiser was bashed in like a boxer's face.

Charlie said to Denice, "What the fuck's up? Moon's in Cancer. On the cusp of herpes, or what?"

"Gimme that," said Denice, as she grabbed the walkie-talkie from Charlie's hand. "Elwood. Are you okay?"

"Yes, ma'am. Can't say as much for the car, though."

"Drive that out into the desert and put as much distance between you and it as possible."

"Yes, ma'am."

"I'm calling Nea right now."

The sound of the Border Patrol chopper cut through the desert air as Charlie and Denice started up the extremely steep, sharp, switchback grade of Wells Spring Mountain.

Charlie mused to no one in particular, "Go, Wood Man. You stud, you."

Denice thought to herself, *Holy crap. This shit's not supposed to happen.*

Esperanza smiled to herself, and in Spanish she said, "He did it for me. He told me. He would make sure we made it."

Elwood's voice crackled through the walkie-talkie. "That's not a fucking helicopter I hear, is it?" He had dumped the Maxima, having driven it straight into a stand of Acacia trees.

But luck was on his side.

There was no more liquid in the radiator to create steam. So wherever he was, he was not visible from the air. As far as the BP was concerned, he could be anywhere within 2,000 square miles of desert.

But at the moment he was in the lobby of the Shot Out Inn and Motel Suites of Borrego Springs, back where they started less than an hour ago. The parking lot was empty, as were the eyes looking back at him from across the counter.

Elwood looked at the Hindu woman behind the front desk and calmly said, "Car's broke down. It's at the 76 up there. I need a room please."

The chopper flew overhead and banked right, skirting Highway 8, westward towards the mountain.

"ID, please," she replied.

"Oh, crap. I left it in the car. But I do have cash." He pulled the bills out of his front pocket.

Her pupils dilated, and the corners of her mouth went from a drastic frown, to a straight severed line. "Fill this out. I need a copy. And then later, your ID." She slid the form across the counter.

"Oh, yeah. Right," replied Elwood.

✠   ✠   ✠

Charlie watched the road ahead, Denice surveyed the road behind. Everyone was still on the floor. Two cruisers with lights on blazed past them in the oncoming lane.

"Jesus." Dee exclaimed.

"You hear my asshole slam shut back there?" Charlie asked.

"That's disgusting, honey."

Charlie was on an adrenaline roll now, "God, that boy's got balls."

Denice said, "Yeah. Where his brains should be."

"He saved our ass. He actually did it. I'm lovin' that hillbilly right about now," said Charlie excitedly.

In the back, Esperanza muttered to herself in Spanish, *He is my hero. I hope he is safe.*

Denice heard her. And even though she didn't understand Spanish, she knew what the young girl what talking about. "Hold on honey, we'll call him in a few," she assured Esperanza.

"Okay, *señora*," came a disembodied female voice from the back of the van.

Charlie proclaimed to Denise, "If you Google 'stud' Elwood's picture would come up." He looked in the rearview mirror, then looked at his wife, "Hand me the walkie-talkie."

Denice was trying to reach Nea on the phone, but handed the radio to Charlie with her right hand. Charlie lit two smokes, and traded her one for the radio. He took a big drag, blew out two huge plumes through his nose. He keyed the hand set.

"How about it, studly? Are you out there?"

Nothing.

✠   ✠   ✠

Woody had just filled out the registration form: *Elwood Haroldson. Cheers. Boston, Massachusetts.* License number: *MST SWLO.* He handed the woman a fifty-dollar bill to cover a twenty-nine dollar single room. He grabbed the key with a promise to return with his ID.

Once in his room, he closed the door, picked up his phone, and turned on his radio.

"Boss-man? Boss-Man? How's about it?"

"I've gotcha, Wood Man, let's get off the air. Call the company phone."

"Ten-four."

Denice was on her personal phone to her daughter, "Honey, the boy left wreckage for a mile and a half."

The company phone rang, she handed it to Charlie.

"You okay, stud?"

"Yes, sir. Just chillin' like a villain, how about you?"

"Smooth as glass. Thanks to you."

"Tell Esperanza she owes me a kiss."

"Ten-four. Look Denice has got Nea on the other line. Hold on a sec."

Denice was saying, "Almost ran into the back of the Maxima..."

"*Oh no he d'ent,*" replied Nea-Nea in her best urban accent.

"Yup. Then the helicopter."

"Charlie interrupted, "Hey, Denice, dammit. Tell her to jump in the goddamn car. And hold up." He spoke hurriedly into the phone, "Where are you?"

"Same place as before," replied Elwood.

Charlie turned his attention to Denice. "Tell her to haul ass. Not now, but right now."

"What room?" asked Nea-Nea, obviously hearing Charlie through the phone.

"Room 100. Honey, bunny," answered Charlie. "And do not dilly-dally."

"Don't worry," reassured Denice to Charlie. "She's already in the car, Brandt's at Lily's."

"Cool."

Charlie spoke quietly into the phone to Elwood, who had been patiently waiting for Charlie's other phone conversation to end. "Watch the parking lot, little brother," he instructed Elwood. "First sign of a cruiser, you take off into the desert. I will come find you."

"Thanks, boss. The helicopter's on the mountain. I guess they haven't found the Maxima."

"Place is gonna be swarming, Woody. You destroyed two cruisers. You crazy fuck."

"Just doing my job."

"I'm giving you a raise."

"Sweet. How's Esperanza?"

"She's digging you a lot right now, stud muffin."

"I want to see her again, Charlie."

"I will make that happen, Wood Man. I'll have Denice talk to Ramona, and tell her it's a love thing."

"Tell Denice I said thanks."

"Goddamn. Woody. We're thanking you right about now."

It's human nature to not look right under your own damn nose. Disappear like a chameleon. Hide in plain sight.

✠   ✠   ✠

So it's over the mountains and through the woods and across the fruited plains.

"Okay, people. We're good. You can get up now. Please use your seatbelts."

You don't want to do an extra 24 to 36 months drinking toilet wine because of an "endangerment" enhancement to your federal prison sentence.

Esperanza translated in Spanish and then asked Denice in English, "Elwood is very brave, no?"

"You could say that."

"I heard him tell you he wants to see me again."

"Yes, I believe he's smitten."

"I don't know this word, *smitten*, *señora*."

Charlie looked at her over his right shoulder and said, "Esperanza, he did that crazy shit for you. He wants a phone number and a big sloppy kiss on the lips. And I think you should give him both. In that order."

Esperanza smiled. For her it felt like the first time in a long time. Her eyes sparkled with mischief, a twinkle that transcended language barriers. She calmly asked Denice, "Do you have a pen, *señora*?"

✠   ✠   ✠

Nea ran over the strange course of events in her head, trying to figure out just what in the hell her mom and dad were doing. The conflicting battle of right and wrong rages on inside all of us. The balance weighs differently depending on a multitude of social factors: environment, upbringing, moral compass, education – or the lack thereof.

As she neared the bottom of the grade, Nea turned up the radio. Big Bad Voodoo Daddy was playing. Keeping time with the music, she lit a smoke, and a small smile crossed her lips as she thought about her family. Never a dull moment with this tribe.

She made a left at the Borrego Springs Scenic Highway and another right at the Krishna Inn. She pulled in front of room 100, and before she could honk, Elwood was out the door and in the car.

"Hi. Good to see you," he said.

"You crazy bastard," she replied.

"Hey, it was your mom and dad. Let's get the hell out of here."

Nea backed up the Tempo. "I'll call my mom."

"Let's head toward Indio. Maybe we rent a car." She turned east on Highway 8 and dialed the phone. "Hey, Mom. We're on our way to Indio."

"Why?"

"Elwood wants to rent a car and finish the job."

"Bless his heart. Hold on a sec." She cocked her head towards her husband and said, "Nea's got Woody. He wants to catch up with us."

"Crazy SOB. Okay. Let me think." After a moment he finally said, "Tell her to have Woody meet us at the Holiday Inn at Cabazon, just past Morongo."

"You hear that, hon?" Denice said into the phone.

"Yeah. I'm dropping Mad Max off here at Enterprise Car Rental. I got to go back. Brandt is at Ron and Lily's. Underfoot, no doubt."

"Okay, kiss his cute little face for me, and thanks, Nea."

"No problem."

Now, had it been something like picking out too small of a purse, Nea would be in complete hysteria. Can't find her lighter? Screaming and yelling ensues. But in times of family emergency, Nea becomes calm and lucid, quietly strategizing her next move. That's why when shit hits the fan, Denice calls in her daughter, the heavy hitter. If you have a malfunction that concerns the DeVille family, you can depend on the fact Nea will make it her concern, and then fix it. Hopefully it's not your fault.

Just ask Larry.

✠　✠　✠

Elwood rented a Toyota Solara convertible using Nea's Visa card. He had the top down and was running about 90 miles per hour over the staggered dune formations that peak and dip on the road to the eastern checkpoint of Indio. It was the long way around to Palm Springs and Morongo, but going back towards the now BP-infested western desert was a cluster-fuck of his making.

His mind was set on seeing Esperanza again. Coming up on Interstate 10 he pulled over and put the top up, and turned on the AC.

✠　✠　✠

The Holiday Inn was a bust; too busy and too much glass. It was also three stories tall. You don't want to chance a room on the third floor, it's too much exposure. Charlie decided on the single level Motel 6.

Charlie parked around the side, and walked into the office.

Denice was on the phone to Elwood, informing him of the change of location. Charlie could hear a TV with *The Price Is Right*. Drew Carey was doing his Bob Barker thing. The office smelled like cayenne pepper and garlic breath.

"Good afternoon, sir. How may we help you?"

Charlie looked around for the part of *we*. "I'd like a room, please. On the end, if you have it. Less noise, you know."

The manager smiled with a mouthful of yellow teeth. "I understand, sir. I believe we can accommodate your request." He slid the registration form across the desk.

Charlie lifted up the chrome bell with the button on top. The one that is essential if you're living in your office, and slid a one-hundred-dollar bill under it. The rooms were twenty-nine-ninety-five. "Love being accommodated. Keep the change, sir."

Charlie filled out the form: *John Holmes of Los Angeles, California*. License number, *DEP DCKN*.

The desk clerk tucked the bill into his top pocket. Bingo. He had a new best friend and preferential lodging for the DeVille Corporation. Finally a break in the drama.

Charlie drove to the end of the building around the backside.

"Hey, look a pool," observed Denice.

Esperanza had been assuming the role of translator and caregiver. She said to the other woman in the truck, "You need to shower, *mija*. Don't be afraid I will look out for you."

This ordeal seemed to affect her more than anyone. She acted like a deer in the headlights. Standing by the bathroom door, she said, "*Señora*, we are hungry. I have some money."

"Okay, let me make a couple calls," Denice told her. Then she turned to Charlie, "Okay, Mr. Large-and-in-charge, run for some supper."

Charlie smiled. Denice threw the phone at him. "Call Ramona. Give her the 411 on our situation."

"Say please."

Denice licked her upper lip, slowly.

"Done deal." Charlie scrolled down and pushed send. "One ringy-dingy. Two ringy-dingy. Ramona? Charlie."

"Seems you've created a stir," she answered.

"You heard?"

"Is everyone safe?"

"Safe and sound. Look. The universe has ten assholes, and I seem to have been standing under one all day. Shit just fell out of the sky."

"Funny man."

"We're close. We need to get a bite and wait for my little brother."

"He's a hero?"

"Totally. Spandex panties and everything."

"He's on his way to you?"

"On the wings of love."

"Huh?" asked Ramona, completely confused by his comment.

"Seems this whole business is a knight-in-shining-armor-type love story, involving a young lady traveling with us."

"I see," replied Ramona cautiously.

"We'll talk at the mall."

"Call me as soon as you can."

"Don't worry. Sleet nor snow, nor dark of night, and all that."

"Cut the crap, Mr. Brown."

"Love you, too."

"Bye."

Denice raised an eyebrow and gave Charlie *The Look.* "*Love you, too?*" she asked mockingly.

"She called me Charlie Brown. You know I hate that."

"Then stop being a Bozo," warned Denice.

Charlie cleared his throat and adjusted his attitude.

"Let's find some food."

"You're the hunter-gatherer."

"Shall I creep up on a Jack in the Box?"

"Let's go Mexican. I'll check the phone book."

Denice called Elwood as she rifled through the yellow pages. "How you doing, hon?"

"I'm straight. A little tired."

"You have any cash?"

"Yeah."

"We're all starving here. We need Mexican food. For ten."

"Gotcha. Mex for ten."

"We're in room number 38."

"Okay. I'm 30 minutes away. Call it one hour, with the stop."

She gave him the address.

✠ ✠ ✠

Elwood could not get her face out of his mind. The way she looked at him with a timid expression in her eyes, that *come-on-with-it* smile, and the tendrils of her long black hair that she continually blew out of her face. He had fallen so fast. He could hear the wind. Or was that the convertible top?

As for Esperanza, she knew he'd be here soon. Why did she feel like this? Her heart was pounding, even though she barely knew him.

✠ ✠ ✠

When Elwood arrived at the Motel 6 he received a hero's welcome, and not just because of the ten pounds of takeout he had in six bags. The group was all smiles, handshakes and pats on the back. Elwood worked his way to the desk near the microwave and set down his load.

Charlie grasped his hand and did the shoulder-bump man-hug.

"Your stock is skyrocketing right now, brother."

Denice came forward and kissed his cheek.

"Thank you, Woody. You put your ass in harm's way for the team."

Elwood looked at his feet. "Thanks, boss. Thank you, Mrs. Denice. Ah, shit. Thanks, Dee."

Elwood felt a tap on his shoulder. He turned around just as Esperanza grabbed his face in both hands, stood on her tippy toes and gently kissed his lips.

"You are my hero, Mr. Woody."

"I could not let them have you." He reached around her small waist and held her close.

Denice put her head on Charlie's shoulder. Charlie put his arm around his wife and whispered, "Mr. Woody. That's some funny shit. Tell Mr. Woody to stand down."

Denice reached over, grabbed his crotch with her left hand, and applied some pressure. "Do not ruin this moment for him."

Charlie nodded his head in the affirmative.

"I will put this thing in my purse if you're gonna use it to think with. Understand?"

Charlie was tethered to the ground. His wife had a firm grip on reality. Also, on his balls.

The group was in excellent spirits as they broke bread together and partook in some social lubricant, in the form of all-American Coor's Light. Sometime later, Elwood and

Esperanza slipped away, leaving the keys to the big Ford Excursion missing from the little table. But the SUV was still parked around the corner. Charlie and Denice slipped out as well, as soon as everyone was asleep, for a quick skinny dip in the pool. With no moon, it was dark and tepid. Love was in the air. The excitement of the day mixed with the danger of the night. The clients were all asleep, California dreamin'.

✠ ✠ ✠

Exiting the seventy-degree pool water, wrapped in terry cloth towels, Charlie and Denice tiptoed back towards their room when Mr. Hamoudi (the motel owner) stopped them dead in their tracks.

He stood there with cases of soda to restock his machines. The bearded man broke the awkward silence, "Ahhh! Mr. and Mrs. Mysterious."

Charlie and Denice were both baffled and perplexed, so mysterious was not far off the mark.

Charlie, fully aware of his nakedness under the towel asked, "Are we in trouble?"

"Not as far as the motel is concerned," replied Mr. Hamoudi.

Denice suddenly recognized him, "You're the manager."

"Correct, ma'am. Owner, janitor, maintenance, etcetera, etcetera."

"Nice place you have here," said Charlie, looking around like it was his first time here. "Water's the perfect temperature."

"Yes, well, not only do we keep a light on for you, but the pool heater as well."

Charlie, for lack of a quick retort simply replied, "Nice."

Denice, remembering her manners, piped up, "My name is Denice, this is my husband Charlie DeVille." Like knowing the fact they were married made skinny-dipping at 1:00 a.m. okay in Mr. Hamoudi's mind.

"Nice to meet you Mr. and Mrs. DeVille. If it's not too much to ask, I'd like to talk to you both. I know it's late, or early. Either way, would you meet me in the office in say, 10 minutes?"

Charlie and Denice glanced at each other and silently agreed, then looking at Mr. Hamoudi, Charlie added, "Okay, how about 15 minutes?"

"Good as gold," said Mr. Hamoudi.

While getting dressed back at the room, Denice asked, "What do you think this is all about?"

"I don't have the foggiest idea," said Charlie. "But it can't be good, who knows what crazy shit that weird beard is gonna come at us with."

They dressed quickly, being quiet so as not to wake the clients. They were out the door, down the stairs and standing in front of the office door in less than 15 minutes.

Just as Charlie started to knock the door swung open and the smiling, bearded face of Mr. Hamoudi appeared.

"*Marhaba*. Hello to you both. Please come in, come in."

Looking around inside the apartment behind the desk, there, standing next to a candle lit shrine of some kind, was a beautiful woman in a yellow, chiffon Sari. Her bright white smile radiated on her dark cinnamon colored face.

"Welcome," she said through that smile.

"Thank you," Denice replied as she and Charlie entered the room.

Mr. Hamoudi pointed to a couch and said, "Please, sit down, relax yourselves."

They sat down but Charlie was anxious, not at all relaxed or comfortable.

Since Mrs. Al-Beduls name was all but unpronounceable, Mr. Hamoudi offered, "This is my wife Anna, and I am called Ham, short for Hamoudi-Al-Beduls."

They shook hands while Charlie introduced himself and his wife. Anna asked, "Would you like some tea?"

Charlie and Denice accepted and Anna left the room for the kitchen. By way of explanation for this late night meeting, Ham spoke first. "Let me tell you a story so that you'll understand why we're here," Ham said, pointing to the coffee table and making a little circular motion. "My family is from the fertile crescent, the South Plains of Jordan. We are descendants of nomadic Bedouin tribes and Christians." Anna returned and Ham took the tea service from her and set it on the table. As Anna began to serve, he continued. "My wife is Hindu, she's from India, and she's the flower of my existence." He shot a smile in her direction. "We met in San Diego at the Asian American Hotel Owners Association Convention. But this story is about me and my family. My mother, father, myself and two brothers came to the United States in a sea-container, smuggled in."

Those words, *smuggled in*, hung in the air thick as hookah smoke. Everyone made eye contact in the awkward silence.

The only sound came from Anna pouring tea from an ornate Middle Eastern tea service. Denice's eye zeroed in on the scrolled etching on the bell-shaped strainer as Anna pulled it from the pot.

Ham looked directly into Charlie's stunned face and said, "I will spare you the horrors of the days at sea, the loss of my Father's legs." Ham closed his eyes, shook his head, as if going back in time behind his eyelids. "Immigration has so many faces, had we stayed, we might have starved and suffered as most of our tribal villages did."

Charlie's mind was racing. *Where was this going? Who was this guy? Was he a Cop? FBI? Shit. I got clients in this motel.*

"My wife and I are one hundred percent American, but have not forgotten where we came from or how we got here." Ham brought the tea cup to his lips, pinky extended, looked over the top of his cup at Charlie and asked, "How many Mexicans this time?"

Charlie with a deadpan expression on his face replied, "Eight adults."

"I noticed you do not hide them."

"I asked them to duck down when we passed your office," explained Charlie.

With a knowing smile, Ham countered, "We have cameras Charlie. Let me ask a question, did you know that Indian-Americans own over half the motels in this country?"

"No, I did not."

"My wife's own extended family owns sixteen franchised motels from San Diego to Fresno.

Charlie was all ears, but bouncing around inside his cranium was, *If the border patrol had surrounded this office, they'd be in handcuffs by now.*

Ham sat back slowly in his easy chair, tilted his leonine mane and asked. "Would it be of service to you to have prepaid locations to temporarily house your immigrants?"

Denice turned her head towards her husband to gage his reaction to this totally unexpected question. Charlie exhaled loudly, smiled broadly and tried unsuccessfully not to show the shock and surprise he felt as the possibilities tumbled into his mind.

"Ham, few things would be of more service. Prepaid? Let's talk numbers."

Denice went to the kitchen with Anna to brew more tea and heat up some pastries. Little triangles of deliciousness with figs, dates, honey, and cinnamon inside. They talked and ate, discussed arrangements to be made with Ramona. They traded stories and laughed. When the evening came to an end, Charlie and Denice were given the room next to #38 and were going to try for some shuteye before the sun came up.

Lying in bed like lovers often do, too excited by the night's festivities and the strong tea to sleep, Charlie staring at the ceiling said, "Hamoudi sure is a cool guy."

"I thought you said he was a weird beard?"

"That was before I knew his story and how much we have in common, but what makes him cool, in my book, is the difference. The bedouin thing."

Sarcastically Denice said, "So the camel jockey crap is over?" As she rolled onto her side facing Charlie.

"Man that guy has seen some stuff. His stories are heart-wrenching. I think he's trying to give back, pay forward."

Denice murmured in his ear, "Anna is Hindu, she says it's a Karma thing, religion is so much a part of their life. Did you see the crucifix over the shrine?"

"Yeah, at first I thought it was creepy. But after knowing them a few hours, the two blended like a mango Margarita."

Denice pulled the covers over her shoulders.

"Anna invited us to dinner at Moon Over Tunis, after the drop."

With a lecherous smile, Charlie offered, "Ham says they have belly dancers between entries."

"Your new best friend, huh?"

"Like I said, he's a cool guy, and just so you know, he rocks that beard."

In the twilight of sleep, just before falling away, Charlie regretfully wondered about the backstories of people he'd met and dismissed, labeling as cultural inferiors. He thought to himself, *life happens so fast. People come and go like so many falling stars. I guess I only scrape the surface before passing judgment. It seems...superficial. Am I lazy? Just being shallow? What do I really know about Ron and Lily? Or, for that matter, Wiley and Julio?* And then, as if another voice entered the conversation, Charlie heard in the back of his thoughts, *Charlie, you need to slow your roll, son. Put away the label-maker, and make time to dig a little deeper.*

Charlie was exhausted. But his last thought that carried him off to sleep was this: *I should spend more time with Valentino. Ask him where Croatia is.*

✠ ✠ ✠

The group was up and loaded before dawn. However, rush hour was not a good time to run, unless everyone was hidden from sight. People are generally nosy, and with the advent of cell phones there are plenty of wanna-be private dicks in L.A., willing to call in their slightest suspicions.

The outlet mall was not busy at 8:00 a.m. Ramona was in a red Chevy pickup. She knew where every single camera was located. The big Ford pulled in along with the Solara, in which Woody and Esperance were cuddling and laughing.

Ramona came to the window of Charlie's truck, at the passenger side, "Tell Mr. Elwood to join me in my truck, and Espy, too. Now."

Denice hit the radio, "Ramona wants to talk to you guys. In her truck, chop, chop."

"Okay," Elwood complied. The couple walked briskly to the Silverado, and got in. Ramona, sat in the driver's seat. "Espy, your uncle is here for you. Right over there," she pointed at a Ford Ranger.

"Yes, Ramona."

Elwood looked Ramona right in the eye, "I want to marry her. I'm gonna make her a citizen. I love her."

"Mr. Elwood, you've only known her for two days."

"I know what I know."

Ramona stared into Elwood's eyes until she bore into his soul. Yet he did not look away. She then turned her gaze at Esperanza. The young girl respected Ramona, but she also did not back down by looking away. Ramona sighed. "Well then, who am I to question?"

"I have her family's phone number," said Elwood. "She gave it to me."

Esperanza leaned forward and got Ramona's attention. In Spanish, she told her, "He put his life on the line for me. He cares deeply for me, and he's the cutest redneck I've ever seen."

Ramona smiled. "Okay, *mija*. Go to your uncle."

Esperanza kissed Elwood quickly, and whispered to him, "Call me tonight. I will talk to my aunt and uncle. As long as I go to school, they will not care."

"Tonight then, at eight o'clock." Elwood hugged his beauty and then watched her get out of the truck and run to her family.

The rest of the clients were delivered to their families, one by one, punctuated by plenty of handshakes and thank yous all around. As usually happens, a kind of bond develops. An unspoken camaraderie evolves when a group arrives intact from a dangerous situation.

"Let's all go to the food court and get some breakfast," Ramona suggested, knowing that everyone must be starving.

Once inside the mall, Ramona handed Charlie $4,000.

In turn, Charlie compensated Elwood accordingly. "Woody, here's an extra bit for your troubles." Charlie handed the young man $500.

"Thanks, boss. I'm gonna go look for a ring." Elwood turned, winked at Denice, and took off, disappearing into the crowd.

Charlie, Denice, and Ramona continued on to Panda Express, where they sat down at a table, away from the other customers.

"You were lucky this time. But this kind of shit must be avoided at all costs," Ramona scolded.

"Woody made a split-second decision, and I stand by it one-hundred percent," Charlie stated with conviction.

"I understand your loyalty, Charlie, but it invites scrutiny and pisses them off. Badly."

Charlie knew whom Ramona meant by "them" but he didn't care. "Screw 'em," he retorted.

Denice chimed in, "Charlie, don't be rude."

"Sorry, Ramona. Look, those assholes don't care whether or not anyone reunites their family. But I do. No one got hurt. Again, I stand by Woody."

Ramona sat back in her chair, tucked her hair behind her ear with two fingers, and stared at Charlie without a word. She seemed to study him as if she'd just met him. She looked at Denice. "You are a lucky woman. I tease him about being the *funny man*, but you've got to respect his loyalty." She turned back to Charlie. "I'm glad we're on the same side. Talk to Woody, tell him that shit is the last option. Can we agree on that?"

"Absolutely. I can't afford $500 bonuses."

"Think he'll really marry her?" Ramona asked.

Denice quickly piped in. "He seems very serious, no?"

"Maybe they'll make a good team."

"In more ways than one," Charlie said.

POOLSIDE PARADISE, PALM SPRINGS
Chapter 23

Nea's trailer was a perfect fit. It was close to the action, yet far enough from danger. She and her little man, Brandt, were protected in many ways that she didn't understand or even know about. Mom and Dad had all kinds of family friends and partners on the mountain, known as *The Network*. Charlie was a favor-trader. If you were in need – and the DeVilles had it – everyone shared.

Valentino was a regular dinner guest. He did not go hungry. He did not need to ask. Thus, Valentino kept his eyes open and his ears alert, without being asked. If Nea needed diapers, and the store was open, her bill was always paid. Ron never asked. The circle of life on the mountain takes care of its own.

No one here is innocent. No one asks and no one tells. Strange are the ties that bind.

✠　✠　✠

Their new home was tucked under two huge white oak trees. When the wind blew, you could hear the acorns hit the roof. With a fenced-in yard around back, "His Nibbs" could dig as many holes as his little plastic shovel could manage.

Charlie and Denice felt a sense of relief to have their daughter and grandson out of El Cajon, and under the watchful eye of *The Network*. Their middle daughter, Becky, and her husband, Allen, had moved their family to Atlanta.

As in most long distance relationships it was tough for Charlie and Denice. They missed their four grandchildren from Becky immensely, more so since their youngest, Crissy, was away at School in Texas. Even though the tribe was scattered. Denice kept her motherly instincts somewhat sedated. *Somewhat.*

Sometimes she'd just burst out in tears, complaining to Charlie how much she missed everyone. And of course, there was the ever-present burden of Grandma being a human trafficker, facing the constant possibility of federal imprisonment. That was sometimes a struggle for her to deal with, as well.

Good thing she had her Charlie. He had more reasons to justify their behavior than he could store in his head. And if that wasn't enough, he would turn on the charm and she'd be laughing and crying all at the same time. Sensory overload.

But if all else failed? Room service. Cheesecake. And an hour's worth of appropriately placed French kisses. Her husband knew exactly where Denice's love button was located, and he was never afraid to push it repeatedly.

✠　✠　✠

While Nea nested and dodged Rudolfo, Charlie and Denice stopped in Palm Springs on the way back from L.A., and enjoyed a much-needed vacation.

Elwood asked for time off to chill in Ventura with Esperanza's uncle, nicknamed *Shmooz.* Elwood hoped to seal the deal on his impending marital bliss, or at the very least, get a thumbs-up from her family.

In the Latino culture, this process is still done the old-fashioned way. Family is the most important aspect of their day-to-day lives. It matters not the color of your skin, but the depth of your love and ability to support your family – Woody's current occupation being a point in his favor. If you're in love with a Latina, like Woody was, you respect the elders of the family. You gain their trust. You go to church and the gathering afterwards. There's no pulling up to the curb and honking your horn, waiting for their little princess to run out to your car.

Hispanic families are tight, loyal, and proud. They take courting seriously. Elwood, with his country charm and good manners, combined with deep love for Esperanza, would be just fine.

✠ ✠ ✠

Palm Springs is paradise. On a spring evening, Palm Avenue is a hip place to play in the So-Cal desert. The Black Iron Mountains that tear through the dusty floor host palm trees and desert flowers, snapdragons and California poppies.

Palm Springs boasts many little bistros, with small tables on the sidewalk. Their awnings overhead spray a continuing mist into the hot evening air. The smell of Italian, French, and Indian cuisine mixed with fresh baked bread and expensive perfume wafts through the air, enticing everyone's sense of smell to come dine with the beautiful people.

Every hotel has at least four tennis courts, and the swimming pools are extravagant and huge. Saunas are standard. Jacuzzis are a must. People who live in Palm Springs always seem to look sexy as hell, even at 70.

That's because Palm Springs is a money town. Its world-class golf courses were started by old money. Sammy Davis, Jr., Frank Sinatra, Dean Martin and celebs like Merv Griffin and Sonny Bono made sure it became a scene. Drive an hour from Hollywood in your drop-top Mercedes to where the stars come to golf, tan, shop, and hide. They lay cucumbers over their eyelids and submerge their thighs in mud. In its hey-day, it was also an awesome place to chase pussy. Apparently.

✠ ✠ ✠

Charlie and Denice weren't golfers or tennis aficionados. But bring on the saunas, Jacuzzis, and massage tables.

Looking drop-dead gorgeous in her white, string bikini and her head-to-toe-tan, Denice tested the water with the tip of her manicured toe.

Charlie, wearing a pair of dated Ocean Pacific shorts, watched her through a pair of wrap-around Ray-Ban sunglasses.

The Palm Springs Marriott was a four-star hotel. Just hold out your champagne glass, and find it magically filled by one of the beautiful service people who do hot laps around the massive pool looking for juicy tips.

The afternoon sun felt delicious on Denice's skin, and Charlie had just slathered her with a tasty layer of cocoa butter lotion. It made her smell like a Piña Colada.

She returned the favor and said, "You are a lean, mean running machine, Mr. Charlie DeVille."

"I am that. Yes."

"What else are you?"

"In love with you."

"Right back at you, man-candy."

Charlie looked seductively at his woman. "If the candy melts in the sun, will you lick me off the chair?"

"No way, that's like ABC gum," Denice giggled.

Nothing like an intelligent conversation to keep love alive.

✠ ✠ ✠

Charlie and Denice swam to the Tiki Bar next to the waterfall, where they sat on submerged barstools.

"Two red trollies, please," commanded Charlie.

The crystal-blue water was at chest-height, while they soaked at the bar.

Charlie wondered, "You suppose someone designed these stools so the water would tickle your nipples?"

Denice laughed, "Well, it's working pretty well."

"God bless that guy."

"I'll drink to that." They raised their cold glasses.

Aside from having your nipples tickled for free, the other advantage of the Marriott was its proximity to the spa casino. A little slice of Indian Reservation smack dab in the center of the Palm Springs shopping district. Even though Charlie and Denice pass on tennis and golf, they do love to gamble.

Walking down Palm Boulevard, Charlie and Denice stopped at Marichano's Cheri for a scrumptious meal of manicotti, chicken Alfredo, and grilled sausage in red sauce. The wine steward suggested a new aperitif, just in from

Sonoma, which was truly memorable. They paid the bill and strolled the boulevard, enjoying the cool mist as they walked along. Listening to live jazz on one block and blues on the next, the noise of traffic and conversation at the small sidewalk tables blended well with the thick desert night air.

After valet parking their behemoth SUV at the casino, Charlie took Denice's hand. "How's the shoe?" he asked.

"Humming like a tuning fork." She let go of his hand and sashayed, rolling her hips. "Ain't no junk in this trunk."

"I'm from Missouri, the *Show Me* state."

"Later, handsome. But for right now, I'm feeling good about the 10×10×10 machine."

Charlie pulled out a one-hundred-dollar bill, and came up behind her as she sat down. He slid the bill into the money slot and kissed her neck. He whispered in her ear, "One for the money. Two for the show."

She looked over her left shoulder and winked. "Three will get me ready."

Charlie smacked her little butt cheek and said, "Then go cat, go." He lit her cigarette, then opened a four pack of Swisher Sweet Milds, and extracted one. Biting off the tip, he swirled it around his tongue. *Flip-click-flame.* "Raise your bet," Charlie insisted.

He sat down next to her on a Lucky Sevens machine, and Denice raised her bet. Charlie watched as the third seven kept sliding off the pay line.

"Raise it again. Max Bet."

As lucky as Denice was, Charlie was calculating. He was always aware of the nuance of a machine. Denice maxed her bet. "Should I put in some more money?" she asked.

"Two for the show," Charlie reached around and slid in another hundred.

"Lower your bet to two bucks. Hit it a couple of times, then Max Bet again."

"Okay, baby."

The server came by and asked, "Care for a refreshment?"

"Two Mai Tais, please."

"California or New York?"

"Cali. Extra cherries."

A California Mai Tai contains one shot of white rum, one shot of gold rum, one shot of Captain Morgan spiced rum, and one shot of Bacardi 151. Legally, they can only serve you two in a 24-hour period. Charlie and Denice would only have one.

Just as the server was returning with their drink order, Denice's machine hit with a vengeance: ten times three, red seven on a three-dollar bet. In this casino, that's $8,000 and some change. Denice did a little happy dance and Charlie crooned, "Go horseshoe. Go horseshoe. Go horseshoe, get your game on, go horseshoe…"

A waitress asked Denice, "Does he always do that?"

"Anything over five grand."

"How long does it last?"

"It's like a spasm. He'll bust out with it all night, until I get him back to the room."

"Sorry 'bout that," the waitress whispered with a grin.

"Oh, don't be, girlfriend. It's like cheerleading for the upcoming game." They both watched for a moment as Charlie moon-walked across the casino carpet.

"The man can dance, I'll give him that," the waitress admitted, and then added, "What's with the horseshoe?"

"Don't ask."

Charlie and Denice tipped everyone: the cashier, the paymaster, the manager, and even the security guy that walked them to the valet.

And then immediately left.

The reasons for this were twofold: First, you never want to hang around with $8,000 cash that every loser in the place knows you just won. And second, and more importantly, winning made Denice horny as hell.

✠　✠　✠

"I love this black marble Jacuzzi tub. It's big enough for two."

"Be right there," called Charlie from the other room. "I'm calling down for some Beef Wellington. I need meat."

"Me, too."

Charlie hummed a little tune on his way to the tub. "It's your birthday. Get your game on. Go horseshoe."

To Palm Springs, from Charlie and Denice (paraphrasing Sammy Davis, Jr.), "You're a classy cat, baby. Stay groovy. Don't ever change."

YEARNING TO BREATHE FREE
Chapter 24

The first contraction began the second the sun went down. Maria doubled over in pain, taking deep breaths. Her husband, Santino, was on the verge of panic.

He said to his wife, "I'm going to kill him."

"He will show," she replied, obviously in pain.

"It's been two days," he shouted.

"He will show. They said so." The pain made it very hard for Maria to speak.

"But not in time, *mijá*, it's going to rain. The baby's coming."

"If the baby comes, it comes. Blessed Mother Mary is with us."

✠   ✠   ✠

Charlie and Dee were back from Palm Springs. They returned the Excursion and swung by home base to pick up the K-5, get more clothes, and check messages and mail. All the normal stuff one does after returning home from a trip.

At the last moment Charlie loaded his nail bags and masonry tools into the truck, thinking he'd finish Nea's kitchen. He did a quick double check to make sure they had enough crap so they wouldn't need to go to Walmart. Charlie thanked his lucky stars that Dee did not have to stop by that four acre big box, pain-in-the-ass place with forty-seven check out cashiers and zero sales people.

They headed back to Live Oaks fully loaded down with more stuff than they would ever need.

✠ ✠ ✠

The massive granite boulders piled up behind the country store at Live Oaks provided more than just a place for lizards to sun themselves. At times they provided a hiding place for beings much larger.

"We can't wait any longer," Santino pleaded in Spanish from behind the boulders. "We don't have a choice. The payphone has taken all my change, those *putos* will not answer. I will not have you giving birth in the mud, in this godforsaken hell hole."

"Help me up." His wife, Maria, was very pregnant and very much in labor. He felt helpless as he admired his wife's strength. They'd just overcome insurmountable odds to come to American soil so that their child would be born an American citizen.

"Can you walk to where those lights are, my love?" asked Santino.

"Slowly, yes," she weakly replied.

✠ ✠ ✠

With the drop in temperature, a storm was on the horizon. Dee put another small log on the fire. Brandt engineered a Lego tower next to it while his mother folded clothes.

"Dad, when will the kitchen floor be done? I'm hoping soon. Mom needs to cook us a real meal."

"Depends. Just pray that I don't get tile adhesive in my other eye this time," replied Charlie.

Denice added, "That would be the embodiment of foolish optimism on both accounts."

Charlie looked up. "Wish in one hand, shit in the other."

"Good come back, Dad," Nea shot back sarcastically. "Little ears are in the room," she said, motioning to Brandt.

Always outnumbered, Charlie thought: *Women are such armchair critics.*

☩　☩　☩

"Stop honey! Oh God...Oh God!" Santino felt useless, but still thought he should do something. "Lean on me, I'll hold you till it passes."

"Damn! It hurts. Oh, sweet Jesus! It hurts!" screamed Maria.

"We're almost there." The trailer was only 50 more yards and the lights inside indicated someone had to be home. But it was up-hill in the freezing mist. The night was still, black as onyx.

When they finally made it to the porch, Maria sat on the steps and her husband knocked on the door.

Inside the trailer Denice jumped with a start. "Are we expecting anyone?"

"Elmo?" asked Brandt.

Nea told him, "I don't think so, honey."

"I'll answer it," said Charlie. He glanced at the 12-gauge shotgun on the wall above the door. Even though it had never been used it made him feel a little better knowing it was there. He opened the door. "Can I help you?"

Charlie immediately took it all in, like a snapshot in vivid color. A picture of helplessness and panic. The woman looked up at him from her crouched position on the steps, her black hair plastered to her face, mud on her peasant blouse.

Her husband's eyes burned into Charlie's conscience, he said something in rapid-fire Spanish. Charlie did not need to understand the words to know this man's urgent plea. He flung the door open, and jumped down three stairs. "Come in *amigo*, come in."

Charlie and Santino helped Maria to her feet. Denice was in the doorway. "Oh my god, sweetie, are you okay?" she said to Maria.

A severe contraction with Maria doubling over in pain was her answer. "Oh my god, Nea, she's having a baby!"

Nea went into her calm, lucid mode. "Okay, mom, I'll boil some water, get some towels. Find a blanket. They both knew the hospital was 30 minutes away. And through the checkpoint.

Santino and Charlie lifted Maria up off her feet, brought her in and laid her out on the couch. Dee shut the door and locked it.

Brandt looked up at Maria and said, "Elephant."

Maria smiled. "*Si, mija, elephante.*"

Another contraction came and now Santino and Maria were speaking in Spanish rapidly. "How do you say hospital in English?" asked Maria to her husband.

"I don't know," cried Santino in frustration.

"We need a birth certificate. Do they have a phone?" cried Maria.

Santino turned to Charlie, and pantomimed by putting his thumb to his ear and his little finger at his mouth.

Charlie nodded in the affirmative. "He needs a phone, babe." He picked up Dee's purse, which looked like a small hammock. "Jesus, honey. Where's the damn phone?"

"Charlie go get Val, he speaks Spanish. I'll find the phone."

Within seconds Charlie was out the door, in the K-5, and heading towards Valentino's trailer.

Back inside Denice handed Santino her cell, he dialed and listened for at least eight rings. "Son of a bitch, they still don't answer."

Trying to make Maria comfortable, Nea spread out a blanket on the floor. Along with some pillows.

Charlie sped up to Val's trailer only to find it dark. No one was home. "Shit. Shit. Shit!"

He jumped back in the K-5 and sped back to the family trailer. Once there, he burst in, blew past Nea, and announced the bad news. "Val's not home. Now what?"

"Cool your jets Dad, Mom's on the phone with Ramona right now."

"Good. At least someone's using their head. 'Cuz I sure as hell can't find mine."

Maria was on the living room floor, close to the fire, with a quilt underneath her. Brandt was giving her a close-up view of a Lego, while Santino blotted her face and hair with a damp towel.

Dee's face was twisted into extreme concern while talking on her cell.

"How far along is she?" asked Ramona on the other end of the phone.

"Don't know," replied Denice. "She had a contraction about nine minutes ago."

"And they just showed up at your door?" clarified Ramona in disbelief

"Yes. Bless their hearts. We're kinda at a loss here, Ramona. I don't think we have time for a hospital run. Even if we could get them there."

"Okay. Let me speak to the husband."

Denice passed the phone to Santino.

"Hello, *señor*, my name is Ramona," Ramona said in Spanish. "I understand your wife is having a baby."

"*Si, señora*, I am Santino and my wife is Maria. The fucking *Anglo* assholes left us in the rocks. I did not know what else to do."

"It's okay. Don't worry. You don't know how lucky you are to have picked the house you're standing in."

"I want to go to a hospital. For a record of the birth."

"I understand, we can handle that for you."

"What you mean 'we,' *señora*?"

"The *Anglos* there. They work for me. I work for a *familia*. You could not be in better hands."

"You are joking with me?"

"No, *señor*. Now listen carefully..." Ramona rattled off instructions in Spanish over the phone.

Maria sat up, looked at her abdomen, and shrieked like a banshee.

Charlie's heart almost stopped, "Holy mother of God," cried Charlie. "She'll wake up the dead." Brandt started to cry, Charlie picked him up.

Denice held Maria's hand. "Shut up, Charlie." commanded Denice. To Maria she added, "Breathe. Woosh. Woosh. Breathe. Big breath. All out."

Maria followed her lead, staring at her mouth. Santino repeated a number and looked gravely at his wife.

"All right, you said your family's in Fresno," said Ramona through the phone. "I'll call and see if I can get through."

"They know the situation," replied Santino. "I had no money to call and did not know where I was."

"Take care of your wife, Santino. Let me speak to the *Anglo señora*." Santino handed the phone to Denice. "Can you deliver the baby?" Ramona asked.

"Between Nea and me...yes."

"Okay. If you call the sheriff or fire department, they will separate the family. I.N.S. will send Santino back immediately, you know my stance on this."

"We can do it, as long as there are no complications," reassured Denice. "Nea and Charlie are running Brandt over to Ron and Lily's right now."

"I heard him start to cry when she screamed."

"Yeah. Not good, we don't need neighbors calling the cops."

"Okay, listen. The word for quiet is *cállate*. They'll understand."

"Gotcha."

Ramona continued, "Here's the plan. I'll get ahold of the family, explain the situation, and get an address. You do what you have to do, and I'll call you as soon as I change phones, this one is no good anymore."

"I'm sorry, hon. I tried Val, I didn't know what else to do."

"It's fine. I'll call you with the new number, look for it, 303 area code."

"Okay."

"God bless us all." Ramona said.

"You can say that again."

And she did. Right before she hung up.

✠ ✠ ✠

"Big Ron. Got a situation," said Charlie urgently, after pounding on Ron and Lily's door while holding Brandt.

"Come in. Come in." Lily took the baby in her arms.

"Hey, good-lookin'!" Lily lit up like a sparkler as she cradled Brandt. "How's my snoogy woogly, cuddle bear?"

Brandt ate it up. Putting his arms around her neck and with a very deep concerned look, he said, "Elephant. *Sí. Elephante.*"

Charlie gave Ron the condensed version of the whole crazy situation as he hurried to the blazer. Just before he got in the car he asked, "Can we keep a lid on this?"

"Charlie, we always have," answered Ron.

"Excuse me?"

"Handle your business, Charlie, We'll watch Snoogy Woogy."

"You never cease to amaze me, Ron."

Ron stared dead into his eyes and said, "The same can be said about you, man."

The night air was thick with humidity. Drops of moisture accumulated on the windshield. Lights reflected off the shiny pavement. The smell of moist earth and wet leaves hung in the night air. Dee had not locked the door and Charlie burst in. "Brandt's good, Lily's ecstatic to have him. And they both know."

"Know what?" asked Denice.

"What we do we do for a living."

Denice looked at Charlie with utter panic on her face.

Maria interrupted their moment with another mighty convulsing contraction. And a scream to punctuate it.

"Breathe. Breathe. In through your nose, out through your mouth," instructed Denice.

Denice had removed Maria's pants and covered her naked lower torso with a sheet. Charlie paced the floor like a feral cat, while Santino held his wife's hand, with a look of love and concern on his unshaven, stubbled face.

Nea laid out towels, a nasal bulb, and roach clips to pull double duty as hemostats.

The contractions were coming two minutes apart when there was a knock at the door. Everybody froze. Inside and outside was dead quiet.

Again the knock. *Bam*! *Bam*! *Bam*! Ron's voice came booming from the porch. "Hey, it's me. Let me in."

Charlie opened the door and said, "Man, I thought you might be the sheriff. Having babies is noisy business."

"I came to see if you needed help."

"Bring any bourbon?"

"No."

"Scotch?"

"No."

"How about a joint. You know...for Nea."

"No!"

"You're no help then. Santino and I could use a drink. Nea could probably puff one right about now."

"A little tense around here, is it?" asked Ron.

Dee said to him, "You boys go in the kitchen. We're kinda busy here. Maybe you'll find a beer in the fridge."

Charlie and Ron went into the kitchen and located the beverages. Both men leaned on the small counter that separated the dining area from the living room. Both rested elbows and forearms on a counter, beers in hand.

At this point all hell broke loose. Maria screamed at her husband. Nea lifted off the sheet. Dee held Maria's hand telling her, "Breathe, honey, breathe!"

"I think she's crowning," yelled Nea.

"Breathe. But don't push. Not yet."

At that moment Charlie came in and looked. But should not have. "Oh, no freakin' way! That'll never work!"

"Thought you said not to look," replied Ron.

"Christ. She's gonna be a cripple after this!"

Santino wiped Maria's forehead. "I love you, Maria."

Maria replied with a stern, "Fuck you! Shut up! Get out! I never want to see you again. Oh god...it hurts!"

"What can I do, *mija*?" Santino pleaded.

"Nothing! Just shut. The. Hell. Up!" Maria hissed in staccato Spanish.

Nea was between Maria's legs. Denice had Maria's left foot on her thigh, sitting, knees on the floor, looking around Maria's leg to gauge dilation.

Charlie looked at Ron, and said quietly, "I can see the top of its head. Should I get a plunger or something to help out?"

"I think you should stay as far away from there as possible," advised Ron. "You're looking pale, Charlie."

The muffled screams started again. Maria sat forward. Denice pushed her back, and Nea was saying to no one in particular, "Almost ready. Almost. Almost..."

Charlie rocked back and forth. Ron watched Charlie. Nea was in catcher's position, like a baseball umpire.

Denice looked at Maria and said, "Okay, NOW! Push! Push! Push!" She puffed through her mouth like she was blowing out a fire, looking right into her eyes. Not 30 inches away from her face, saying again. "Breathe. Push! Push! Push!"

Maria screamed bloody hell.

Santino let go of her hand and knelt in the *pray-to-Jesus-help-us-all* position.

Denice had Maria's undivided attention. Their eyes had interlocked and welded together as one. Nea yelled, "Here it comes!"

And Charlie's mouth fell open when he saw what was coming.

At that second the baby's head and shoulders abruptly emerged, and the rest of the baby quickly slid into home plate, face first.

Right about then Charlie hit the kitchen floor face first.

Thankfully, the newborn began to wail.

"It's a girl. It's a girl." Nea exclaimed, holding her while she cried and the baby gurgled. Dee cleared the infant's nose with the blue nasal bulb. Santino stared into space like he'd just seen God. And in a way he probably had.

Dee quickly cut the cord with the razor blade and roach clip hemostats and secured it with a big blue plastic paperclip.

Ron looked over Dee's shoulder in complete amazement.

Nea quickly dipped the baby's feet into a bucket of cold water, prompting the little bundle of joy to take her first breath, her first breath of freedom; she used it to scream loudly. Very loudly.

Maria watched Nea intently wipe her baby down.

Ron quipped, "The Discovery Channel ain't shit compared to this."

Dee wrapped the baby in a Winnie the Pooh blanket and set Celia Dee Jean Piñia on her mother's chest. "Charlie. Come see the baby," Denice pleaded.

So much for big tough Charlie DeVille.

"Honey?" Denice looked around. Charlie was lying on his back now, his eyes rolled up in his head. "Charlie. It's over, baby. Wake up."

Everyone except Maria and the baby were gathered in a circle standing over Denice, who was sitting on the floor slapping her husband's face gently. "Wake up, honey."

Charlie opened one eye. "Who's the ugly guy standing behind you?"

"That's Ron, honey."

"I'm gonna let that pass," said Ron. "Seeing as how you've lost your mind, and all."

Charlie sat up, and accidentally put his hand in the wet tile adhesive that was still out from his kitchen remodel. "Perfect."

Nea said to Charlie, "You okay, Dad?"

"Not after what I just saw." He crawled on his hands and knees and looked around the bar at Maria and the baby. Maria was smiling, nursing Celia with the proud papa looking on. Santino had a goofy grin on his face. At least *he* didn't pass out.

Everyone took a collective breath. "What now?" Charlie asked.

"We call Ramona," said Nea.

"Can't do it, phones are no good," replied Denice.

"I'm hungry," Charlie chimed in.

"Now that's something I can handle," said Ron with a smile.

"Not much here," responded Denice. "We haven't gone shopping yet."

"I own a restaurant, maybe you've heard of it. Live Oak Inn."

Charlie, always looking to have the last word, piped up with, "Well, then what are standing around here for?"

✠　✠　✠

Ernest Hemingway said, *"What is right is what feels good after."* How can bringing a new life into the world be wrong? All because you didn't involve the police? Some things just boil down to choices made in the moment, and what your heart tells you to do. And if it feels good afterwards it's easy to defend your actions and live with the consequences.

When the lights came on at two in the morning at Ron and Lily's restaurant, the only people awake were at a large table in front of a modest fire. Drinking coffee and winding down.

Ron was in the kitchen doing his magic, and judging by the smell, he was doing an outstanding job.

The lights were dim, the fire crackling. Charlie was quiet and pensive, as Brandt chose a crayon. Nea was teaching him *Eenie Meenie Miney Mo, catch a monkey by the toe.* Which just goes to show how things change and still stay the same.

Denice looked at Lily and thoughtfully asked, "Are you angry?"

"For what?"

Charlie added himself to the conversation. "Ron made it pretty clear that you both knew about our present profession."

"It's not ours to judge."

Denice grabbed the pot, poured Lily more coffee, and said, "We never have and never will endanger you, Ron, or your business with our profession. We consider this place our haven, our safe port. We did not know Santino and Maria were hiding in the rocks.

"We did." Lily continued softly. "We don't like it, but it's beyond our control. We've only owned Live Oak for two years and this has been going on for generations." She blew across the top of her mug of steaming coffee and added, "Sometimes I see them late at night using the pay phone. Sometimes I leave food behind the store." She shrugged her shoulders and looked into the fire. "Ron and I cannot jeopardize our investment by hiring them. But that does not mean we don't feel for them."

Ron entered from the kitchen pushing a loaded-down pastry cart, buffet style with breakfast goodies: scrambled eggs, sausage, bacon, hash brown potatoes, biscuits and gravy, the works. He handed Nea a couple of containers and told her, "Pile up two plates for the happy couple."

"Thanks, Ron," she replied. "It looks delicious."

Ron sat down and joined the conversation. "Heard you talking from the grill. And I've got to say, we worry about you two."

"This is not what we chose, Ron," confessed Charlie. "We just kinda fell into it out of necessity."

"I know," empathized Ron. "I was there. Remember?"

"Brother, I will never forget."

Ron smiled and said, "We do not consider you guys criminals. But when you consider the alternative, what *could* happen, for example *the van thing*, and all those people dying..."

He left it uncomfortably hanging in the air, like a chuckle at a funeral.

Lily made an attempt to break the somber moment. "You seem to have made quite a name for yourselves. In certain circles around here."

"Yes," Denice replied. "*The Network*."

Ron laughed, "You don't spend time on this mountain and not hear things."

Charlie forked in some eggs, took a bite from his biscuit, and tried to say something about Indians, but his mouth was too full to enunciate clearly. He swallowed and said, "Sorry man, that was rude." He wiped his mouth and tried again, "You have an ear to the ground on the reservation?"

"Kind of," admitted Ron.

"What do the drums tell you?"

"That depends on who's beating them. There are many facets to the Indian diamond. But generally we don't involve ourselves. We live in peaceful coexistence."

"Us, too," Denice replied.

They all sat in silence for a moment until Lily asked, "So. What happens to the new family?"

"We're waiting for instructions from the Big Kahuna."

"You have one of those?" Lily inquired.

"Huge one."

"No shit." Ron said.

Charlie confirmed, "That's the thing about legends, bro. Sometimes they're true."

✠ ✠ ✠

The phone sounded like a fire alarm, bouncing around in Denice's purse. She went elbow deep into the small hammock and extracted the phone. "It's Ramona."

The other adults in the trailer crowded around, except Maria. She was fast asleep on the couch. Baby too, in a custom-made diaper.

"Hi Mona. It's a girl."

"Everything went well, I take it?" asked Ramona.

"Very. Except my Big Hunk passed out on the kitchen floor."

"Men are such a pain in the ass, bless his heart. Did he bruise his pride when he hit the ground?"

"No, he landed on his face."

"Kiss his boo-boo for me."

"Savin' that for later."

"Okay, let me speak to Santino." Denice handed the phone to the new father.

"Congratulations, *señor*." said Ramona to Santino.

"*Gracias*," he replied.

"You're all set. No questions till you get here. Do exactly as you're told. Your new friends know what they're doing. Trust them. Now let me speak to Denice, please." Santino handed the phone to back to Denice. "Call me at the 405 and Highway 10."

"Will do. Can't give you a E-T-A yet."

"Not a problem."

"Okay, bye."

"Bye."

Outside there was no rain yet, but the air was swollen with humidity. The first light was three hours away, Charlie put on a fresh pot of coffee. Extra strong. "We'll stay up. Wait for rain. Get past Temecula. Then pass out the rest of the trip."

"I'm exhausted," said Denice.

"Me, too, but it feels like rain. *I GOT THAT RAINY DAY FEELIN AGAIN*," sang Charlie, poorly.

"Hush-up. You'll wake the baby," Denice commanded.

Charlie smiled. "You're so cute when you're grouchy."

WHICH IS JUSTICE AND WHICH IS THE THIEF?
Chapter 25

The sky opened up. Time to run. Trailer Trash Triage was history, and so were they. After packing bags, and good-bye kisses all around, Brandt even woke up at the last minute to say "Elephant," while pointing at Maria.

They quietly loaded the new family into the K-5 blazer. Charlie unlocked the emergency brake and coasted to the intersection at Old Highway 8.

The rain assaulted the windshield, with the wipers putting up only a vain attempt of keeping it clear. The darkness was almost total as Charlie started the motor.

No words were spoken when they got on Interstate 8, and then merged onto I-15, heading north in complete silence. The tension fogged up the windows, but broke when Denice said, "Look. Lights."

Those lights were what they feared the most. However, the glow of the checkpoint started to fade, one light a time. They could almost hear the *click* as each million-watt floodlight turned off, one by one. The Border Patrol had decided to call it a night.

Charlie said, in a very somber and respectful whisper, "Thank-you, Lord."

Santino and Maria seemed to catch the gist of what was happening, due to the smile on Charlie's face.

Mother and baby were quiet, the Blazer K-5 rumbled and settled into a purr as they approached the closed checkpoint.

Shakespeare said, *"Which is justice and which is the thief?"* With every run the line that divided the two became more blurred. Charlie noodled that around inside his head for a moment and decided what he was doing, what he did now for a living, is a good thing. *He was justice disguised as a thief.* This allowed him to justify his actions so he could focus on the task at hand.

The rain came down as the miles went by. The vibration and whine of the big tires lulled the baby into a peaceful bliss.

☩   ☩   ☩

Ramona lived in Brentwood, nestled in the hills on the backside of Topanga Canyon and Mulholland Drive, facing the San Fernando Valley. She had given them directions after hitting the 405. Charlie and Denice had never been to her home. They considered it a sign of trust and respect to have been invited, even under these unique circumstances.

"O.J. Simpson's house is somewhere around here," Charlie said to himself, loud enough for everyone else to hear.

"Yeah, thanks for reminding me," said Denice sarcastically.

They found the address and pulled up into a semi-circular driveway that fronted a 1970s ranch-style home, with tongue-and-groove wood siding, and cedar shingle roofing. There was a BMW 750 IL in the open garage, and a red Silverado next to the house.

Charlie said, "That's a 12-cylinder BMW. Think she'll let me drive it?"

"Let me think," mocked Denice. "NO!"

Charlie put the truck in park. Denice opened her door, and Santino, Maria, and the baby sat motionless. Before Charlie could open his door, he noticed there was a very serious man standing three feet from his driver's side. Charlie got out slowly.

Have you ever wondered what happens to gang bangers who live long enough to sport gray hair? They end up working security. And they do a damn good job of it.

The middle-aged man staring at Charlie's back wore a gray Brooks Brothers shirt that did not quite cover all his scary tattoos. He also had on pressed gray slacks and highly-polished Armani shoes. A little gray at the temples of slicked back hair topped off his professional look. He was handsome in a severely serious, Secret Service sort of way.

When they shook hands, Charlie noticed the man's nails were impeccably manicured.

"Charlie."

"Jorge. Ramona is expecting us."

"I know."

Charlie pointed to Denice. "My wife, Denice or Dee for short."

Jorge's black eyes looked at Denice and possibly smiled, with no expression on his mouth. "*Señora.*" He turned his attention back to Charlie, "*Señor*, do you have a gun?"

"Don't need one," replied Charlie without a hint of his trademark sass.

Jorge smiled and asked, "Does *señora* have one?"

Charlie pointed to his zipper. "Right here."

Jorge smiled, "I must search you, *señora*."

"The fuck you will," Charlie shot back.

Jorge's smile vanished. "*Señor*. I strongly suggest you be reasonable."

"You can search me. But you *will not* put your hands on my wife." Charlie turned to Denice, "Dee, call Mona. Get her out here. Now."

Ramona emerged from the entryway, in Spanish she said, "Jorge, I told you. It's okay."

"Just doing my job, *señora*."

"Please, Jorge. Apologize to my guests."

"No." In English Jorge said to Charlie, "Just doing my job."

Charlie smiled and said, "*Está bien*."

Jorge's responsive grin looked a little reptilian, but it was safe to say that all was now good.

"Okay. Now that we have the tough guy stuff out of the way, maybe we can get mama and baby out of the hot car?" asked Ramona rhetorically. She then turned to Denice and added, "Men are such a pain in the ass."

Once inside the house, Ramona spoke Spanish to Maria. "Oh my, isn't she adorable?"

"Yes, but she needs a birth certificate," replied a worried Maria in Spanish.

"All that's been handled. Your grandfather will be here soon to pick you up. I'll explain later."

Santino relayed the whole story to Jorge, ending with, "They saved my baby's life, I'm sure of it."

"These *gringos*?" asked Jorge surprised.

"Those *gringos* are little Celia's godparents. Or will be."

"No shit?" said Jorge looking at Charlie and Denice in a new light.

"No shit," confirmed Santino.

Ramona slipped $2,500 into Dee's hand and said, "Put this in your purse."

"Are you sure?"

"Give Nea $500, and tell her to call me on my new number. We have work. By the way, is she okay with Rudolfo?"

"He's an ass. But she can handle him."

"He is loyal, and knows how to keep his mouth shut. Except around certain women."

"Yes, well. He's still an ass," Denice reiterated.

"Very true."

"Charlie and I are exhausted. We won't be ready to run for a couple of days. We don't even know where Woody is."

"I do." Ramona told her.

"You do?"

"Venice Beach."

"Doing what?"

"Getting a marriage license."

"A real one?" asked Denice with a grin.

"He's got some friend who has a little beach house near the boardwalk. He's close to Ventura and Esperanza's uncle's house."

"I'll call him in a couple of days and leave a message," said Denice.

"I can work with that," confirmed Ramona with a smile.

Everyone gathered in the living room, taking turns giving Eskimo kisses to the baby. Handshakes all around, and hugs for the ladies with a promise of phone calls and updates.

Jorge looked at Charlie, extended his right hand, and said, "We're cool?"

"Definitely cool," replied Charlie.

"Just doing my job, *señor*."

"Right. Just doin' your job."

"See you, *gringo*," said Jorge with a smile.

"Back at ya, *vato*," replied Charlie with his own smirk.

In this business respect is rarely given by proxy. It's earned the old-fashioned way. But it seems Santino's telling of the events of the last 24 hours left an impression on the toughest of the tough, that being a fifty-year-old Latin King.

✠   ✠   ✠

Rolling down Interstate 15 South, Charlie and Denice were uncharacteristically quiet. Each processing the events of the last forty-eight hours. Maybe a little shell shocked from bringing a new life into the world and a new family to L.A. Proud but tired.

Denice smiled at her husband. "Let's check into the new Hotel at Pala Casino. Give it the once over."

"Take room service for a test drive?"

"I'm exhausted. It's been a brutal couple of days."

"I kinda got my second wind, honey," said Charlie playfully.

"Yeah, I don't know..."

"What? No slap and tickle?"

"No slap. For sure no tickle."

✠　✠　✠

The Pala Indian Hotel Resort and Casino is in a beautiful little valley, green and lush. Small lakes join the edge of the road, and the actual reservation itself could be easily missed, but not the 10-story, gold, glass hotel and spa. Dee checked in while Charlie valet parked and supervised the bellman. God help them both should her comfy pillows or a piece of luggage get misplaced.

They went straight to their room, then straight to the shower, then straight to bed. And amazingly, then straight to sleep.

✠　✠　✠

Bright white sunshine cut through the heavy curtains, and reflected off of the flat screen TV. Charlie looked at the digital clock next to the phone. It was 11 a.m. the next day. They had slept for 18 hours. "Baby, you awake?" asked Charlie.

"I am now."

"It's tomorrow."

Dee rose right up out of bed, and said, "What?"

"Remember, we were going to nap, then hit the casino?"

"I remember."

"Well. It's the next day," explained Charlie, as he opened the curtains.

"No way!" said Denice in disbelief. "I'm starving. Let's go to the café."

"No. Room service," Charlie countered.

"I'm hungry now." Denice insisted.

Of course, Dee won out, so they got dressed. Charlie put on his signature black Justin pointed-toe boots, black boot-cut Levi's, and black leather belt below a sleeveless shirt that read, *Get more ass than a toilet seat.*

When Denice saw his shirt her face fell. "Dammit Charlie, take that off."

"Why?"

"Because people will think I'm a tramp, it's just gross."

Charlie smiled and asked, "How's the shoe?"

"Couldn't find it with both hands and a compass right now. I'm in a coma. My husband looks like an idiot. I think I'm going to cry."

Needless to say, Charlie was wearing Hugo Boss with a silk undershirt by the time they walked into the café. After having eggs benedict they were ready to lose every freakin' penny they earned in the last 48 hours. And did. It was like stubbing your toe a hundred times on the way to the bathroom in the middle of the night. You get pissed off with every step, but you still have to pee.

A Byzantine Roman named Petronius once said, *"Moderation, in all things including moderation."*

But an even smarter fellow, Charlie's dad, once said to Charlie, "No good deed goes unpunished."

Charlie considered his ass whooped as he stared at the ATM screen. He looked at Dee. "Spent all our cash. If we hit that button we're going backwards."

"The shoe's pooped," Denice said.

Charlie replied, "Good one, baby-cakes."

"I miss Kenny Rogers."

"He's hard to miss, what with all that cosmetic surgery, and all." Charlie was ever the smartass, even when the chips were down.

"No, I mean I'm comfy there."

Denice said the word 'comfy' with her bottom lip pouted out, looking at her man underneath her left eyebrow, head slightly cocked to one side.

After three lowball, five-dollar tips they were done and on the run. Pulling into Platinum Club Valet, Denice looked at Charlie with a smile. "I need a shower. A steak. A beer and my blankee, in that exact order."

BEEN FOOLED OR JUST BEING ONE?
Chapter 26

"Woodmeister, what the hell ya doin?" Charlie said into the phone. "Where you at, young man?"

"After close examination, I believe I'm in the lobby. Couldn't find you down in VIP," replied Elwood.

"We're in room 401, come on up."

Elwood was at the door in his 501s and t-shirt, sleeves rolled up. Looking like the cat that ate the canary, Charlie mused. "Are you hungry?"

"Always."

"Me, too. Hungry like a hostage."

"Should I call down and order some club sandwiches?" asked Denice.

"Yeah and some sweet tea," replied Elwood.

Charlie chimed in, "This ain't Alabama, cuz."

"It's just sugar, man. What? Ya-all don't put sugar in your tea?"

"We don't *drink* tea. Next you'll want a Mint Julep or some sissy drink like that. Christ."

"That'd be awesome," Elwood mused.

Denice asked as she pulled a six-pack out of the mini-fridge, "How bout some Rolling Rock pale ale?"

"Good call, babe. When we want a Mint Julep we'll send Junior here to Disneyland."

Elwood's eyes beamed. "That would be so cool, maybe for my honeymoon."

"Yeah. What's the deal with that?"

Denice set the phone down after ordering three clubs, six beers, and potato salad, and asked, "Set a date yet, hon?"

"Naw." Elwood took a beer from Denice and twisted the cap off the bottle. "Need to make some money and Espy's got to be in school. Her uncle's a pretty stubborn man."

"Sounds like he's smart," Denice replied.

Looking uncharacteristically serious, Elwood took a swig of beer as he shifted awkwardly in his chair. Then thought, *screw it*. He smiled hugely and looking at both of them announced, "I got a freakin' brilliant idea I want to run past you."

Charlie smiled, "I knew I smelled something burning."

"Got a friend who works at a nursery. Delivers trees in a box truck, takes the truck home on the weekends." Excited now, trying to talk with a mouth full of Rolling Rock, he choked, swallowed, banged a closed fist on his chest, belched like a sailor and continued. "Got a big graphic thing on the side, you know. Like Shmoz Tree Farm, or some shit."

"Go on. I'm listening."

"Anyway. When you roll up the big door all you can see is trees and bushes. Man, you could hide a gang of people back there as big as Tijuana, they'd have to unload a ton of trees just to get to them."

Charlie and Denice glanced at each other, then she smiled at Woody. The young man could tell his mentors were impressed. He stuck out his chest with pride.

"Genius," proclaimed Charlie.

Elwood agreed, "Yup."

"I'm thinking, T-shirts and cargo shorts. The Full Monty," said Denice

Elwood added, "Full Monty. Don't that mean naked?"

"He's right, hon. We should wear pants."

Denice mused, "Speak for yourselves." But her mind was reeling with ideas for disguises, right down to the gloves. Going for the *feng shui* feel of it. She could visualize the whole scenario. The idea had a certain *Je ne sais quoi* to it.

Charlie disrupted her train of thought. "Smells like a money-maker, little brother."

"Don't it, though?" agreed Elwood.

"Is there any problem using that truck over the weekend?"

"Hell, no. Nothing a couple hundred dollars won't fix."

"Where's this guy live?"

"El Cajon."

"Perfect."

After a while in this business, you develop a void where your adrenaline glands used to be. It's a bonus, because Border Patrol Agents are trained to recognize any kind of nervousness, prone to be displayed on people's faces when they're doing something illegal. If they don't perceive guilt, you don't show guilt. If your 'give a shit' is broke, you're probably good to go.

✠ ✠ ✠

Ramona answered the phone on the third ring. Knowing it was Denice, she picked up and said, "Good afternoon, girlfriend. All rested up?"

"I believe so."

"What's the good word?"

"Six to eight."

"Excellent. I'll call you."

"Bye, now."

✠ ✠ ✠

Camacho's phone rang. "Bar and grill," he slurred.

"It's me," said Ramona. "How's it going there?"

"Hot. Sandy. Pokey. Itchy and poisonous."

"How's Pelón?"

"Half blind and all the way bald," said Camacho without missing a beat.

Ramona rolled her eyes and chuckled. "Eight for the great white hope."

"Eight?"

"*Sí.*"

"They must have some crazy shit planned."

"Two days?" asked Ramona.

"Yeah, I think so. Let me check with Lon Chaney behind the bar."

✠ ✠ ✠

Denice bought cargo shorts and beige golf shirts at Banana Republic. Charlie waited on a bench in the mall, pretending like he was not looking at all the beautiful California girls. He tried to hold up the pretense that he was not a sexist pig. Which he was not. But he wasn't dead either.

"Let's go down to the T-Shirt Hut and get these lettered," Denice said to Charlie.

"You need a bodyguard and escort? Lots of beautiful people around."

"You noticed?"

"Part of my job, ma'am," kidded Charlie. "Vigilance."

"Really. Your zipper's down, hotshot."

"Dammit!" Charlie scrambled to pull it up.

After "West Coast Landscapes" was applied to the shirts and shorts, Dee promptly made some additional modifications to her uniform. She made the shorts shorter and the shirt a little tighter. Big chest, small sweater creates illusion, delusion, and BP confusion.

✠   ✠   ✠

Elwood waited at Nea's house. "Mom and Dad should be here for dinner," Nea told him.

"Okay, I just came a little early to hang with the little guy," Elwood said, referring to Brandt.

"He'll love that."

Elwood. Uncle Woody. Male influence extraordinaire – he had no problem driving Tonka trucks through mud puddles, as he (Uncle Woody, that is) had no problem sitting right in the middle of mud puddles. He also loved pushing Brandt all over the place on the toddler's Big Wheel while making stupid motorcycle noises, and basically spitting all over the back of Brandt's head. When Woody was done hanging out with the little guy, everybody needed a bath.

The sun had gone down, and crickets and katydids competed in the chaotic night air. Insects buzzed around the meticulously placed streetlights. Summer was around the corner, but only just.

Inside the Live Oak Inn Restaurant, the mood was jovial. It was a good crowd for Thursday night. Word was starting to get around downtown San Diego about Ron and Lily's little resort and restaurant.

That evening the din of conversation, clinking of glasses, and the occasional laughter warmed Denice's heart. "This is nice," she said to no one in particular, even though Charlie was sitting next to her.

"Good to see things are busy," Charlie added.

"Not *too* busy. I like the solitude of weekdays," Denice confessed.

Lily sauntered up to the table with a twinkle in her eye. "So. You went legitimate?" she asked, referring to the landscaping business uniforms.

Charlie replied, "Too legit to quit."

"Landscaping? Please." Lily wasn't buying it.

"You think I don't have a license to drive a shovel?"

"Let me see your fingernails?" asked Lily wryly.

"No," replied Charlie hiding his hands.

She looked at Denice and pointed to Charlie. "What a wuss."

"Remind me to dig a hole, Dee," said Charlie with a straight face.

"Are you serious?"

"Dead serious." To Lily, he added, "Thanks, sweetheart. Your little jab probably kept me out of jail."

The little things. Yes, it's the little things that trained eyes don't miss, like landscapers with manicured nails.

Dumb-ass.

✠　✠　✠

Wiley had eight men under the Bridge of Sighs just outside Jacumba. The bridge hides many things at night, not just humans. It *sighs* in frustration, because so many have become "Shadow People" as the Kumeyaay Shamans used to describe them. Walking shadows. Shine a light, and they disappear. Move the light away, and they're back. At the Border Patrol shift change, Wiley would move these particular shadows to his cousin's house.

✠　✠　✠

"This is the most gutless piece of shit I've ever encountered in all my days." Charlie was foot-to-the-floor, pedal-to-the-metal in an Isuzu tilt-cab diesel box truck. Pulling a little six-foot trailer with a lawnmower, a weed-wacker, and miscellaneous "landscaping equipment."

The two had stopped at Nursery Land and spent about $300 on six-foot bushes, three of which were in cedar containers that looked extremely heavy. But in actuality they were not too heavy to move aside.

"God help us if we need to outrun somebody," said Charlie as they climbed the steep grade to Nea's house.

"You mean like a tortoise?" Denice added.

"Hey, babe, since we have all this time on our hands, call Elwood for me, would ya?"

"Okay." Denice rummaged around for her phone in her purse that doubled as a small bedroom closet. "It's in here somewhere."

"Love your uniform," complimented Charlie.

"You do?" she eagerly replied with a coy little smile.

"Those shorts would give a dead man an erection."

Shoulder-deep into the black hole of a purse she replied, "Thank you. I think."

"No. Thank you." He leered. "I have an idea. Let's pull off the road, and jump in the bushes." Charlie pointed with his thumb behind him.

"Look! Found it!" she said, holding up her phone.

"So?" he said as he stared at her cleavage.

"You said you wanted to call Woody."

"Oh, yeah. You were digging around in that sack of a purse for so long I can't remember why I wanted to talk to him."

"Probably to tell him to pick us up at the Acorn? And that you're going to park in the truck stop."

"Oh. Right. And *then* the bushes?" Charlie asked.

"No!" she said annoyed. But then demurely added a second later, "Well, maybe..."

✠　✠　✠

It was almost dark when they crawled out of the bushes and jumped back into the cab of the truck. Charlie thought Denice would look good in a pith helmet right about now. He chuckled at the idea of big-game hunting in a small truck.

Denice was in the front seat looking in the side mirror, pulling leaves and debris out of her hair.

"You're an animal, Mr. DeVille," she chided playfully.

"You are what you eat."

"Speaking of which, are you going to buy a girl dinner, maybe a drink? Our little safari has left me famished."

"Yes, I believe that's a *bushman*'s custom. Or so I'm told."

Charlie handed her a cigarette and *flick-click-flame*, she had a lit Marlboro Red in no time, all while brushing leaves out of the back of Dee's hair with his left hand. "You know how much I love you?"

"Right back at you, big fella," said Denice with a smile of gratitude.

"Adventure keeps love alive."

"And my man satisfied."

"There's a song in there somewhere."

They got out of the truck and hand-in-hand strode to the side entrance of the Acorn, where he held the door for her. "Do you know where we could find a pith helmet?"

"A what?"

✠   ✠   ✠

Inside Charlie talked to Elwood on the courtesy phone, so their conversation had to remain fairly generic and cryptic.

"Elwood."

"Hey, boss."

"Look, I'm calling from the Acorn so listen up. Keep both phones on *[which means the radio too]*, *and* we'll be done here around 11:30 *[in other words, ready to roll at the BP shift change]*. Dee will check in by phone about the grandkid – *so stay put until you hear from us and we're ready to roll."*

"Okay. Got it. Later."

"See ya."

When Charlie was called to the paging phone, they were already cashed out and ready. Denice hit the walkie-talkie the moment they were in the truck.

"How about it, Woody."

"Gotcha, boss."

"Go-go, gadget."

The box truck rumbled down the Highway 8. Elwood's eyes were scanning both sides, straight ahead and behind. Slowing down to 35 miles per hour through Jacumba, he dodged shadows and tried not to think about apparitions wandering the night. Out of town, just past the airport. He made a right and parked at the Shell gas station, "Boss man, boss man. You copy?"

"Go ahead," replied Charlie.

"All clear. Good to go."

"Ten-four."

Charlie and Dee pulled into the post office parking lot. Charlie jumped out and rolled up the back door. He already made a place behind the trees for the people to sit.

They came single file in fast pace, up and into the back. No more than 30 seconds, tops. Charlie rolled down the door, jumped in the driver seat, and pulled out onto old Highway 8. The whole encounter took less than a minute.

Across the street, from the elementary school, Wiley Coyote watched as the *gringo's* taillights faded from view. He dialed his boss, Ramona. "Lots of landscaping going on out here tonight in Sand-land."

"Good, we could use more green."

"You ain't kidding, sister."

✠   ✠   ✠

Because it was almost midnight, almost too late to be on the road, and definitely too late to be going through a checkpoint as a landscaper, they headed toward Indio.

Question: What word has the most alphabetically consecutive letters? Give up? It's the word *almost*, as in horseshoes and hand grenades. "*Almost" don't cut it*," as Charlie would say. Landscapers landscape in daylight. The Borrego Springs exit was *almost* too fresh in his memory, so it was on to the pride of Sand-land, which included the Indio Desert Inn and Motor Lodge. Hopefully Mrs. Cabbage Patch would be on duty.

As luck would have it, the big, pink vacancy sign was lit up. So Charlie did as the little sign on the door instructed and pushed the button. Mrs. Cabbage Patch opened the door looking like a Shar-Pei in curlers. She motioned Charlie inside. The haze of cigarette smoke filled the office, made bluish by the reflective glow of her illuminated television. It created a dive bar feel, like a middle-aged stripper could casually saunter by any moment. Charlie noticed the rabbit ears on top of the TV had only one ear.

"Hello, *Elvis*," Mrs. Cabbage Patch said sarcastically.

"Hey, good lookin'."

"Landscaper now, eh?"

"Busy as a beaver."

"You're full of shit on both accounts."

"But not when I tell you you're a looker, though." Charlie turned on the high-wattage charm.

"Yeah. Maybe 100 years ago," she shot back, as she slid the key across the counter. "Room 100. And I don't need one of your pornographic registrations. Chuck about had a coronary last time."

"Your husband's name is Chuck?"

"Yup. Don't give a fuck Chuck. Been not givin' a shit for 'bout 30 years now."

"Magin' that. Can't understand it," said Charlie ironically. He slid $200 across the dusty blue counter. "Here's a little gift from me and the missus. Find a cabana boy and get yourself a massage."

"Hell's fire, two hundred dollars? Landscaping's been *that* good, huh?

"Definitely. See ya, good lookin'."

"Later, Elvis."

Charlie pulled the gutless wonder around the side of the motel, while Elwood pulled into the parking space in front of the room. Denice took the key and opened the door. Charlie went to the back of the truck, opened the roll-up door about a foot, and asked, "Anybody speak English back there?"

"I do, *señor*," came from behind the bushes in the back of the truck.

"I'm going to leave this backdoor open two feet. We're at a motel."

Charlie waited for translation.

"Quietly roll out one at a time, two minutes apart. And go into room 100."

"*Si, señor.*"

"I'm going to sit in that car and watch. If I bang on the side of the truck, stay where you are. Understand?"

"*Si señor.*"

The off-loading went smooth as silk. But the room was crowded and smelled like ass. Denice said quietly, "Honey. Lover lips. Could we get another room, please?"

"Woody, you and Dee go find us someplace nicer than this. And pick us up some food." He handed Denice some cash, and then she and Elwood were out the door, leaving Charlie alone with this latest batch of hopefuls.

The men in the group could not be happier about the break in their travel itinerary. "My everything hurts," said one of them in Spanish. Once the ice broke the questions and comments flowed like a melting glacier.

"Can we bathe?"

"Holy mother of Mary. My *culo's* killing me."

"Hey, Martinez. The *gringo* say anything about food?"

"I like the kid's car."

Charlie addressed the crowd. "Who speaks English?"

Martinez spoke up. "I do, *señor*."

"Tell your friends to keep it down, shower if they want. Food is coming. We leave in six or seven hours."

Denice located a room at a chain motel, handed her Visa to a size 10 woman squeezed into a size 6 dress.

"How many?" the woman asked her.

"Two beds, please."

"No. How many guests?"

"Three," replied Denice with a completely straight face.

The gum-smacking desert debutante raised an eyebrow. She cast a glance at Elwood who was buying a fossilized Snickers Bar from a snack machine in the lobby. A bit confusing, but not completely off the mark. "Here. Fill this out, room 220," she said, as she slid the registration card over to Denice.

Dee used her real name because of the Visa card, but she listed her her license plate number as *IM EZRU.*

Miss *Sand Storm 1990 Behind-the-Front-Desk* blew a bubble and popped it as she read the card. "Some girls have all the luck," she commented, and slid a key card across the counter.

Elwood winked at her on the way out. "Ma'am."

Denice drove them around looking for somewhere open in which they could buy food. "Nice," she commented, referring to the car, "but nowhere near as nice as my Camaro."

They found a Jack in the Box near the intersection of Highway 8. This one still had a clown head on the drive-up menu and one in the pick-up window. It looked like he had been living on Ben & Jerry's Meth Monkey ice cream and crack-head soup.

Denice shouted their order into the scary clown mouth, and the crackly, disembodied voice repeated their order back so fast all she heard was a low hum. Denice looked at Elwood. "Any chance he'll get that right?"

"None whatsoever," Elwood said chuckling.

Denice and Elwood pulled forward to the pick-up window, where an arm that resembled a stick tossed bag after bag at Denice. Then a head with missing, crooked teeth, and exhausted sunken eyes popped out the window like a tree squirrel and slurred, "Have a wonderful evening."

"Let me make a suggestion," replied Denice with a tight smile. "Try ingesting something that doesn't come in a plastic baggie. And get some SLEEP."

The burned-out kid slammed shut the drive-up window. Elwood was impressed. "Pretty cool, Mrs. DeVille."

"I have my moments."

It was a glorious moment when Denice and Elwood returned with food. It goes without saying that even a semi-warm Jumbo Jack and rubbery fries taste fabulous to a starving man.

Everyone devoured the nasty food as if it were their last meal. And truth be told, they knew that it could be.

"Mr. Martinez," inquired Charlie while everyone ate.

"*Si, señor.*"

"We're going out. Do not answer the door. I have a key."

"*Si.*"

"We'll be back at daylight. Be ready to go." He continued.

"Stay quiet. Turn off the light. Do not go outside. Understand?"

"*Si, señor.*"

And do not EVER use the motel room phone.

✠ ✠ ✠

The next morning it was already 80° as the sun came up. The *landscapers* were up before the dawn, loading client cargo deep into the depths of the box truck bushes, after which Charlie, Denice, and Elwood had a little planning session. "Hey, Elwood. Dee and I decided to go balls out. We're goin' straight through.

"Okay. Me, first?"

"Doesn't matter."

"Okay."

"We need you for the temporaries they set up out there."

Denice said, "Just follow us till we're through. You got your shirt on. You work for us."

"Why not just go the long-way around? I can run the point till it's closed," Elwood offered.

"Too hot, Woody. Those people will roast back there."

"Okay. Then let's do this."

They took a left out of the parking lot and crept through town, heading towards the Salton Sea to the checkpoint, about three miles west of town.

The sun had not quite crested the purple mountains that surround the desert floor. Until you've seen the blue and amber of predawn in the western U.S. desert, you just haven't lived. The colors change moment by moment, and it fills you with humbling awe. It was a perfect way to start the day.

✠　✠　✠

Charlie pulled up to the stop sign at the checkpoint, with agents at both driver and passenger windows.

Dee had her left foot on the dashboard, painting her big toe bright red, causing her short shorts to all but disappear. She had her knee pressed against her chest to accentuate her cleavage. Add to that her huge boobs and push-up bra and the effect was outstanding.

The officer speaking to Dee's chest said, "Destination, please."

"Palm Springs," Charlie said.

"U.S. citizens?"

"Yes, sir."

His partners' eyes were on Denice, and never left the nonexistent inseam of her skimpy shorts.

"Any fruit trees back there?"

"No, sir."

"Mind if I check?"

"Go ahead, you'll need this key."

"Mel, go check the back."

And without moving an eyeball, or even blinking for that matter, Melvin said, "You look."

Searching for the hint of a nipple in Denice's deeply low-cut T-shirt, there was a moment of awkward silence. Denice pushed her knee harder against her breast, causing a little more double-D to protrude. You could almost hear the blood draining from those poor fellas' brains. Peeping Tom, *a.k.a Officer Tom* said, "Have a nice day, drive safe."

"Thank you," replied Charlie, not questioning why they didn't want to look in the back after all.

Denice flashed a flirty, coy smile, and a bimbo finger wave. "See ya, boys."

Charlie checked the rearview mirror as they waved Elwood through without incident.

Back at the checkpoint Officer Melvin grumbled, "Lucky bastard," referring to Charlie.

"You see her looking at me?" asked Officer Tom. "She wanted me bad."

"Yeah, chicks dig law enforcement officers."

"Melvin, chicks dig *me*. Period. Someday I'll share my secret."

"Is it the donut sprinkles in your mustache?"

"Really, man?" said Officer Tom, quickly wiping his face.

"'Fraid so, stud."

"Shit."

Back in the cab of the truck Charlie said to Denice, "God, I love it when a plan comes together."

Denice started singing, "…all I need's a buxom woman and an occasional brew."

The radio came alive. "How about it, boss man. That's what I'm talking about," said Elwood through the receiver.

"And the Academy Award for best actress in the big boobs-small shirt category goes to…Denice DeVille!" exclaimed Charlie.

He handed the walkie-talkie to Denice. She keyed the mic, "I just want to thank everyone who supported me. Charlie, Elwood, and my inspiration, Daisy Duke. I…I…I just love you all!" she cooed while blowing kissing during her mock acceptance speech.

Denice handed the radio back to Charlie, "Do that voodoo that you do, Wood Man."

Elwood squealed the tires catching second gear as he passed the tree truck, and then disappeared into the shimmering mirage that was a thousand shades of beige.

✠ ✠ ✠

On the way home, as Charlie and Denice passed the rock tower, Denice flashed back to a week ago when Charlie wanted to recon the road down "The Backside."

There was no better place than the Fieldstone Rock Tower that clings to the precipice of the rim of the world. Like a lighthouse in a sea of desert sand, you can see all the way to Arizona.

Denice recalled in her mind when Charlie had found the perfect flat rock among the boulders that afforded an unobstructed view of Highway 8 to the desert floor. Perched on top of the world, he put the binoculars to his eyes. "When I was a kid," he told her, "we'd come to this mountain, eat mushrooms, lay on a flat rock like this one and watch clouds. They've got the best clouds up here."

Denice pondered that for a moment. "You ever notice that when you look at clouds they seem to always take the shapes of animals?"

"The shamans call them cloud people...man, back then I was free. Unleashed and unbridled. Big bong bubbles, no life troubles." Charlie removed the binoculars from his face, looked at Denice, and gesturing with an all-encompassing sweep of his hand said, "All this emptiness reminds me of the futility of our chosen occupation."

"What'cha mean baby?"

"No rational person would believe that they'll never get arrested. There's a thousand of them out there and only two of us."

Charlie put the field glasses back up to his face and continued his search.

"A thousand of who?" Denice asked.

"Law-dawgs. Border patrol. CHP. Sheriffs. Hell, this whole valley is a national park. I never even considered the game wardens. I feel like I'm still looking for a rush, but in the wrong place."

A warm breeze blew Denice's hair into her face. She tucked it behind her ears, a familiar gesture Charlie found so endearing.

Charlie spoke into the breeze, "My baby girls are having babies. I'm turning a corner in my soul and I don't recognize the territory. You know. The cosmic province, not the GPS territory."

He smiled.

These kind of inner reflections from her husband came few and far between. Denice understood he was standing on his personal precipice, giving her a glimpse of what he sees in his abyss. She remained quiet, looking up at the stone sentinel that clung to its own abyss.

Charlie, trying to articulate his feelings, stumbled on, "The kid inside me says *this is living life. Balls out.* But the man inside me asks, *What the hell are you doing, Grampa?* How about you, Pumkin?"

She thought a moment.

"As far as the Cosmos goes, it's all about heaven for me."

Charlie nodded his head. "The cosmic jury is still out as it pertains to *my* Karma. On the plus side, getting grandma Izzy home wasn't a bad thing."

Denice smiled at the memory of her husband face down in the kitchen. She added, "Bringing Celia into the world safe and sound was good, too. She's such a doll. I can't think the world would be better off without her."

Charlie pulled the binoculars from his face and handed them to Denice.

"Look at the Border Patrol unit in his hidey hole behind the runaway truck ramp."

Denice focused the binoculars on the spot. "I see him."

He's waitin' for us, like a deer hunter in a tree stand."

"If we were runnin' right now we'd be toast," said Denice.

She handed the field glasses back to Charlie.

"There's a million ways to screw the poodle out here. Bound to go down one day. I can't help thinking we're on borrowed time."

Denice contemplated her husband's words, a warm breeze blowing on her face. Charlie picked up a beautiful wild orange California poppy and placed it in her hair behind her left ear. He kissed her full on the mouth and said, like all smugglers do, "Someday. Maybe. But not today. Let's ride, baby-cakes."

GET YOUR KICKS
ON ROUTE 66... THOUSAND
Chapter 27

Standing under the *porte cochere* of the Golden Acorn Casino, the hot wind blows off the desert floor and shrieks past the three-story rock view tower. It picks up speed and dust, and then mixes with the moist ocean air coming from the west. They meet in a frenzied competition for airspace, causing 50 to 60 mile per hour gusts that end up blowing sideways through the huge parking lot. Leaves from the Jacaranda trees, pieces of wild oat grass and Devils comb, and refuse left behind by mindless travelers all dance in the hot wind. Thousands of bugs try to seek refuge by flittering around the incandescent and neon lights of the Casino Truck Stop gas pumps.

Charlie opened the first set of doors of the casino for Denice. "Elwood is missing a hell of a sandstorm."

He opened the second set of doors and his wife passed through saying, "He better not convince Espy to elope. Ramona and I have wedding plans."

Charlie considered that a moment, then dismissed it as girl stuff. "Doubt her grandpa would allow an elopement, anyway."

They took in the busy scene, and decided to play on the machines in front. The clamor of hushed conversation, mixed with the plethora of gaming machine noise stirred the senses and made Denice's horseshoe kind of tingle.

Charlie pointed out, "Look there's the old bird, The Colonel, surrounded by peroxide."

"That is so disgusting," said Denice. "He's got to be at least 80. And the casino tramps flutter around him like it's a military payday. Jesus."

Charlie never got in trouble keeping his mouth shut, so he said, "Larry sells him a sack of dope most every weekend, a little something to attract the humming birds."

"That is so gross," said Denice, making a sour face. "He freakin' smells bad."

"Hey, whatever blows your skirt up."

"What the hell does that mean, *Charlie David DeVille?*"

Ah-ooh. The big three. As given by his mama. Think fast.

"Means he's a pig," said Charlie. "The worst kind, baby. An old lecher. Preying on the…"

"Put a cork in it," Denice interrupted in disgust.

"Love you, Pumkin."

Denice stuck out her hand, palm up in his face, and said, "Just sponsor my gambling, or you'll never have enough wind to blow this skirt up."

If you can't talk your way out, then buy your way out. "I'd like to introduce you to my buddy, Benjamin Franklin," said Charlie, as he handed Denice a hundred-dollar bill.

There's a game called *Wheel of Fortune.* It's a dollar one-armed bandit that has a progressive tally and a loud, screaming feature that consists of a raspy-voiced broad who shouts, "*Wheel! Of! Fortune!*" when the machine hits a pay line. Then a giant mechanical wheel turns above you, and stops on a bonus dollar figure of up to $1,000. In the past, there have been huge progressive winners on these machines to the tune of $1.2 million. In the early days of the Acorn these payouts almost broke the bank. That oversight has since been rectified.

Sitting at a very exciting row of these machines was a solemn Charlie and a smiling Denice.

Denice turned around to survey the room and unexpectedly came eye-to-eye with Valentino. She jumped with a start. "Holy crap, Val, you scared me to death."

Valentino's beady little white eyes drifted side-to-side like his ears were playing the old Pong video game with them. "Good evening, Denice." He tipped his fedora, complete with checkered headband.

Charlie was momentarily blinded by the Casino lights glaring off Valentino's small, shiny, bald head. "What's with the trench-coat, Val?"

"I'm not really supposed to be in here," he replied.

The Pink Panther theme rattled around inside Charlie's head. "Okay. You're kinda creeping me out, Val."

Denice handed Valentino a twenty-dollar bill. "Your favorite machine is open, right over there." She pointed across the casino floor.

"Thanks, doll."

"Oh, come on," chided Charlie to the old man. "Tell me you didn't just say, 'Thanks, doll.' Really, Val. Really."

Valentino leaned in close to Charlie and whispered, "Disguise is all about staying in good character. I'm on the down low."

Valentino's breath smelled like a combination of curried tuna, clove cigarettes, and Mentos. Charlie gagged a little and changed the subject. "Seen Larry?"

"Heard he's hanging at Sycuan, looking after his sister. Nobody's seen him on the mountain since Dick Rod proved what an asshole he was." He then turned his attention to Denice, and in a normal tone said, "Thanks, Dee, for the twenty." He tipped his hat again and vanished into the crowd like Harry Houdini.

Charlie looked at Denice, "Where'd he go?"

"Who cares? He's really creepy sometimes."

"What's that crap about a disguise, and being on the down low? He's so short he's got no choice but to be on the down low."

"That's why I never wear a skirt around him," Denice deadpanned. "I hope he was dressed under that freaky trench-coat."

"Ew. Thanks for that eyelid movie," scolded Charlie sarcastically.

"Notice he never took his hands out of his pockets?"

Charlie returned the visual favor. "Probably cut the pockets out."

Dee chuckled. "Ugh. Now I need a shower."

✠　✠　✠

The good thing about truck stop casinos is that they have excellent, huge, and extremely hot showers available for only two dollars. The customer pays to get through the first door that opens into a hallway, with three doors on each side, six showers altogether. Very private and very clean, and a good place to scrub the creepy Valentino aura off.

Charlie, never one to pass up naked time with Denice, picked up on the "I need a shower" comment and without skipping a beat said, "Let's do it in the...er, I mean *take* a shower."

"Really."

"Yeah. We got bags in the Blazer. I can scrub your back for you. Not like Nea's shower, there's room to, um, you know. For both of us."

"Shower and a late dinner. Sounds fantastic."

Back on track, from zero to hero, thought Charlie. "Words cannot express my love."

"And a two dollar shower can?" asked Denice skeptically.

"You can bet your horseshoe."

"You ain't touchin' my shoe."

Charlie looked at his beautiful woman and said, "That's the thing about horseshoes, baby. You only gotta get close to score points."

✠ ✠ ✠

Nothing makes a person feel lucky like a good orgasm, that's why they call it *getting lucky*. Walking out of the showers, through the truck stop, and onto the casino floor, Charlie and Denice felt refreshed *and lucky*. They strolled into the Acorn Café with big, goofy smiles on their faces.

Charlie lit a cigarette for Denice and said, "I'm a happy guy."

"Me, too."

"Nope, just got a real good look. You are not a guy."

Their regular server, Sherry, came to the table, "Hey, guys."

"Hi, Sherry. By the way, I just checked. She's not a guy," Charlie said, pointing to his wife.

"Funny, Chuck."

"Don't call me Chuck, I'll have you know I go by Stud Muffin now, isn't that right, honey?"

"Sherry, don't let this stud rattle your cage. He's hungry. Let's get a steak in him. His testosterone will subside."

Sherry thought about that momentarily, and said, "What if he doesn't eat meat? Like, you know, a vegetarian."

"Then we assume there's something very wrong with him, and we'll help him work through it. Like any vegetarian, it's not their fault they're handicapped."

Charlie chimed in, "I am a carnivore, and to prove it I'll have a raw rib eye and three as-yet-not-born baby chickens. And mother's milk from a cow."

Denice looked up from her menu and said, "Me, too, but cook my steak and no mother's milk for me, from any animal, thank you."

Sherry stuck the pencil in her ponytail and headed to the kitchen, saying "You guys are so, like, weird."

During dinner they ate and talked about nothing of importance, keeping an eye peeled for *Inspector Valentino*, in case he thought to join them. Not that they didn't want to feed him, but the trench-coat thing was just creepy. And the smell of curry tuna made Charlie throw up a little in his mouth.

About 4:00 a.m., which was about an hour before the casino audit time, Charlie and Denice sat down at a bank of triple diamond Keno machines. The desktop-type machines were lined up four in a row, back to back, eight altogether. The video display screens were set at a slight angle to diffuse light, and were 18" x 24" square. Oh, and they accepted nickels, dimes, quarters, and dollar bills – and paid tickets and gold tokens that represented one dollar. The odds varied with the amount of numbers picked.

The designers of this particular Keno game located the *Max Bet* button conveniently so that your forearm would easily and unknowingly push it.

In this case, Charlie put twenty dollars in after lighting a cigarette and setting his drink where he would not knock it over. He was losing steadily and was down to his last five dollars. He looked at Denice and complained about it. So being the sweetheart she was, she stuffed a gold coin in his machine and smiled. "There ya go, handsome."

Charlie's forearm accidentally hit *Max Bet* on dimes for five dollars. All five dollars. That's when it happened. Provenance. Divine intervention. The Keno game subtracted five dollars and for some unknown reason 22 balls hit 22 numbers, none of which were Charlie's. But the machine promptly put six dollars back on the credit line.

"Holy shit. Did you see that?"

"Yeah. What's the deal?"

Charlie whispered, "Shhh, not so loud. Give me a coin, please."

Denice handed Charlie a coin, and Charlie put in another twenty. Now the machine was loaded with twenty-six dollars total. He hit the Max Bet button, and dropped in the coin at the same time he pushed *Play Max Bet*. The machine subtracted five dollars. Won nothing, but put six dollars back on. He had bet five dollars, lost, and now had twenty-seven dollars on the machine.

Angels were singing in his head.

He looked over at Denice, and said, "SWEET!"

He tried it again, but his timing was off. The machine did not put the five back on. He looked at her again and said, "Glitch in the program."

He tried again, this time his timing was perfect. The only difference was he hit six numbers on Max Bet for $700, and five dollars.

Denise whispered to Charlie, "Oh my God. Oh my God. Oh my God!"

Both sat very still and very quiet for a moment while they processed this new information, and the ramifications of what they'd just witnessed. Charlie murmured, "Holy shit. We can't lose."

Charlie hit the button with no coin, and the game played normally. He hit three out of eight for even money. He tried it on a quarter, and then on a dollar. It only malfunctioned on dimes.

"Try yours." Charlie said.

Denice switched to dimes. She hit the Max Bet button and dropped in a gold dollar. They both watched as Denice's machine spent five dollars, lost, and credited the pay line with six dollars. They looked at one another with a smile and each had their second orgasm of the evening.

"Do not let anyone see what you're doing," instructed Charlie.

It was a foregone conclusion that they were going to milk this like a cash cow. The duo played slowly at first. For any win under $200 the machine would pay in coins. The buckets were stacking up under their feet. Dee's machine was out of coins after 15 minutes, and Charlie's within a half an hour. The cashier runners were enjoying fat tips as they cashed-out for paper tickets under $1,200. Any hit over that was considered a jackpot and would immediately draw attention, not only from the staff and cameras, but from the other players as well. It was hard not to draw attention when you could not lose.

Charlie ordered coffee for both himself and Denice. When the coffee arrived, he lit her a smoke and one for himself. He then ran a couple full buckets to the cashier cage and sat back down, giving Denice her half.

"What are you up to?" he asked.

"Twelve thousand, I think."

"I've got about $10,500."

"We should go. Audits about to start."

"Okay."

He took a long pull on his smoke, blew out a long plume of smoke toward the ceiling, and took the last dregs of his coffee in one long swallow. He then said to Denice, "Let's smack down a couple more times, and then we'll go see Nea."

His smile was devious and knowing, the kind you present to your opponent when you beat them soundly and completely.

Then the horseshoe, not to be outdone, chimed in. *BADA-BING!* Seven out of ten on a Max Bet, which yielded $8,800. *BAM!* They hit their cash out buttons at the same time. It was 3:48 a.m. Twelve minutes to audit. A good time to saddle up and skedaddle.

Denice signed the tax forms for the jackpot, and then they quickly made the rounds, giving hundred dollar bills to every cashier, runner, waitress, and even the cashier at the truck stop store, on the way out the back door. "Thanks for the shower," he said to the cashier. The guy stood there staring at the one-hundred-dollar bills in his hands.

✠　✠　✠

Charlie accelerated the K-5 up the steep incline towards the top of the grade shouting, "I am the king and you are the queen!"

"You bet your ass."

"What do you suppose the legal ramifications are?"

"It's gambling. They took a risk putting that game on the floor," reasoned Denice.

"Yeah, but there is a sign that says, '*Malfunction voids all play.*'"

"That's not a malfunction. I think that's for when the power goes out or you spill your drink on the buttons," said Denice, as she counted, putting together stacks of one thousand dollars on the seat and floorboard.

"So what you're sayin', cuteness, is that a program error is their fault?"

Dee replied, "I would think so. They must have approved it at some point. Some kind of game certification."

"Kinda screws up the odds being in favor of the house."

"Not if you don't play dimes."

"Bingo."

"Keno."

Charlie looked over at his lovely wife surrounded by money. "Got a chubby, right now."

"Little moist myself."

They were quiet for a moment; the only sound was the rumble of the motor and Dee counting, "...eight hundred, nine hundred, one thousand."

Charlie turned right onto Highway 67 exit/Lake Hodges Road, and followed it into Lakeside. He then turned right, onto San Vicente and the rodeo grounds, and on up the mountain to Barona Indian reservation. Denice looked at Charlie as they began the climb up the mountain. With complete disbelief she gave Charlie the total of her tally: "$31,400."

"Yahoo and thank you, Jesus!" shouted Charlie.

Denice smiled. "It's good zombie."

"What?"

"Good zombie, that's what Corn Hole calls things like that, good or bad zombie."

"Kinda spooky, babe."

"It's the mountain, the Mother Spirit and how she perceives your presence. And whether good things happen to you."

"Well. Whatever, we figured it out."

Denice was very serious now, and when she was sure she had her husband's attention. She said, "No, Charlie. It was not an accident. We did not figure out SHIT. I dropped in a coin as a joke, and you accidentally hit Max Bet with your elbow *like a dumb-ass*, you said so yourself, and that seems like good zombie to me."

They were quiet again for a moment while both came to terms with this new hypothesis. Never ever discount The Supernatural, unless you're one hundred percent positive it's false. Just because you can't see it, does not mean it's not there.

Denice continued, "Mother Earth must be respected and praised for her gifts."

Charlie was solemn now after pondering this for a bit. "I was scared the whole time, thinking casino cops were going to come out of the woodwork," he finally admitted.

"You see what I mean?"

"We have to get a room. Stash the cash, and go back, maybe tomorrow. Definitely before the weekend crowds."

"Okay, but now we need to think of how we're going to give some back," Denice declared. "Do something good. I feel strongly about this, honey."

Charlie said, "I'll go with the flow, Pumkin, whatever you think. I'm not one to piss off the Mountain Spirits. Too spooky."

Denice may not have been too far off the mark.

Strange things happen in and around the reservation, for that matter all over the mountain. The legends persist from the days of settlers, and their caravans of covered wagons coming up the Butterfield Stagecoach Road. To the smugglers and smuggled that perished here, to the Indians forced onto this land, Mother Earth giveth and she taketh away. Who really knows how the score is ultimately settled?

✠ ✠ ✠

Pulling in to Barona at 5:00 a.m., valet parking was a breeze, even though it was now Friday. They were provided a room immediately, an advantage of tipping big – employees remember your face, not just your Platinum card.

They loaded the electronic safe and Denice looked over her shoulder at Charlie. "Hey. We should call Elwood. Take him with us, he needs honeymoon money."

"That's a good idea." Then Charlie changed the subject. "We need to have a plan of attack. They're gonna get wise if they haven't already."

"Weekends. Not good," Denice responded. "Too many customers and lots of staff."

"We hit the perfect timeframe. Midweek and two in the morning."

Denice programmed the digital lock with a four-digit pin, shut the safe, handed $500 to Charlie, put $500 in her bra, and patted her breast. "Ammo," she said softly.

"Big golden bullets. Let's go kill 'em."

THE LIST TO DO, DON'T FORGET
Chapter 28

Denice badly needed to make a to-do list. For her, making a list and checking items off brought normalcy to their otherwise, stressful lives. People to call, things to do, reminders, shopping lists. It represented progress and stability of some sort.

First on the list, celebratory lobster tails, and the best was served at Anthony's Fish Grotto. Of the two locations, Mount Helix and the Embarcadero, the Embarcadero was by far the best in ambience. The entire restaurant hung over the water, right next to the 110-foot, three-mast Ironside Maritime Museum, which by the way was as haunted as the Whaley Mansion in Presidio Park. If you've never been to either of these museums, do not go at night. Or you'll have to bring adult diapers.

Having made reservations for three at Anthony's Fish Grotto, Elwood waited at a table right at the window. The sun was moments from setting as the maître d' escorted Charlie and Denice to their table.

Charlie exclaimed, "Nice table, little brother."

"Only the best," replied Elwood.

Charlie pulled Denice's chair out and winked. "My queen."

"Thanks, handsome."

The maître d', whose nametag read *Carl* offered, "I'll send your server over for your drink order."

"Thanks, Carl." Charlie then turned to Woody and asked, "How's life, Junior?"

"Good."

Charlie quickly moved on to the topic at hand. "Man, have we got a story to tell you." Their server, a handsome young man who was sporting an English-style short jacket and said his name was Peter, inquired, "What would you all like to drink?"

"Champagne. Moet, if you have it." Charlie responded. "We have an occasion to celebrate, Peter."

"Yes, sir."

Anticipating the possibility of a large tip, his smile was huge and his step was brisk. Woody was intrigued. "So what's up, boss?"

"All in good time, son. But let me just say, today's your lucky day."

The champagne came iced in a huge silver bucket, the lobster tails were fresh and tasty, and Elwood's Newburg was *kickin'* (as Elwood described it).

Dee was pleasantly champagne-sedated. And over the Boston cream pie, Charlie filled Elwood in on the windfall, and the game plan for the next scrimmage on a triple diamond Keno.

"I can't believe you all are gonna include me."

Denice said, reaching out and covering his hand, "You saved our ass out there, Woody. Charlie and I don't have too many people in our lives that give a shit about loyalty or trust. Besides, Brandt loves you."

Charlie added, "Kids and dogs, good judges of character."

"Don't pay attention to him. He's got more money than sense right now."

Elwood smiled. "That ain't a bad thing."

"Seriously, partner. Got a lot of love for you, because you do as you say. Plus, you're good at what you do, and you have brass balls. We need you focused. Ramona and the girls have some wedding plans, but it's gonna cost you some cash." Elwood folded his hands, looked out at the harbor with a misty faraway stare.

When he turned back and looked at Charlie, he said "Six months ago. I didn't have a pot to piss in, or a window to throw it out of. Now I'm getting married. I got a nice place, beautiful friends, and a purpose.

"Purpose?" Denice asked.

"You should hear some of the stories Esperanza tells. I know it's illegal, but I'm proud of what I'm doing."

Charlie calmly said, "I know. But it won't last forever."

Elwood, not seeming to hear, said, "Brandt calls me Uncle Woody. Comes out UN Woo. I love that kid."

"Me, too," Denice said.

Charlie, wanting to lighten the mood, picked up his champagne glass and raised it in a toast. "Here's to weddings, grandkids, and video programmers with tunnel vision."

Elwood raised his glass. "Here, here."

Dee joined them and with all three glasses touching, she added, "Nothing succeeds like success."

"CHEERS!"

✠   ✠   ✠

Sunday morning on the Kumeyaay reservation was an idyllic seventy-six degrees. The sun was bright, and the white puffy clouds made the sky look bluer than it should have been.

Children at the Kumeyaay Day Care, part of the church complex, giggled and chased each other around the colorful playground where a warm desert wind gently followed.

Charlie and Denice parked the Blazer right next to the front door. Charlie came around and opened the door for Denice. She jumped down out of the truck carrying her hammock-purse.

Charlie opened the glass doors of the church for Denice, and followed her through to the front desk. The young Indian girl behind the counter smiled, using her left hand to tuck a strand of long blue-black hair, behind her ear. "Can I help you?"

"Hi, I'm Denice and this is my husband, Charlie. I was wondering if the manager was in?"

"You're looking at her." She extended her hand to Denice.

"Name's Natalie."

"How do you do," said Denice. "We would like to make a donation."

"Really?"

"Yes."

"Most donations are made through the church and then filter down to the daycare." She made an expansive gesture with her hand, palm up. As if to say, *not much filters down.*

Denice said in a firm tone, "We would like this gift to go to the children for education supplies, lunch programs, and such."

Natalie looked through partially squinted eyes, not sure just what these people represented, or if they should be trusted. In her world, white people talked big and smiled nice while knifing you in the back. She tilted her head to the side and inquired, "What kind of *gift* are we talking about here?"

Denice reached down into her hammock-purse, pulled out a cashier's check for $3,300, and presented it to Natalie. "This kind of gift."

Natalie looked at the check, speechless. Her eyes met Denice's and then she whispered, "How did you know?"

Dee did not miss a beat. "Spirit Mother told me."

Charlie was quiet and would uncharacteristically remain so.

Natalie took the check, came around the counter and put her arms around Denice, whispering something in her ear. Then she came to Charlie, and gently kissed him on the cheek. She said something to him in her native tongue that he did not understand. She bowed her head in front of both of them and said, "The children thank you, also." There are times when nothing more needs to be said, and this was one of them.

Charlie and Denice then left in silence.

In the Blazer Charlie asked, "What did that girl whisper in your ear?"

"She said, 'Thank you, grandmother. The wind will always speak your name,'" Denice answered.

"Really? How cool is that? We're sailing into the mystic on a wind that speaks your name."

Denice's tone was reverent, "We've been blessed Charlie. That whole experience back there, it just made me feel so... happy. We did good, honey."

"Well, Pumkin, that's what we were shootin' for. Doing some good. Bullseye, Pumkin."

There are so many mysteries on this mountain, so many complex, interwoven histories, so many walking shadows, and conflicting zombies. Friedrich Nietzsche once said, "The most common form of human stupidity is forgetting what one is trying to do." Don't forget it. Live it.

✠   ✠   ✠

Monday night and Tuesday morning brought butterflies and nerves of steel. Charlie and Denice sat down and played and planned. Jack in, one hundred dollars. Play down. Then use the trick to go down to twenty dollars. Alternating back and forth, not cashing out for the coins.

The metallurgy of the receiver tray is designed to emit maximum noise on an old coin pay machine. Walk down the aisle dropping a coin into each tray. *Bing. Bing. Bing. Bong.* Play that machine, especially if it's close to the entrance doors.

Keeping as incognito as possible, Charlie, Denice, and Elwood played to get paid. Eight, nine, and ten numbers at Max Bet. With the impossible-to-lose-it-all factor, the big payouts came quickly. Elwood, who usually only gambles to get the girls, popped up over the top of the screen at Charlie, who was sitting straight across from him. "I'm up to nine freakin' grand," he said, and then ducked back down. Charlie was reminded of the clown that pops out of the music box.

"That guy over there keeps staring at us," Denice said from the machine next to Charlie. "He hasn't moved in 10 minutes."

"Okay." Charlie said, "Let's roll out, just like we planned. I'll go first."

"Okay. See you at Nea's."

Charlie cashed out, waited for the attendant, and then collected his cash. He quietly went out the front door and began the half-mile hike to his daughter's house.

Next was Elwood. Out the front door and into the Toyota mini-truck. He also headed to Nae's.

Last was Dee, who took her winnings, went out the side door at the pumps, and hopped up into their jacked up, blue Blazer, all under the watchful eye of Acorn Security.

Even though they were all being scrutinized, they made it out safely with their winnings and met up at Nea's house.

Nea was beyond being surprised by her parents showing up. Being that it was 4:00 a.m. it was as good a time as any for a visit if your parents are professional gamblers. Charlie, Denice, and Elwood came in the door to dead silence. Nea said, "Hi mom," as she rubbed the sleep out of her eyes.

"We did it," Denice said.

Charlie and Elwood pulled their hands out of their pockets, and started throwing hundred dollar bills all around the room. They whooped and hollered, dancing a money jig.

Denice joined in, throwing money in the air and laughing till she cried.

"What the hell?" questioned Nea. She picked up a bill examining it closely – scooping bills off the floor, she added, "I've never seen so much money."

Brandt, awake now, sat on the floor pantomiming his mother. He put a bill in his mouth, decided it tasted terrible, and reached out to Grandma to be lifted up and cuddled.

"Don't like the taste of your college fund?" asked Charlie.

They gathered up the money and counted it. Thirty-three thousand and some change, for a total of $66,000. Charlie handed $9,000 to Elwood. He stood dumbfounded, staring at the stack.

He handed $4,000 to Nea. "Make some big plans, and stop sweating the small stuff." He hugged his daughter, knowing the hardships that faced a single mom. Nea kissed her Mom and Dad as Woody looked on with a smile.

SEND IN THE CLOWNS
Chapter 29

The next morning Charlie and Denice awoke to the sound of the company cell phone. Charlie answered it with his typical aplomb, "Hello, good looking."

Ramona, never caught off guard answered, "Is that the way you address your boss?"

"Denice prefers it, yes."

"What are you guys doing?"

Charlie looked at Denice, laying next to him.

"Hang'n out like a hair in a biscuit." Charlie handed the phone to his wife.

Denice, cranky and still half asleep, spoke slowly into the phone.

"Sorry hon, he's like bad hair, I can't do anything with him."

"Good morning, Dee, I'm glad he passed the phone to you. Look, I've got two VIPs I need in L.A. in less than three days. They're at Bobby Peg Legs' house in Jacumba right now."

"Okay, we'll call Bobby."

Ramona reinforced this request by saying, "This one's important. I need you guys to give this your complete concentration, put a plan in motion and call me with a delivery date and time. Let's do the drop at the mall near Brentwood. You know the place?"

Denice answered in the affirmative and promised to call back with the info.

Denice looked at Charlie, "You hear that?"

"Yep, call Woody and invite him to a mandatory breakfast, then let's call Bobby. Tell him we'll be there this afternoon. No matter how this goes down, I want the clients here at Nea's. God only knows what might happen to them at Bobby's."

✠ ✠ ✠

While waiting for breakfast, Charlie played with Brandt and in a moment of complete clarity, staring at his grandson's angelic face, trying to create a tower of building blocks, guilt suddenly ambushed his compassionate heart. This young boy needed his grandfather, depended on him for male influence. However, the uncertainty of Grandma's and Grandpa's daily life jeopardized his little world. Charlie knew this, and as time went on it was a growing concern that refused to stay put in the back of his mind.

Very few moments of Charlie's life were assaulted with feelings of apprehension and anxiety. *Every time we run we put moments like this at risk*, he thought. Brandt smiled at Charlie and gave him a close up look at the blocks in his right hand. Charlie's internal struggles intensified to the point of confusion – an emotion Charlie was not familiar with. He pushed the doubt and inadequate feelings aside, to be contemplated another day. Today would require strength and resolve.

A knock at the door brought Charlie out of his reverie. He strode towards the door. "I'll get it ladies." He scooped up Brandt and said, "That'll be Uncle Woody." Brandt squirmed in his arms, escaped, and hit the floor running toward the front door. Not yet tall enough to reach the doorknob, Charlie opened it for him.

"Morning Wood Man." Woody took one step into the house and Brandt assaulted his leg with a fierce hug and did not let go. Woody hobbled into the kitchen with Little Man still attached to his calf.

"Hey y'all, what's for breakfast?"

Denice and Nea both chimed in, "Banana pancakes!"

✠ ✠ ✠

After breakfast came the planning session. Charlie said, "My thinking is we bring them here and wait for rain."

Woody agreed, but was skeptical about the weather. "It's looked like rain for a week, but nothing."

"We've got three days max," reminded Denise. "If no rain tonight, then I say we go down the backside and wait it out at the motel."

"Sounds good to me," Charlie finalized.

Nea interjected into the conversation, "I'll run to the checkpoint every couple of hours, see if it closes."

"Thanks, honey." Denice then asked Woody, "Would you run to Bobby's and pick up the clients, bring them here to wait it out?"

✠ ✠ ✠

Everyone was surprised to see that the VIPs were a young couple. They held hands as they walked up Nea's stairs to the porch. Nea opened the door for them and Woody brought up the rear. Introductions were made and to everyone's delight, the couple spoke excellent English.

The young man half of the couple, Mr. Lopez, shook hands with Charlie and then said, "Mr. and Mrs. DeVille, we want to thank you for bringing us to your daughter's home. Ten more minutes with Peg Legs and I'm not so sure I wouldn't have strangled him."

Charlie laughed. "You're welcome. Bobby has that effect on people."

Mrs. Lopez spoke to Denice and Nea as she took off her jacket. "Mr. Peg Legs' Spanish is awful. And he stuttered like... um, well...like..." Charlie finished her thought for her. "Like a bitch."

"Exactly."

They all sat down and as Charlie ran down the game plan, Brandt fell madly in love with Mrs. Lopez. He bestowed his charming smile and best goo-goo eyes while filling her lap with toys. Nea and Grandma looked at each other and shared a knowing smile. A little charmer just like his grandpa.

After a light lunch, Nea left to check the status of the Highway 8 checkpoint and Mr. and Mrs. Lopez laid down in Brandt's bed for a much-needed nap. Charlie, restless, thinking a run down the backside of the mountain was almost inevitable, turned to his point man and said, "Woody, let's go down to El Cajon and rent a van, maybe a twelve-seater. Are you okay with using the Toyota to run point?"

"Sure, Boss Man, no problem."

Nea returned, coming through the front door with, "Still open – three Border Patrol Agents: two stopping cars, one in a Bronco behind binoculars." She waited for her dad's instructions on what to do next.

"Great, just great," was all she got.

Denice, holding her sleeping grandson, told the guys, "Run down to the valley and get the van. Nea and I will start dinner."

✠   ✠   ✠

Charlie and Elwood returned with a twelve-seat maxi van, white with tinted windows. Charlie commented after kissing his wife and throwing the keys on the counter, "Checkpoint's open, skies are clear, it's not looking good to go west."

Brandt held up his arms to Charlie, "Up, Papa. Up." Charlie bent down and scooped him up, much to the toddler's delight.

Woody sat down on the couch and said to no one in particular, "Looks like it's down the backside, hotel, motel, Holiday Inn."

"Well, we can't wait for the rain, we've got a deadline," Denice reminded everyone.

Charlie added, "There's no way we're going through the Salton Sea checkpoint. So it's hanging at the No-Tell Motel. Through the dunes checkpoint and maybe Hamoudi's place to wait for dark. Sound good?"

Everyone responded with the affirmative. Everyone except Mr. and Mrs. Lopez, who had just awakened from a catatonic sleep.

Mr. Lopez's first question was, "No tell motel?"

✠ ✠ ✠

The usually reliable Indio Desert Inn was showing a *No Vacancy* sign. "Oh, hell no," groused Charlie. He got out of his van and entered the smoky office.

"Hey, good looking!" he cheerfully greeted Mrs. Cabbage Patch. He still had no idea what her real name was.

"Hey there, Elvis. New van. Got out of the landscaping business, huh?"

"Yeah, you know me, a mover and a shaker."

"Bullshit," she said knowingly with a sinister smile.

"Yeah, pretty much. Look, I need a double room, and before you ask, yes, I saw the sign. But that doesn't include your premium customers, does it?"

"Good grief, you *are* a piece of work." She turned and grabbed a plastic tabbed key, circa 1960 and handed it to Charlie. "That'll be one hundred and twenty-nine dollars, and before you ask, that's double our price for our premium customers."

Pulling a cigarette out of a fancy, yet beat-up, case, she put the cancer stick between her dry, cracked lips. But before she could light it, *flip-click-flame*, Charlie's lighter was glowing and accommodating the business end of her cigarette.

"You're a doll," she rasped after she took her initial drag.

With smoke encircling her right eyelid, she said, "You're full of shit, Elvis," and turned to answer the ringing phone on the wall.

Charlie strolled to the van, nodded at Elwood and opened the van door.

"That woman loves me," he said as he handed the key to Denice.

"Let's get inside, it's a hundred degrees out here."

Once everyone was settled in, Woody offered, "I'll run out to the checkpoint, see what the status is."

"Good idea," replied Charlie. "I'll grab some food and meet ya back here."

On the way to Alberto's Mexican Food, Charlie's mind drifted back to his encounter with Officer Rodriguez, and wondered if it was a good idea to have Woody driving the Toyota. Pulling into the line for the drive-thru window, the song *Smooth Operator* by Sade came on the radio and immediately sent him back to the time when he and Woody stole the pool furniture. They had the balls to bolt that furniture down in the back of a rented moving van, and then use that outfitted rig to transport innocent people comfortably, safely, and free of drama.

Now, ten-thousand-dollars-a-job later, the adventure of risking everything, and coming out a winner *every time*, Charlie had to ask himself, *How cool is that? I have a great job. I'm doing good, right?*

But years of running that gauntlet left him with an ever-deepening sense of conflict in his soul. Never lacking confidence in himself, it was more of a moral dilemma of *What is truly right, what's considered wrong, and who's gauge are we using? God's, the government's, our own personal heartstrings, my grandkids?*

This feeling of apprehension was new, growing, and becoming harder and harder to shake off. It left Charlie contemplative, which he didn't necessarily appreciate. Dig deep and you won't always like what you find. Waiting in line at the Alberto's drive-thru window, Charlie moved the rearview mirror to glance at his reflection. *Who IS that old guy lookin' back at me?* He thought. *I don't feel a day over nineteen. This casing still contains a teenager.*

But the passing of time was evident at the corners of his eyes, the laugh lines around a smile he used so often to get himself out of a jam. Strands of determined gray hair mirrored the frequent foreboding he couldn't seem to shake.

Back in the day I wouldn't think twice about something going wrong. I was fearless, invincible! Does gray hair bring fear with it? As time goes on you accumulate more to lose; family, friends. And what about broken promises?

This much I do know: When I was a kid, I sure as hell didn't talk to my reflection. Dammit.

When you bare your soul, know what you get? The naked truth. But can you see the truth between the lines of *need to do* and *want to do*? Hopefully, as you age you learn to distinguish the difference.

Charlie pondered. *This path I'm on, is it the one I was destined to take? Or have I taken the proverbial wrong off ramp? What about when I'm gone? Will I have left something of myself behind? Who will miss me? Has what I'm looking for been here the whole time? What if a smile and a kiss are what it's all about? Something as simple as love.*

Charlie rolled down his window to let in the hot desert air filled with the smell of fresh soil and car exhaust, though the scent of his confusion still lingered.

The sound of music from somewhere outside rushed in the open window and Charlie glanced in his side view mirror. It was a tune he did not recognize coming from the kid's car behind him. They were passing around a joint, smiling, laughing, bouncing in the their seats, doing what young people do. Charlie had the impulse to go up to their window and ask, "Hey, can I hit that?"

But you don't find what you're looking for by going backwards. At his age the correct road lies ahead.

He put the vehicle in drive and pulled forward to the pick-up window. "That'll be fifteen-seventy-five, sir," said the young, Hispanic cashier with a pleasant smile.

✠　✠　✠

When Woody returned, it was bad news. "Checkpoint's still open."

"Dammit!" exclaimed Charlie. "We have no choice. We have to go the back way." He tried to hide the fact that he didn't have a good feeling about this plan, but it didn't matter. They were on a deadline. Ramona had come to depend on him, and he wasn't about to let her down now.

They pulled out of the Desert Inn at 6:00 a.m. the next day, still hoping for rain and a closed checkpoint. Neither happened. The group headed out towards the dunes of the southern California desert and the small border patrol checkpoint twenty miles from nowhere.

Woody was a half-mile behind the van watching as it crested each dip in the pavement.

Mr. and Mrs. Lopez, lying in the back behind the third row seats covered in a blanket, were not visible from the driver-side window.

Charlie and Denice wore their warmest smiles as they pulled up to one of the Border Patrol's tiny booths. The officer in the booth greeted them with his standard, "Good morning."

Brandishing her best smile, Denice cheerfully replied from the passenger side, "Good morning to you, officer."

Her goodwill was not returned. "What's your destination?" gruffed the officer.

Charlie answered, "Palm Springs."

"Any fruit to declare?"

Charlie thought to himself, *Cool, we're good to go*, "No, sir, no fruit," he said without a hint of stress in his voice.

What happened next was anything but cool, and completely startling. Just as he put the car into gear, expecting to be waved through the officer suddenly said, "Pull over into secondary, please."

Charlie and Denice looked at each other and knew instantly that the ride was over. Charlie's first thought was *Run for it!* But he didn't. Instead he did was he was told, even though his mind took off racing.

Elwood saw the van slowly pulling over to the side and without hesitation slammed the pedal to the metal, shot over into the oncoming lane and ran through the wrong side of the checkpoint at seventy miles per hour.

Charlie muttered under his breath, "Shit, shit, shit."

Denice, not sure of what would happen next, turned around facing the back and urgently commanded, "Sit up, guys, put on your seatbelts, *now!*" just in case a wild ride ensued.

But it didn't.

Charlie rolled to a stop in secondary. Another officer tried the back doors of the van and found them locked.

Elwood looked into his rearview waiting, *praying* to see red and blue lights. However, nothing but retreating desert asphalt followed him.

Charlie saw Woody out of the corner of his eye run the checkpoint as the second officer glanced over his shoulder, but paid no attention to the diversion. He kept walking towards Charlie and the open driver-side window.

"Keys, please, sir," said the officer in a voice that sent a shiver down Charlie's spine.

Charlie solemnly turned off the ignition and handed him the keys, which he then threw to his partner. Denice's phone rang, showing Elwood's number. She quickly pushed answer. Not lifting the phone to her ear, she said loudly, "We're done. Do not come back," and hung up.

Mr. and Mrs. Lopez sheepishly exited the van through the rear doors and were led into one of two trailers in the secondary parking area. The officer, who now at the passenger window, asked for Denice's phone as she got out. The other officer holding the door open for Charlie had his hand on his 9-mm service revolver as he ordered, "Please exit the vehicle and put your hands behind your back, sir."

Charlie complied, but over his shoulder asked, "What gave me away?"

The officer smiled and said, "See those new yellow poles? Those are sonar heartbeat detectors; two bodies, four heartbeats. Technology kicked your ass, sir."

Both Charlie and Denice were handcuffed, escorted to the second trailer and put into a holding cell. Next they were fingerprinted and photographed. Then yet another officer led just Charlie to a small room with a desk, two chairs, no windows, and a very surly bigwig. "So, Mr. DeVille," said Officer Bigwig, "How long have you two been smuggling illegal immigrants?"

"Leave my wife out of this," replied Charlie quietly.

"Well, she *was* in the vehicle with you. I'd say that involves her pretty deeply."

"She's got nothing to do with any of it, let her go."

Officer Bigwig suddenly changed his tune, and became a bit friendlier...which was even scarier. "We might be able to work that out, *depending*."

"You do that," replied Charlie. "I take full responsibility."

"Okay...let's talk about that," mused Officer Bigwig.

"When I see her drive away in that rental van, *then* we'll talk."

Officer Bigwig motioned for the subordinate patrolman in the room to come to him. They whispered in hushed tones until the junior officer said to Charlie, "Okay, let's go."

Charlie stood up and the patrolman led him back into the holding cell, where he found Denice crying huge gushing tears running down her lovely cheeks. "Send in the clowns," she said. "Christ, what a major cluster fuck, look at me."

Charlie put two fingers under her chin and lifted her face to look in her eyes. "We knew this was coming."

"Charlie, I'm scared…"

"I'm riding the beef on this one. I'm almost positive they'll let you go. If they ask you any questions, you know nothing. It's my deal. You'll want to get an attorney right away. I was driving, I'm responsible, you understand?"

Denice nodded and tried to put on a strong game face through the tears.

✠   ✠   ✠

Denice drove the rental back towards Jacumba. The first of many phone calls she made was to Woody. She asked him to meet her back at Nea's. The second call was the hardest. It was to Ramona. This was the call she hoped she'd never have to make. Denice agonized for long moments while dialing. Once she'd entered Ramona's number into her phone, she stared at it for a second before she finally hit send. On the third ring Ramona answered. "Hey girl, you in L.A.?"

Denice gulped and held back tears before she spoke. "No, we lost this one. Charlie's on his way to Metro Correctional Center and Mr. and Mrs. Lopez are on a bus back to Mexico."

"What? AH! No! Dammit!" Then silence.

"Ramona?"

"I just need a moment to digest this. Thinking about other things impacted…"

"Being VIP I knew there was a lot riding on success," Denice quickly interrupted. "I'm so sorry."

"I'm stunned they arrested Charlie and are prosecuting," reasoned Ramona with a hint of panic in her voice. "Usually they book you and let you go."

"Charlie's not talking. He's holding his mud no matter what. His words not mine."

"Okay, good." Ramona immediately went into warrior mode. "Got some calls to make, one of which is to an outstanding Federal lawyer. And the ACLU. Plus, some others I can't tell you about yet. Keep me posted. You should hear from him within 48 hours, that's how long it takes to get a PIN number. Let me know when he contacts you. I need to go." The line went dead.

Denice hung up feeling alone, overwhelmed, and scared to death.

✠   ✠   ✠

Charlie was booked into M.C.C., the Metro Correctional Center, and medically cleared for general population. They issued him an orange jump suit (too tight in the crotch, too long in the legs) and a shower kit. Then a guard led him to a long row of cell doors and unceremoniously pushed him into a stark white cell that contained the custom stainless steel toilet found only in prisons.

He sat on the edge of his four-inch mattress with its grey horsehair blanket, stared out the four-inch window and wondered where Denice was and how she was holding up. Charlie was physically and emotionally exhausted. He collapsed onto his cot. As he fell to sleep, his hands instinctively searched for a pillow that wasn't there.

A little while later Charlie awoke with a start to the sound of a food tray being slid into the four-inch hole of the cell door.

"Chow," some trustee yelled as he pushed it through the opening.

Dog chow went through Charlie's mind. But what he actually received was fried baloney and watery oatmeal. Must be breakfast. Had he really slept that long?

Charlie completely lost track of time, but the next sound he eventually heard was keys hitting home in the lock mechanism of his cell door. The bored monotone voice of the corrections officer, a.k.a the C.O., said, "Lawyer visit, Mr. DeVille. Turn around, I've got to cuff you."

"For a visit?"

"For escort in the elevator. I'll remove them in the visiting room."

✠   ✠   ✠

"Mr. DeVille, my name is Chad Kinkade," said the man in the fancy suit waiting for him in the visiting room.

Charlie shook his hand. "Charlie DeVille."

"Mr. DeVille, I'm a Federal attorney, possibly your attorney of record. My services being provided by the woman you know as Ramona. That being said, do you agree to have me as your attorney?"

"What's my other option?"

"The Federal Defender, which might be your only option after this consideration is concluded."

"Why's that?"

"My job is to represent you and Ramona's best interest. If your decision involves being a confidential informant, it would constitute a conflict of interest for myself and my firm."

"Mr. Kinkade, I have absolutely no desire to include anyone in my, shall we say, *dilemma*."

"Okay, Mr. DeVille, we're on the same page. Let's talk about where we are in the big picture. First, the detectives are going to offer you a deal to work with them."

"Not gonna happen," replied Charlie.

"If we take it to trial, you're looking at eight to ten years if found guilty. The feds have a 98% conviction rate, Mom, apple pie, and America versus the illegal alien smuggler."

"I was caught red-handed," confessed Charlie. "I'm not going to waste everyone's time."

Mr. Kinkade got down to brass tacks, "Then it's a plea deal we're looking for. That all depends on how the prosecutor sees your crime, and what he knows about you and your dealings in Jacumba."

"My dealings in Jacumba? What the hell does that mean?"

"That means we have to go to the investigator's meeting, hear them out, see what they know, what info Homeland Security has. Believe me when I say, they probably have an extensive file on everyone in and around Jacumba."

Charlie sat back against his chair to digest Kinkade's last remark. His head was swimming. The last few weeks had been an emotional hell. Charlie was reaching critical mass. Not unlike the time he got lost at the zoo as a child. The terror was immediate and increased in intensity with each moment that he could not find his mom and dad.

Charlie's heart pounded much the same way right now as he thought about the correlation between *his dealings in Jacumba* and *prison*.

Charlie had heard it said that going to prison is like dying with your eyes open. Your life unfurls before you moment by moment. Not in a blinding flash, but slowly, over time, each night before you fall sleep. Tiny time capsules you pull from memory flash in your brain like still pictures – a lifetime of single moments. The unraveling comes stitch by stitch until you're inside out.

One of the gauges of sanity is the ability to tell how much time has passed. One hour? Three hours? The atomic clock of incarceration has no hands and no numerals, only moments, each unto itself. "Doing time" is analyzing those moments, either with regret or savoring the joy found within each one. Every night is a new adventure in trying to find the sleep those moments allow by way of dreams.

Sitting in that visitation room, snippets of Charlie's life played out in the theater of his skull: *Dancing like a gypsy with frosting from the wedding cake still in her hair. His new bride looks up at him with trusting and vulnerable, big brown eyes.* Charlie recoils at the thought. He is not worthy of that trust. He'd failed; failed to keep his family safe and grounded. He pictured himself sitting on his cot, in his cell, and whispering into the darkness, "I vowed to protect her and I failed."

Loneliness suddenly floods in and brings with it little clips of time: *Driving home, Charlie's little pig-tailed princess asks, "Papa, does God have a wife?"*

"I don't think so, baby girl."

"Then where did Jesus come from?"

At the time, the innocence of that moment makes Charlie smile with fatherly pride. But the threat of prison fades that beautiful memory to black. It breaks his heart knowing he'll be locked away from making any more of those kinds of moments. Time only flows in one direction. When you try to stop it, or dam its flow, it overwhelms its banks, muddying the water, drowning everything left behind.

At this point all Charlie can do is try to find center and hold on tight, hold fast, like his sanity depends on it, which in a way it does. Engulfed in despair and helpless, Charlie tries to keep a grip. For a man like him vulnerability is a small death... with eyes open.

Charlie snapped back to the present and found Kinkade staring at him, expecting him to speak. After careful consideration, Charlie finally said, "In the past, I've been stopped by California Highway Patrol for suspicion of trafficking, briefly held at the Salton Sea checkpoint for questioning, and then released. That's it."

Kincade opened his brief case and shuffled through some papers. Finding what he was looking for, he looked Charlie in the eye. "What you need to be concerned about are people like Larry, who have informed on you, and anyone else who could throw you under the bus to shorten their own prison time. Conceivably, it's possible they have a huge amount of information on you, anything from personal statements to phone records. Just so you know what we're up against here."

Overwhelmed by his lack of knowledge, Charlie asked, "What's the next step?"

"I dig around, ask some questions, try to get a feeling for what the prosecutor knows, what he's thinking."

"When will we talk again?"

"I'll see you at the end of the week."

The two stood and shook hands. Kinkade gave Charlie a business card, waved his hand in front of the camera, then banged on the door. Before it opened he said over his shoulder, "I'll put a few hundred dollars on your books on the way out. Call your wife. She's worried. But say nothing on the phone, and keep quiet around other inmates."

Out the door he went into the big, free world, leaving Charlie with his pants around his ankles (metaphorically speaking). Not good in a prison setting. However, he felt a little better having not ironed his orange jump suit like the dork at the next table over.

Since formal charges and indictments were sworn out for Charlie, they moved him from the holding floor to a pretrial cell on the eleventh floor, overlooking the San Diego skyline. That is, what you could see of it through a four-inch window.

The new cell was institutional yellow and smelled of unwashed feet. The top bunk was unoccupied and the lower bunk was straining to support another inmate, whom Charlie thought looked like the Wookie, Chewbacca, from *Star Wars*. He was out cold, snoring like a farm animal.

Charlie was never so happy to see a pillow in all his life, with a pillowcase, no less.

The C.O. slammed the door shut and ran the locking mechanism home, a sound like no other, the sound of incarceration. Charlie stood there in the center of his ten-by-twelve listening to the other cells being locked down for the count, followed by the reverberations of incarceration; the echo of the locks, angry voices, a quick laugh. Charlie could feel the tears well up behind his eyes again. He thought to himself, *Genghis Khan. Winston Churchill. George Patton. Stone face. Can't let my guard down, not in here. Stone. Cold. Killer. That's me.*

He paced the cell, back and forth. *Shit, I'm no killer. I'm a grandpa, for chrissake.*

He added his voice to the other animals in their cages and screamed, "This fucking sucks!"

Nights in prison for Charlie were full of ghosts, thoughts and memories of faces, people inside his circle: Denice and family, of course. Still shots flash on the back of his eyelids of people and places the last three-year journey had taken him.

It's easy for a person to attribute noble motives to his actions to try and validate his crimes. Not so easy to weigh the consequences to the innocent, like baby Brandt; his friendships, like Ron and Lilly. They were all on the right side of the law according to the values of the status quo. Charlie felt the same respect for the people in his life that are considered criminals. It further justified his resolve to roll with the punches. Maybe he'd lost his center, maybe it *was* time to "straighten up and fly right," as Charlie's father had told him on so many occasions. When sleep finally found Charlie, it was thin and fractured.

Next morning it was up the elevator to the roof, twenty-two stories above Front Street and the rooftop cages that constituted a recreation area. The chain-link and guy wires were to keep the John-Gotti types from making a mad dash via helicopter.

Stepping off the elevator after coming back from the roof was like the descent into the first circle of hell. All the upper and lower level cell doors were open for the indoor part of "recreation." Convicts of every description competed for televisions, card tables, and any available oxygen left in the room. Charlie had the immediate sensation of breathing everyone's exhale. Making his way through the sea of orange jumpsuits, he headed straight for his cell.

His "celly" was not actually a Sasquatch, but an investment banker. Charlie overheard him tell his story to another inmate, whining about his 18- to 24-month sentence for bilking millions from retirement funds under his supervision. Then and there, Charlie categorized him as a thief and a piece-of-shit, knowing how many foreclosed mortgages and ruined retirements this man's greed caused. *How many folks will have to eat cat food four or five times a week because of you?* Charlie thought. *Surely I'm not that kind of criminal?* Who sets the bar? The government? Society? God? My God or your God? Charlie jumped on his bunk, buried his face in his only possession (a flat pillow) and tried to figure out if he was more angry, emotionally exhausted, or just plain disgusted.

✠ ✠ ✠

In the underground basement of the Metropolitan Correctional Center, the opening of a tunnel runs a quarter mile under downtown to the Federal Court Building, where the prosecutor waited with detectives to meet with Charlie and his lawyer.

Shackled to fifteen other inmates, it was a slow procession through the stark white halls of the narrow tunnel. The industrial government linoleum was freshly waxed but you could still see the thousands of scuffmarks made by prisoners' chained feet as they shuffle back and forth daily.

The walls closed in a little tighter as the elevator doors of the court building came into view.

The elevator opened up inside a massive and plush office area. A bailiff unchained Charlie and gave him over to his attorney, who led him to a conference room. Kinkade introduced everyone around the table to Charlie, as if they were all simply meeting for tea. The prosecutor opened the pre-sentence festivities with, "Welcome to the jungle, Mr. DeVille."

Charlie's eyes flashed around the table.

"Seems more like a zoo to me," Charlie said in a bit of a daze.

"Call it what you will, Mr. DeVille. All the same you're in a world of hurt."

Silence.

"My client understands his position completely," said Mr. Kinkade.

"Good. Then, Mr. DeVille, I assume then you'll save yourself a ton of grief and tell us who you're working for."

Mr. Kinkade added, "At this point my client would like to make a statement."

Charlie drew in a deep breath and spoke. "My wife and I were on our way to Palm Springs. I spotted Mr. and Mrs. Lopez walking on the side of the road in the heat of the desert. They told me they were illegals. I made the decision to help them. I'm guilty of transporting. End of story."

"Jesus Christ! Do you know who you're fucking with, Mr. DeVille?" barked the prosecutor.

Silence.

The detective at the table, playing good cop bad cop, said in his best nice-guy voice, "You want to walk out that door right now? Cooperate and you could be home with your family for dinner tonight."

Charlie remained quiet for a moment, and then said, "I can't help you. I can't do anything for you. That's it. End of story."

"You're going to regret this, Mr. DeVille," hissed the detective, obviously pissed that Charlie could not be intimidated into helping.

Mr. Kinkade stood, all six-foot-two of him, turned to the detective, and asked, "Is that a threat, detective?"

"That's a fucking prom—"

"That's enough, John," the prosecutor loudly interrupted. "You heard Mr. DeVille. He *wants* to go to prison."

Charlie thought to himself, *What I want is to get this shit over with! What I want is to punch Detective John Smooth in the face. What I'm going to get is most likely three-to-five years of mystery meat, communal showers, and facial tattoos.*

But what I really want...is to go home.

✠   ✠   ✠

After six months of complete boredom sitting in a cell, Charlie took his last stroll through the tunnel of shame, so he could stand in front of the honorable Judge Tourino and receive sentencing. *Six months* they dicked around deciding what to do with him. Now that Charlie had a taste of prison, he was anxious to start his official sentence so he could look forward to when he was getting out.

Over that six months, Charlie was reminded daily that sadness is everywhere in prison. It feeds on any joy that's left over after being locked in a cage. That joy is a double-edged knife; memories haunt you, but dreams can be your salvation. Hope is your tether to the free world.

Each night that sadness engulfed Charlie in despair. He was both disgusted and disappointed in himself. Those joyful moments he held on to marched through his mind and stopped only long enough to play out. *Click, click, click*, another goes by and brings Brandt's cute little face into view. Charlie crumbled like a castle before a siege. *Oh Jesus. Ah, God. Brandt...my little man.*

Charlie envisioned little hands reaching for him from the floor, *Up, Papa. Up?*

Charlie's heart seized upon a hundred questions. They rushed from his empathetic mind and through his tormented soul:

Who will sit with him in the mud and fill his little dump truck with dirt?

Who's going to fix his bike?

Who will take my grandson to Cub Scout meetings?

Who will show my grandson how to be happy?

While these questions may sound silly coming from a convict, they're a matter of great importance to Brandt and his grandpa. Four simple, easy questions, and Charlie can't answer any of them, not a one.

The guilt was so all consuming that Charlie couldn't comfort himself. The excuses he used before now fell on his own deaf ears.

So, not knowing what else to do, Charlie did something he'd never done. He gave himself permission to cry.

Having come unstitched, with every nerve exposed, the tears came like a typhoon. Pouring out through his eyes until his insides were parched. Shattering every window to his soul. Laying waste to every dwelling. Flattening every blade of grass in his field of dreams, which was now scattered with emotional debris. It will take years to clean up the mess left in its path.

For now, as the tears dry up and the gasping for air subsides, Charlie realizes that over the last six months, not knowing how long this will go on, he has emotionally bled out. Right there on his bunk. Which has left him *dead with his eyes wide open.*

But now the waiting was finally over. Having signed a guilty plea in exchange for 24-to-36 months, he knew there was an end in sight. This hearing was just a formality. And Charlie was ready to get it over with so he could get on with his formal sentence and start counting the days to when he could get back to his life.

Still handcuffed and in his best orange jumpsuit, Charlie faced the bench and assured the Judge that he understood he had zero rights and he was at the mercy of his court.

Charlie replied in the affirmative and after five solid minutes of legal speak, he heard this, "I hereby sentence you to *forty-two months* in the custody of the Bureau of Prisons and three years of supervised probation. Does Mr. DeVille have anything he'd like to say?"

Charlie was stunned, confused, and pissed. This was *not* the plan he agreed to! "Yes sir, I do."

"At your convenience, Mr. DeVille."

Charlie looked at his lawyer, but saw no sign of intelligent thought. At that point he knew he was on his own, adrift at sea with no life raft. "Your honor, I signed an agreement with the prosecutor for 24 to 36 months..." He let the statement hang in the air, like maybe it carried some judicial weight. It didn't.

The judge smirked like he was addressing a child. "Mr. DeVille, I am not bound by any deal you and your attorney made with the prosecution. According to your presentence report you were less than cooperative. Would you like another forty two?"

Charlie glanced at the prosecution table, smiles all around. Obviously, there was no deal. This was a huge win for the prosecutor and he wasn't about to give it up. Charlie turned his confused gaze to Mr. Kinkade, who shrugged indifferently, as if to say, *Hey, you win a few, you lose a few.*

Charlie looked over his shoulder at Denice, who was trying to be stoic, but her tears betrayed her.

Finally he faced the honorable Judge Torino, took a deep breath and straightened his spine. "Forty two is good, sir," he said respectfully. "Forty two is fine."

EPILOGUE

Twenty-four Months In, Twelve to Go

At mail call Charlie hears his name. It's a letter from Elwood and Esperanza. Inside are a note, a picture, and a copy of Esperanza's high school GED. Charlie studies the photo; it's a picture of success. Woody and Esperanza stand on the Santa Monica pier, Woody's arm proudly wrapped around his wife's thin waist. He glows with a lopsided, hillbilly grin, as he points to a pink puff of cotton candy in Esperanza's hand. Charlie reads the accompanying note, which says, "Thank you, Big Daddy DeVille." A huge smile completely takes Charlie's face hostage.

He lies back on his shabby jailhouse rack and brings out his old-school photo album in which he lovingly saves such treasures.

Charlie opens his album to add this new picture, but immediately gets captivated by a picture of Denice and him embracing Miss Isabelle. It was the day they reunited her with her son, Carlos, and the rest of her family. The old woman's glorious Cabbage Patch doll smile says it all. Charlie thinks, *"If I died tomorrow, standing at the gates of heaven, I would be proud of this."*

Turning his gaze to the opposite page, Charlie studies a photo of Denice in a summer dress leaning on the fender of her '71 Camaro. Bright red Revlon lips frame a sultry smile thrown in the direction of her husband behind the camera. Is this the same girl, head on a swivel looking for Border Patrol? He hears her voice in his head: *"All clear, handsome."* His heart responds sincerely: *We got a million miles on our life's odometer baby, you and me till the wheels fall off.*

Charlie carefully turns a page and sees Wiley in his linemen boots, shoulder holster rig with the grip of his 9-mm peeking out from under his right arm. His same hand holds his hat in front of his face, while his left hand gives Charlie the finger. No one has a picture of Wiley's face. *No one.* This man, Charlie's friend *and brother*, represents to Charlie the *get-em-there-safe* struggle. Charlie's friendship will always be there for Wiley. *Always.*

Turning a page, Charlie's heart warms when he sees teeny little Denice Pena's beautiful brown face peering out from her white satin christening gown. The DeVilles are her godparents and considered part of the family. The infant's tiny arms reach out to Charlie from the photograph, fully embracing his heart.

Charlie knows he'll never transport another undocumented person, but the issue of immigration in his mind is far from over.

And finally he comes to a picture Renea took of Brandt riding piggyback on Lily, laughing uncontrollably, his hands digging into her hair as Ron chases them around an oak tree. Renea makes sure Daddy has pictures of everyone on every holiday. It's what keeps Charlie's heart full, leaving less room for sadness.

Although these photos provide comfort, the paradox for Charlie only deepens each time he meanders through his cherished memories. What's important to him now is family.

Being locked away from his girls and grandchildren brings a deeper understanding of what is essential in this life. It's called *caritas,* a Latin word meaning love and charity towards family. His. Yours. The family of man.

Experiencing these images never fails to make Charlie misty-eyed. He gathers a tear on the end of his finger and flicks it to the floor. Justification never seems to end in prison and sometimes it can be your savior. It's what's inside you... when it's just you.

Charlie reflects: *The skin on my hands is scarred. The ink on my tattoo is faded. My hair has more grey than ever. My eyes need glasses to read. After all this, and prison too, would I do it over again?*

Charlie looks down at his goddaughter's angelic face and the Santinos' proud smile. "Hell yes, I'd do it again," he whispers to an empty cell. Because in his heart he knows, when you engage in the world, when you take a stand, when you make a conscious decision to pray for rain...sometimes you gotta deal with a little mud.

ABOUT THE AUTHOR

David Charlton Taylor has tumbled through life like a pair of nine-sided dice. He's been a husband, a father, a grandfather, a lover of nature, and an outlaw. Currently, he's serving a 10-year sentence in federal prison for the latter.

In David's own words, he says this about himself:

I have a muse. Her name is Angelica. She came to me here in prison four years ago. She showed me how to kill the cannibal in my head that was eating me alive. She filled that empty dead space with words and story. She makes me laugh and cry at the same time, as I put my hand to pen and paper. She once quoted Nietzsche in my ear: *Dave, he who has a 'why' to live for, can bear with almost any 'how.'*

I have a sneaking suspicion my mom sent my muse to me. I love you, Mom.

Life's journey often starts out in the opposite direction of our creative destiny. And I'm happy to say, I'm so far from done I can't even see the finish line.

Oh yeah, and Angelica says, "*Smile every chance you get.*"

In other words, David was a writer all along, but never knew it. He found his Nirvana being a wordsmith...from prison.

For more about David, and to read his blog posts, visit David's blogsite at www.PostcardsFromPrison.net.

Follow David on Twitter at @JacumbaConnect, and on Facebook at facebook.com/davidcharltontaylor.